HEART SPRING MOUNTAIN

HEART SPRING MOUNTAIN

ROBIN MACARTHUR

THORNDIKE PRESS
A part of Gale, a Cengage Company

Farmington Hills, Mich • San Francisco • New York • Waterville, Maine
Meriden, Conn • Mason, Ohio • Chicago

Thorndike Press, a part of Gale, a Cengage Company.

ALL RIGHTS RESERVED
Thorndike Press® Large Print Reviewers' Choice.
The text of this Large Print edition is unabridged.
Other aspects of the book may vary from the original edition.
Set in 16 pt. Plantin.

**LIBRARY OF CONGRESS CIP DATA ON FILE.
CATALOGUING IN PUBLICATION FOR THIS BOOK
IS AVAILABLE FROM THE LIBRARY OF CONGRESS.**

ISBN-13: 978-1-4328-4608-4 (hardcover)

Published in 2018 by arrangement with Ecco, an imprint of HarperCollins Publishers

Printed in the United States of America
1 2 3 4 5 6 7 22 21 20 19 18

For my children,
and theirs

The land is a being
who remembers everything.
You will have to answer to your
children, and their children,
And theirs —
— JOY HARJO,
"CONFLICT RESOLUTION FOR HOLY BEINGS"

Be like the fox
who makes more tracks than necessary,
some in the wrong direction.
Practice resurrection.
— WENDELL BERRY, "MANIFESTO:
THE MAD FARMER LIBERATION FRONT"

CONTENTS

PROLOGUE:
BONNIE

4 P.M., August 28, 2011
Tropical Storm Irene

Maple and oak branches lash the window-panes, sirens scream all over town. The power went out an hour ago, and all Bonnie and Dean can see are those branches, their wind-thrashed, mottled leaves, and heavy rain. A hurricane! They said it was coming on TV, and here it is. Here it is.

"All yours, baby," Dean says, handing Bonnie the needle. She's on the couch, shaking, not hungry, thinks she might vomit in the kitchen sink. Instead she lifts the sleeve of her nightgown, winds the band around her left arm, and searches for a vein not hardened. She slips the needle in. Ah! There it is: immediate heat, warm breeze.

She tips her head back against the couch cushion and closes her eyes. Poppies from Afghanistan: she sees them waving in a

11

bright field in her mind. The mysterious source of this magic. Bonnie smiles and she's a young mother again, Vale in her arms, spinning on the shore of a lake, fireworks in the distance, laughing. She puts her chin into the rolls of fat at Vale's neck and breathes in. That sweet-sour milk: homegrown yogurt.

Divine, Bonnie thinks, smiling, her eyes still closed, listening to the rush of wind.

"I'm going out to wet my feet," she calls out to Dean, rising from the couch. "Explore the fray!" He nods, lining up packs of smack and fentanyl on the table. Bonnie slips out of her nightgown, tugs on jeans and a sweatshirt with a neon-pink wolf across its front, pulls Reebok sneakers over her bare feet. How long has she had these sneakers? They are Patti Smith sneakers. Motherfucking Joan Jett sneakers. She laughs. Glances at her face in the mirror. What's happened to it? Pockmarked. Drawn. Ghost version of her former face.

"I'll see you," she says to Dean, walking out the door and down the three-story exterior staircase to the ground below.

The water of Silver Creek, usually running languid twenty feet away, has climbed the concrete embankment and crossed the parking lot, is kissing the soles of her sneakers. "Holy water," she whispers, kneeling to touch it. It's cold and rust orange — a color she's never seen water before. It's climbed ten feet, at least, maybe fifteen. It crashes against the basement windows on the far side of the building, deafens the air with its roar.

There's a woman across the street standing on her rooftop taking pictures. She waves to Bonnie, shouts something Bonnie can't hear, and Bonnie waves back. Grins. Turns and walks parallel to the creek.

A barrel shoots by. A child's plastic truck. Three car tires.

A hurricane! Just like they said on TV. Bonnie and Dean had filled the bathtub with water and waited all day for the wind, but it was peaceful, eerily mild, just a steady rain and the branches gently striking the windows. But the river — who knew? The storm they'd all been waiting for. Bonnie does a little dance, her body warm, electric.

She walks onto the Estey Street bridge — concrete piers, green iron — and stands in the middle of it, facing the surge, her arms spread out on either side of her. Like Jesus on the cross, Bonnie thinks, raising her face to the rain.

She's found him of late: Jesus. The tall preacher, in that concrete church at the edge of town where Bonnie makes it some Sundays, hollers: "For by grace you have been saved through faith." His blue eyes flickering.

She sits in the back row, her head in her hands, nodding.

Bonnie looks upstream at the roiling river. Rain pours down her cheeks, her neck, her lips, slips under the collar of her sweatshirt. A warm rain! A Bahamas-scented rain. A southern-scented rain. Like in that city where her daughter lives — too far away. Bonnie tips her head back, bares her teeth, lets the water seep through onto her tongue. *Whoever drinks the water I give them will never thirst,* it says in Matthew.

Bonnie wrote that on her wall with a black Sharpie.

"Wild, baby girl!" she shouts into the roar and din, imagining this same rain pouring down Vale's neck and chest in New Orleans. The water answers back. A deep and glorious bellow. The asphalt below her feet shakes. Bonnie laughs. Whispers, "Holy water," heart thundering below her rib cage.

PART I
RIVER

VALE

Vale is tending bar in New Orleans — pouring lavender bitters into juniper-infused gin, flicker of wrist, carmine leather, Beyoncé's "Diva" playing on the dust-covered speakers in the corner — when she gets the call from Deb: *High water. A bridge. Your mother.*

For twenty-four hours she's been watching the storm on TV. Hurricane Irene touched down the night before in New Jersey, downing trees, flooding rivers, causing seven deaths. One and a half million people without power. It landed next over Long Island — roads, houses, streets destroyed, sewer plants overflowing in Long Beach. Then headed north into New England, where it lost its intensity and dropped to a tropical storm. Just heavy rain, the news said. Winds slowed. Sighs of relief at the bar. "Baby gone to sleep," Monty whispered,

17

laying his palm on the cigarette-marred mahogany of the bar top, watching the footage of search and rescue missions along the coast of New Jersey. *Someone going to turn this bar into a guitar someday,* Vale can hear Moe, the piano player who comes in on Thursdays, say in her head. She wasn't here for Katrina, but the residual trauma has soaked into her bones, here where they know the power of wind and rain all too well. When storms come there is a magnetic, dread-sickened buzz in the air. They turn the music up. Overdrink. Dance more recklessly. They are waiting, every day, for the next big one, not an *if* but a *when*. Tonight Vale mixes drink after drink and, alongside the others there in Marigny, breathes a sigh of relief for their brethren in Brooklyn, brethren in Queens. Awful. Destructive. Yes. But not near as bad as predicted. The end of the world has not come.

The bar is full, and she loves the flickering motions that take over her body on busy nights. She steals shots, dances in slow motion to Shorty and Missy and Kanye.

But later that night, eleven thirty, other footage starts floating in: cell phone videos from northern New England. The winds dropped, yes, like the news said, but the rains picked up. The screen shows images of roads torn up, trees downed. "Just think of the ghosts unearthing," says Monty, who found his cousin's body, bloated in two feet of water, at the house where he was born, four days after the storm. Vale taps her glass against his bourbon. Says, "They'll be just fine there." Vale is from Vermont — a blue-walled apartment above the river. Hurricanes don't hit there. It's one of those places that is oddly immune: to poisonous snakes, poisonous spiders, tornadoes, earthquakes, landslides. But the next shot is of a double-wide — green vinyl siding, black shutters — being swept downstream. "Shit," Vale whispers, passing another Maker's Mark to Monty, who starts to shake visibly. Vale's mother, Bonnie, is in one of those river towns being torn up, right now, by floodwater. The storm, according to the news, has dropped eleven inches of rain in eight hours. Creeks have surged. River depths soared. The screen shows a 250-year-old covered bridge collapsing and going under. Vale reaches for her phone and calls Bonnie's landline, but the number is disconnected.

She gets the call from Deb, her aunt, a near stranger, an hour later. Deb's voice is scratchy, barely audible. She must be standing at the top of the field above Hazel's

19

house, the only place there's cell reception there on the farm. "Bridge . . . missing . . . eight hours —" she shouts, her voice breaking up in places.

Vale feels a cold stillness. She takes the phone outside into the street's warm air. The branches of a thick-trunked magnolia rise above her. Sirens wail in the distance. She must have misheard. "What?"

Deb repeats herself. Is shouting over the sound of the rain. Vale's mother, she says, walked out into the storm eight hours ago. Was seen by a neighbor walking toward a bridge that collapsed. Hasn't been home since. "They'll find her. I'm sure," Deb says, the last word rising like a question.

The images register in Vale's mind, piece together slowly. The first time she saw her mother with a needle in her arm Vale was sixteen years old; claw-foot tub, wood floors, smell of incense and bathwater. A slow progression of wine, then Oxy, then heroin in that blue-walled apartment above the river.

"Okay," Vale says into her phone before hanging up. Vale was doing her own stuff back then, too — pills of all kinds. At eighteen, eight years ago, she got clean and left home. She hasn't seen her mother since. She looks up into the branches of the

20

magnolia rising above her. Puts her forehead against its thick trunk.

She loves this city — its warm heat, its music, its light. She hates home — its silence, its whiteness, its holes, the people she left there.

"Bonnie," she whispers.

The next morning she slips into boots, packs a bag, gathers her cash, and walks herself to the bus station on Loyola Avenue.

LENA

May 17, 1956

Dearest Pines —

My sister's husband's eyes are the color of moss, the color of fern. I've never seen eyes that color, certainly nowhere in this town or on this mountain. Earth-colored, speckled with light. I'm living in what used to be my grandfather's hunting camp, one room made of hemlock and spruce, still dank with the smell of whiskey and deer hides, a place where I keep my bird books and this notebook and the photographs I cut out of *Outdoor Life* and *Field & Stream.* The Battle of Taejon took my father, and Lex, my sister's husband, came back from that war distant, drinking too much, averse to shoveling shit and milking cows. Who wants anything to do with a world like that? Sick with killing — nuclear.

My place? Wool blankets hung over the

22

windows to keep out the drafts in winter, a battery-operated radio that plays Little Richard and Patsy Cline and Louis Armstrong. Buckets of creek water lined up near the door, and Otie, my one-eyed barred owl, found on Route 100, hit by a truck and barely breathing. I brought him home on a cool night in March, built him a nesting box from an old apple crate, and here he is, two months later, one-eyed, unable to fly, fervently alive.

"Fervently alive, Otie," I call out. He purrs. "He" because he's smaller than others I've seen; according to my bird book, males are significantly smaller than females.

And so it is just he and I, and these letters I chicken-scratch, while Satchmo sings "Mack the Knife" on the radio.

"Mouse!" I call out, laughing and handing Otie a live one, pulled from the trap, by the tail. He swallows it whole, blinks his thank-you. In the daytime: clings to my shoulder wherever I go. The barn, the fields, the woods. Anywhere but near houses or towns — their cool stares and many eyes. Their imposing expectations. Every one of which I've failed.

I avoid my sister's house below, too. Its polished floors and clean lines and Lex's fiddle on the back porch late at night —

one-hundred-year-old melodies leaking up into the sky.

I'm like the three-legged coyote that lives nearby, the one that crosses the field in the evening, sticks to the darker edges.

Like this morning. Dawn, mist rising out of the valley, over the sunburnt trees, over the orchard and Silver Creek and the pines — you, my friends — who stand upright at the top of the hill.

"Good morning!" I call out, stretching. White pines: straight-backed ladies, winsome. You bend with the wind, sing in the strongest storms, smell like earth when the sun shines and like sugar when it rains. Hear that? Like sugar when it rains.

"What am I good for, my friend?" I ask Otie, who blinks and asks the trees. Me: twenty-seven years old. One wandering eye that won't behave.

I laugh. Bring my cup of coffee — black, no sugar — to the granite slab outside my door, Otie by my side. The coffee burns my lips; I rub them together, feel the chaff there. Tip my head back to face the sun. A bear was here last night circling the trash can, sniffing the food-scrap pit. Her muskiness still in the air. Otie hops across the yard until he finds her scat, full of acorns and last fall's apple drops, steaming near the outhouse door.

"Good work, Otie," I call out, laughing.

Smoke rises from the farmhouse below. And faint but undeniable: the sound of a fiddle. He must be drunk at dawn.

"Go to sleep, Lex," I whisper toward the trees. You shiver in response. Shake your heads. Say nothing.

VALE

August 29, 2011

Alabama. Tennessee. Virginia.

Factories. Strip mines. Blue mountains.

Billboards for Smoky Mountain Motor
Lodge, billboards for Dollywood. "Damn, I
could use me some tits like those!" Bonnie
cooing from the couch as they watched
Dolly sing on the *Grand Ole Opry.* "Beaute-
ous fake babies. Not like your mama's little
knockers." Laughing and kissing Vale's
head, sipping her Chardonnay. Vale is seven.
She curls up on her mother's lap — her
favorite place to be: lavender and salt,
always warm. "You and me, baby," Bonnie
whispers, reaching for Vale's feet, pulling
them onto her lap, brushing her fingers
across them slowly.

Flicker of bus lights. Pounding wheels.

Deb called earlier to say the police and
National Guard are still searching but have

found nothing. Her broken-up voice, spotty reception.

"My mother is not dead," Vale whispers.

Deb might sound doubtful, but eight years or no, Vale still feels her mother's particulate matter in this world. Somewhere: a wet field. A cold barn. An empty house, window cracked open, next to a roaring fire.

Vale closes her eyes.

A story Bonnie used to tell, quoting Vale at four: *Mama, you know how we get love?*

How?

When you're in the mama's belly you hear the heart. And that makes your own heart. And then when you come out you have that love. The mama is a love factory.

Bonnie laughing, grinning, reaching for Vale, "The mama is the love factory!"

Bonnie, Vale writes in neon script across the dark sky of her mind, as the bus crosses the border into Vermont.

She's shocked by the destruction: a garage collapsed, a pine uprooted, a black sedan wedged into the low branches of a large oak tree. Vale eyes it all slowly, looking for familiar limbs — five feet tall, dark hair, walking or sitting.

Vale checks the local headlines on her phone: 2,400 roads, 300 bridges, and 800 homes destroyed or damaged in the state.

Some 117,000 people without power. Two dead. One missing.

One missing, Vale thinks, turning back toward the window, eyeing the streets of this town she left eight years ago swearing she'd never return: *my own.*

The man at the bus station in Nelson laughs when Vale tells him where she's trying to get: ten miles out of town, uphill.

He has one blue eye and one brown. Points, with eyebrows raised, toward Vale's boots: thin soles, cracked leather.

Vale shrugs, throws her backpack over her shoulder, walks to the edge of the road, and sticks her thumb out.

Tomorrow she'll go to her mother's apartment, that place above the river where Dean will no doubt be, heating a nugget of smack on the stove, that sickly sweet, damp vinegar smell. Tomorrow she'll go to the bridge where Bonnie was last seen.

Right now Vale needs food and a bed to sleep in. She needs to get uphill to Hazel's old farmhouse, that place where Bonnie grew up. That house — cold white rooms, white pine painted clean again and again — where Vale's ancestors have lived for two hundred years. Joyless in old photographs, their mouths thin lines. "How many years can you go without joy before the whole shit show crumbles?" Bonnie saying years ago, pinching Vale's side, laughing.

She catches a ride with an elderly man in a red pickup truck.

"You walking? Those roads are destroyed. No way in or out. I can only get halfway."

Vale nods. "Halfway is good." She looks at her phone. There's a message from her boss at the bar, Freddie, to whom she told nothing. *WHERE YOU AT, SUGAR CAKES?*

"Crazy storm," the man says. "A woman is missing. You hear that? They still haven't found her."

Vale says nothing, slips her hands under her thighs and holds them still there.

They pass the fire station, rain-wrecked cornfields where Vale used to lie down between the tall stalks and get stoned, the 7-Eleven where she's stolen cigarettes, candy, bottles of wine. She was sixteen; she would stick them down the front of her shirt and flash a grin. Every piece of the landscape contains a memory; they attack her chest, claw there. Vale opens the neck of her sweater, seeking air.

They don't pass the ruins of that green bridge or the apartment where Bonnie lives

29

above the river, but Vale keeps her eyes peeled.

The last time Vale saw her mother was in that apartment. Plum-colored bruises up and down her arms. One hundred pounds, barely. Vale told Bonnie she was leaving and not coming back. She had a social worker then who said: *Your mother's life is not your own.* Bonnie walked her to the door, handed her a plastic bag. Inside were two oranges and some photographs. She gripped Vale's arm too long; when Vale finally pulled away, some strands of Bonnie's hair came out in her hands.

The pickup passes a mustard-colored trailer tipped on its side fifty feet from the creek. There's a pink curtain blowing through a broken window, a woman's bra hanging from a tree branch.

Vale does a double take. Not Bonnie's.

In New Orleans Vale tends bar three nights a week and works as a stripper the other two. Similar acts, in some ways: costume, makeup, performance, verve. Her drink specialties contain hints of sage, lavender, rose. Her dancing: strut, swing, coyness, refrain. She's never told Bonnie about the strip club. About the way she can make four hundred dollars in a night.

Nor does Vale tell her friends in New

Orleans about Bonnie. About needles or hardened veins or the love factory. Not Shante, not Freddie, not Jack. Not anyone at the club where Vale spins and dances, shakes her hips, reveals the dark orbs of her nipples one at a time.

Vale raps her knuckles on the glass window and points to the liquor store. "Here is fine," she says.

The man pulls the truck over. Eyes her. "You sure?"

"Yes," Vale says, hopping out.

Vale buys pretzels, instant coffee, gin, and wine, stuffs them into her backpack, and starts walking.

The back roads are a mess — downed trees, twenty-foot-wide gullies where culverts once lay — but by foot, passable. The creek bank that runs alongside her is lined with detritus — boulders, barrels, plastic toys, a washing machine: the things parked behind trailers and barns, all washed downstream. Vale sees a kid's high chair crumpled against a ledge. A fur coat, snagged on a branch of a still-standing pine tree, six feet up in the air.

The higher in elevation she gets, the less damage there is, though the culverts are still washed out. Her legs ache. Her throat is parched. She stuffs pretzels into her mouth, keeps walking.

It's late afternoon by the time she reaches the roadside spring. Clear water trickling out of a copper pipe by the side of the road three seasons of the year. The brass plaque says HEART SPRING, the name of Vale's family mountain, the place Ezekial Wood and his wife, Zipporah, settled in 1803, when it was nothing but wild forest inhabited by Abenaki and bears and moose and mountain lions. Heart Spring, they named the mountain and this spring, ever running. How deeply unfitting, Vale thinks, bringing her lips to the copper pipe. But the water is clear and mineral rich and deliciously cold. She splashes it on her face and neck, wipes a wet hand across her chest.

Bonnie used to bring her here once a week to fill plastic jugs. "Clean water," Bonnie would say, tipping her head back, putting her lips against that copper, laughing, drinking. "Love me the taste of some hillside spring water! Don't give me any of that chlorinated town water, honey-cakes."

Bonnie hated the hillside where she was born and grew up, but she was drawn to it, too. Deep trees, clean water, the trickling pools of Silver Creek. Vale bends to the water and fills her mouth, again and again.

For as long as she can remember, Bonnie

cut the horoscopes out of the newspaper and taped them to the bathroom walls: *The magic is yours, Gemini! You will be loved. Today is the start of something astonishing and new.* Little flakes of white paper scattered, eventually, across the black pine floor, spewing good fortunes.

Vale wipes her mouth, turns, and continues walking, blisters crackling on her heels.

By the time she arrives at the bridge to Hazel's house the shadows are long. It's been forty-six hours since she's slept; her legs ache, her shoulders ache, her eyes burn as she turns to face the view.

This high up you can hardly tell there's been a storm at all. Hazel's house at the top of the hill: a blaze of tin, traces of white paint lit by late-afternoon sun, ghost-gray clapboards fading into hillside. Behind the house stand the old chicken coop, the empty barn, empty storage sheds. All squares and rectangles, damp earth and shivering pines. Vale closes her eyes and thinks of New Orleans's heat: of her sometimes-boyfriend, Jack, in his tree house overlooking the city, of the Gypsy fortune-tellers with their dark voodoo, of Shante with her ukulele, of the room in the ramshackle house (once hotel, once whorehouse) where Vale sleeps, camellias outside the open window.

"I don't want to be here," Vale says out loud.

Uphill of the farmhouse Vale can just barely make out the wooden walls of the cabin where Deb lives. Bonnie: "Beware of hippies, my love," smiling and bringing a cigarette to her chapped lips. "They are slippery!" Turning David Bowie up on the stereo, closing her eyes and starting to dance, bare feet on cold linoleum.

Vale doesn't want to go to Deb's cabin, or to Hazel's house. She doesn't want to face their cold pity. She turns to her right and there is the teal-blue tow-along camper down by the creek where she lived for a summer when she was sixteen, butted up against the trees at the edge of the field.

She can't believe it survived the storm, that it's still here, creek-side. A miniature, pale-blue tin miracle.

The door pops open with a hard tug, and a pool of brown water runs out onto the ground in front of her feet.

The smell nearly makes her gag: mildew and mouse and creek water — but she's slept in worse places before. The camper hasn't changed much in ten years: a two-burner stove, a table, a bed in the corner. Water-stained yellow paper glued to the walls. Vale pulls open a kitchen drawer and finds mouse shit, a pipe, sugar packets, mildewed condoms. Detritus left over from when she was sixteen. On top of the shelves sit her collection of owls from that summer she lived here, ones she found at thrift stores. Plastic talismans. Purposeless idols.

She remembers Hazel once telling her back then, in a moment that surprised her: *My mother always said owl sightings mean the death of something old and the start of something new.*

Hazel had never said anything like that to her before.

"Hello, owls," Vale whispers, pulling the bottle of gin out of her bag and unscrewing the top. She goes to the front step, takes off her boots and rubs her aching feet. Two blisters — bleeding — which she brings to the air.

The gin is cheap, but she feels it settle into every inch of her bones. She takes another sip. And another. Is grateful for its burn. She is just here for a day or two. Until she finds Bonnie.

Vale reaches for her backpack and pulls out a thick black journal, slips a photograph out from between its pages. It's one Bonnie gave her before she left: a photo of Bonnie and Vale at the river. Full summer, July or August, Bonnie standing waist-high in the water, strands of dark hair blowing across her eyes, her arm across Vale's shoulders, her lips planted on Vale's seven-year-old plump cheek.

"Baby, come in the water with me!" Bonnie said, stripping, jumping, hooting, laughing.

Her love: intoxicating. They lived at the outskirts of town then, a room above the laundromat, and would sneak down the riverbank at night to cool down. *Water, baby. Night swimming.* Vale has never known who her father is. *You don't need a dad, honeycakes. You've got me. Me! All yours.* Laughing and reaching toward Vale. Putting her lips against Vale's ear and singing the chorus of R.E.M.'s "Night Swimming."

"Where are you," Vale whispers. The night is so quiet: just the sound of the creek and the shuffle of pine needles across the camper's pocked tin.

DEB

June 14, 1974

Deb hitches north in a beat-up van with a guy she barely knows — a friend of a friend named Ron. She thinks. Or maybe it's Ran; he says it with some kind of southern drawl though she's pretty sure he's from Baltimore. The drawl matches the clothes he's wearing — weather-beaten overalls and a torn plaid shirt as if he's straight from the tobacco plot, as if he's six generations deep in some backwoods holler, except that his blond hair is long and pulled back into a stringy ponytail and he hasn't shaved for days. She's pretty sure no tobacco farmers have ponytails.

The world is a mess and she's looking for salvation. Nixon's tapes released. The oil embargo. India building the next nuclear device and naming it, of all appalling things, the Smiling Buddha.

Deb's heard about the communes from a handful of old friends. They say all you have to do is drive north until you hit the Vermont border and you'll find one. Find a town along 91 and ask any ponytailed person around. Ron or Ran is driving his van north to find one, too, and said he'd happily take her along. He said, "It's a free world, honey," passing her a joint, and does she have twenty bucks for gas? Deb is twenty-one, has just dropped out of Swarthmore, and is not going back to her parents' house outside of Pittsburgh, her father working at a factory that makes parts for helicopters, her mother's dutiful complacency.

Two of her friends died in Vietnam. The war might be over, but the toxins are everywhere: Patty Hearst's shootout in San Francisco. Nixon's lies, ongoing. Every time you open a refrigerator door you are complicit, Deb read somewhere.

It's Deb's grandmother, Zina, from a village outside of Vitebsk, she wants to be. Zina died when Deb was ten, but Deb still remembers the way she spoke of the farm where she grew up before the Germans came: cows, ducks, sheep, chickens. Since then Deb has dreamed of getting back there — to fields, farm animals, to doing the good work and using her hands, her arms, her strong legs. To a world apart from wars. She takes the joint from Ran's thick fingers and puts it to her lips — breathes in. Relax, she tells herself, face into the sunlight. Dresses, fields, farming — self-reliant, purposeful, free. Her grandmother's warm eyes would grow moist, look out the window: *Nothing like waking up on a farm in the morning,* she would say to Deb, eyes following a passing crow or swallow or blackbird.

In her backpack Deb has paperback copies of Thoreau's *Walden* and Helen and Scott Nearing's *Living the Good Life.* Her bibles. The Nearings: "The value of doing something does not lie in the ease or difficulty, the probability or improbability of its achievement, but in the vision, the plan, the determination and the perseverance, the effort and the struggle . . ."

The pot makes Deb's mind lift in a cloud, and she looks out her window at the fields flying by. They're in Massachusetts now, and already she can breathe easier. Smell the earth through the open windows. Smell the Connecticut River gliding by them like a silver belt, lit by sun. Janis Joplin comes on the radio, and Deb tilts her head back and smiles. Her mother will be arriving home from the club, half-wasted from three martinis. She will see the note on the counter, surrounded by a ring of purple clover gathered from the backyard: *Off to live the good life. Love and peace. D.*

Her mother, who has never done anything unexpected or, Deb thinks, brave. Deb wants to be brave. The road north feels like it fits the bill, there in the van listening to Janis's pitched yearning, feeling the wind in her long hair, feeling the sun on her cheekbones. But Ron/Ran is suddenly putting his fingers on her blue-jeaned thigh and turning to give her a stoned grin, and so she is torn from her reverie. She slaps his hand away and says, "Lay off, asshole. You can let me off here."

Freedom.

It feels different when you're alone, without wheels underneath you.

Deb finds the back road that runs parallel to the highway and starts walking.

She passes: farms surrounded by cows and crumbling outbuildings, trailers with dogs out front, some cabins tucked up against the trees. She gets a chill along her spine. Likes the way the landscape feels wild, unfettered, free.

There's a creek running alongside the road, its water flickering. Deb climbs down the bank and splashes her neck and face. It tastes sweet on her lips. She wets her hands and rubs the cold water against her armpits. How real, Deb thinks, as she starts walking. Her heart lifts into her upper chest. How serene.

It's near dusk when she sees the sign on her left. White with a rainbow surrounding the letters: FARTHER HEAVEN. Smaller letters in blue: *welcome.*

There's no house or farm in sight, just a long driveway, steep and rutted, weaving up through some fields and, farther up, tall trees.

At the top of the hill she stops.

There is a big old house, white paint fading. There are barns, sheds, apple trees. Under the apple trees to the right of the house are two women in blue jeans and loose blouses doing something with their hands. To the left of the house are three men, shirtless, moving hay bales. The late light catches their long hair, their sun-loved chests. The scene is so quiet, liquid in the late light, like a scene from an Ingmar Bergman film. She recalls her film class last spring: Liv Ullmann amid the stone cottages; Tarkovsky's fields of tawny wildflowers.

There is a child, too, she sees now, in the grass close to the women. Naked. Rolling. A dog in its arms. No. Something smaller. Pink. The child is laughing. It's a pig. A little naked pig in a naked child's arms.

My God, Deb thinks. She falls down on her knees. Her legs are so tired. She starts to laugh. Though maybe it's a cry. A pig in that child's arms. She thinks of Zina in Vitebsk. *I have arrived.*

LENA

May 25, 1956

Honey B —,

It's all honey. All honey, Honey Bee! I wake up to the song of Otie, his low caterwauling and clucking, faster each time around. According to my book, descending trill and whinny calls serve as contact song among family members, establish territory.

"So you love me. Good," I say, rising and making coffee. Coffee and more coffee: this thing I do. I sit with it at the table, pull out my notebook and pencil, draw a picture of Otie. Brown and white striped plumage. Eyes, umber. Talons looking two hundred years old. Under the drawing I write: golden fury!

"Golden fury, Otie. Is that you?"

He doesn't reply.

I finish my coffee. Down some crackers. Slip on boots, say, "Come."

We walk toward Adele's cabin. Adele is my only friend barring Otie and the animals that stalk these hills: bear, fisher, deer, moose, fox, owl, coyote. Coyote: the three-legged one I spy most evenings crossing the far edge of the field, the one I hear calling upstream nightly. A night creature, she or he is, like Otie and me — remarkably good at going unseen. Its tracks littering the banks of the swamp come morning.

There are ghosts, too. In the cellar holes and at the cemetery where my ancestors have been buried for two hundred years. Gray stones rising out of the earth with faintly etched names: Henry, Ezekial, William, Zipporah, Eunice, Philena, Phebe. More recently: my grandmother, Marie, and my mother, Jessie, who died in the upstairs bedroom one morning in June when I was nine years old. Some days I bring her jars of wildflowers: Indian paintbrush, phlox, Queen Anne's lace. I plant them in the rocky earth, lie down in the grass, and close my eyes. Dream there.

But not this morning. "Buck up, Otie. Don't let the world get you down!" I call out to the bird on my shoulder, smelling woodsmoke, following the path through birch and hemlock and spruce.

The path ends at Adele's house: roadside,

tucked up against the trees. Two rooms, white paint, a long porch, piles of wood stacked everywhere.

When I was a girl her uncle, Buck, lived in a house made of tin and tar paper a ways back in the woods. He logged with horses, lived on canned beans, threw the empties out his back window into a pile that reached halfway to the roof. I snuck to his cabin once alone and stood, quiet and unseen, at the edge of the clearing. Smoke rising from the chimney. A pair of rawhide snowshoes nailed to the wall. From within those walls came a soft and beautiful singing — a ballad about a lost lover and roses twining over gray gravestones.

I sat there in those leaves, listening, until the song came to an end.

"Indian," my father always called him. "Gypsy-nigger." My father's blue-eyed grimace, his smell of grease and cow and copper.

"Hello," I call out on Adele's porch.

She comes to the door, grinning. Dark hair pulled back into a ponytail, polyester pants, men's boots with softened leather. "Otie! Lena," she says, opening the door wide. "My favorite fools." Inside there are herbs drying from the ceiling, coffee brewing, a pot of venison stew on the wood stove. In the corner a nephew lies sleeping on a floral couch, the TV on without volume. Above his head: a wind chime made of bone.

"Here," Adele says, bringing me a steaming cup of coffee. "And for you, Otie — *gohkohkhas* — who is better than anything — this," she says, going to the pantry where she keeps her traps, returning with a live mouse, held by the tail.

He downs it fast. Blinks at her. Adele cackles, pulls a pack of cigarettes from her pocket. "It's a good smoky dawn," she says, lighting one. "You coming fishing with me today, Lena and Otie?"

"Too shy," I say, looking out the window, downing my coffee. Suddenly itching to be elsewhere: field, woods, hill, creek.

Adele shakes her head. Whispers, "Squirrel," with a smile on her lips, as Otie and I nod our thank-yous, slip out the door.

We take the long way home, around the backside of Heart Spring Mountain. How deep the woods must have been in 1803, when my ancestors moved here! Old-growth forests, Indian foot trails. I try to imagine clearing this forest with an axe and a two-handled bucksaw. I smell the log cabin where Ezekial and Zipporah slept with thirteen children while building themselves their house on the hill. Parting the trees for light. Parting the trees for air. How grave their God must have been back then, Otie! How severe.

Hazel

September 1, 2011

This girl walking up the driveway. Which one is she?

It seems a trick of her mind, this girl in gray, rising out of the mist. Something the storm dragged in. Hazel steps closer to the window and looks out. Disheveled dark hair, a red dress, tall boots, dark eyes. It *all* seems a trick of her mind these days. What is happening to it — her mind? The past slipping in and out. All that rain. The torn-up roads. And Bonnie missing.

"A bridge," Deb said, knocking on her door in the early morning several days ago. "High water." Tears in her oblique eyes. No word since then and the power still out, like it used to be when Hazel was a girl here, eighty-some years ago. How quiet the house is without electricity. How long the nights.

And now the knock on her front door,

sturdy and real.

Hazel goes to the door and opens it.

The girl is standing there, dark hair in a braid down her right shoulder, dark makeup around dark eyes.

"Hello, Aunt Hazel," she says, a thick gray sweater wrapped tight around her waist. "It's Vale."

Hazel's mind spins. Fishes for that name. Oh! Vale. Bonnie's daughter. It's been so long. How long?

"Vale. Hello. Come in," Hazel says, opening the door wide. The girl looks like a drowned cat. Like a ghost. Is she? Hazel wonders for a moment too long, standing there in the open doorway.

"Thank you," the girl says, voice cool as silver, cool as the dark rooms in the back of the barn, where someone hid, years ago. Who was it? Hazel's mind — a leaky ship, full of holes.

Hazel goes to the table, picks up her white teacup, carries it to the sink. The girl follows her inside.

"I'm staying in the camper," Vale says. "For a few days. Can I have something to eat? And borrow some blankets?"

Hazel looks at the girl. "Oh, yes." Yes, blankets. Yes, food.

But what does she have to offer? Three

49

days since the storm, and there is so very little in her cabinets.

"Of course," Hazel says, placing the cup in the sink. "Bread? Butter?"

"That sounds good. Thank you."

The girl eats quickly. Does not talk or look up. When she's finished she asks if she can go upstairs for some blankets, and Hazel nods, and so the girl disappears, the clunk of boot soles on pine.

Like Bonnie, when Bonnie was young. Coming home late, climbing the stairs to that room with low-hanging eaves at the top of the stairs. Hazel pretending to sleep but not sleeping; the radio flicking on until ungodly hours of the night. Awful music — full of rage. As if the house was not made of two-hundred-year-old thin bones. Hazel had no idea what to do with this girl — her sister's daughter — not her own.

But she did her best, didn't she? Food on the table. A warm bed.

Vale returns, arms loaded with wool blankets. She asks if she can take one of the jugs of rainwater lined up near the door, and Hazel says, "Oh, sure," keeping her body turned toward the sink, and then the girl slips back out the door, calling over her shoulder, "Thank you."

Hazel calls back, "You're welcome,"

though she doesn't think Vale hears. What Hazel doesn't say is: Wait. Come back. Nothing is right here. Not the roads, not the creek, not the weather. Not me. I'm so sorry about your mother. They will find her. Won't they? Also: I think I am dying. I am sure of it. In every single bone.

The others don't know — Deb or Danny or her doctor — but Hazel knows. It's been happening for months, these spells of confusion, these potholes in her mind. Two days ago she rounded the corner of the house, expecting to see the barn, and instead found the well shed, unused for sixty years. This morning she went out the back door to use the outhouse, stood in the wet grass, barefoot in nothing but her threadbare nightgown, but the outhouse wasn't there. She could see it perfectly when she closed her eyes — that building she used every morning for the first thirty years of her life — a quarter moon carved into the door. The smell of it — not a bad smell — human waste, sawdust, pine shavings, moss. But it was gone. For how many years? Just a patch of overly ripe green grass.

Hazel hasn't told Deb, who comes every morning and every evening since the storm to check on her, that she is afraid. That she can feel death like a bear lurking at the edge of her fields.

She wants to chase that bear with her broom, her scythe, her tractor. She doesn't want to die. What will happen to this house and this land when she dies? Who will care for this mountain, as she has? Heart Spring Mountain, the place her great-great-grandfather, Ezekial Wood, and his wife, Zipporah, settled in 1803, a man who walked for three days with a horse and an ox and a wagon from Cornwall, Connecticut, until he came to a place where no one else lived, a place no one had yet claimed: a piece of land with a brook running through it and a south-sloping hill, springs scattered throughout the bedrock, little white flowers called bloodroot. How do you choose a house site? The way one has always chosen a place to live: water, white pines, land you can dig with a shovel. Higher ground, above floodplain. He chose this slope and Hazel is happy for it. She has lived every one of her ninety years here and is sure Ezekial chose the perfect spot: the spot that catches sun earliest in the morning and sits downhill of the deepest spring. In August when her neighbors' wells run dry, spring water still trickles through the pipes into Hazel's basement and into the roadside spring down the hill, too. Eternal water: Heart Spring he named it.

Hazel looks out the window. She looks toward the barn and cannot help but think of those dark rooms in the back of it. And who was just here? Bonnie?

No, Bonnie is missing. Heart Spring, the headwaters of Silver Creek — is where those eleven inches of rain settled, grew, began. The headwaters that became the river where Bonnie was last seen. Heart Spring Mountain. Because the heart springs eternal here, she had told herself as a girl, and as a young woman, and in middle age. But was that true?

And Bonnie — where is she now? Hazel turns and calls out toward the living room: "Bonnie?"

VALE

September 2, 2011

Vale dreams she is back in New Orleans. A party at the edge of Lake Pontchartrain, the deserted beach where the amusement park used to be. Shante plays her ukulele, wears a blue dress that shimmers in starlight, has a pair of black wings tacked to her shoulders. She howls, the lyrics to her song guttural punctuations, indecipherable. Flicker of headlights crossing the causeway. Vale and Jack and others are there, too: they are dancing in slow motion to Shante's song. There is a bass drum — they move their hips to it. Sirens. Flashes of far-off lightning and the steamy, fish-heavy air of mid-August. Jack puts his lips against Vale's spine, inches them up toward her neck. Vale laughs. Turns. Twists away. Shante sings louder — cackles of laughter. Shrieks of verve. Vale steps into the water, pulling her dress up over her knees, and opens her lips to say something — the word, pearly and half-formed, the color of milk, birthing itself on her tongue —

But Vale's heartbeat is suddenly loud as thunder under her ribs and the world returns: the stench of the camper. The rushing hum of creek water.

The sucker punch: *Bonnie.*

Yesterday Deb called the police from a neighbor's phone, but they still hadn't found anything. Four days she's been missing. Vale's stomach tangles. "My mother's life is not my own," she whispers.

It's dawn, according to the cast of pink in the eastern sky.

Vale wants to return to the dream: Jack's lips rising up her spine. Jack, a friend she sometimes sleeps with: a left-handed illustrator of hawks and eagles and peregrine falcons, half-Creole, who sleeps in a tree house in the backyard of a house full of musicians in the Ninth Ward. She doesn't love Jack. It's the easy coupling of their bodies she returns for; that tree house, the sounds of the city through its open windows. When the levees broke in 2005, Jack stayed put there in that house tacked to trees while the water rose around him.

What tree is Bonnie in? What abandoned

55

apartment/trailer/spot-below-a-train-bridge has she called her own?

Vale rises. Pours water into the rusted teakettle. Strikes a (miraculously) dry match and the stove's front burner bursts into flame.

When the water boils she makes a cup of instant coffee and reaches for her backpack. She pulls out her black notebook and slips the photo of Bonnie and her out from between the pages. Rubs her finger over her mother's narrow shoulder bones.

There's another photo, too, which she places on the table next to the first one. It's of Bonnie's mother, Lena, who died of a fever a few days after Bonnie was born. In the picture Lena stands outside the door of her cabin — a place set back in the woods somewhere on this hillside — in a dark fedora, a one-eyed barred owl perched on her shoulder. She wears a threadbare flannel shirt, blue jeans and tall boots, has a dark braid reaching halfway to her waist. Who the hell, Vale asks herself, looking at that photo and at that bird.

She only knows what Bonnie knew: that Lena lived in the one-room hunting camp at the top of the ridge overlooking the swamp with that owl named Otie. "My mother? Lunatic, bat-shit crazy, unwell,"

Bonnie would say, shrugging, laughing. "No wonder we're a little odd, V-bird." Vale wonders: Bipolar? Schizophrenic?

Three years ago Vale got a tattoo of an owl on her left shoulder in honor of that bird of Lena's: same markings, same eyes.

Vale finds thumbtacks in a drawer and tacks the photos to the wall above the table.

Bonnie never knew who her father was, either. "Who cares," she said, wrapping her arms around Vale in that bed where they slept together most nights until Vale was thirteen. "I have you and you have me." Sheets covered in yellow roses. Bonnie's long neck, the soft and warm skin of her belly.

The last time Vale spoke to Bonnie was two months ago. Bonnie was breathless. She told Vale about the love of Jesus and how it had found her. Her voice jittery and quaking — her thoughts disconnected — high on something — junk or Jesus or both. "His love is bright burning, honey. All-loving. Holy!" A hoarse laugh that turned into a cough. She said she'd joined a church somewhere. Told Vale it had changed her. That everything was finally making sense. "A new leaf, Vale-honey. I'm cleaning up, I swear."

"Are you?" Vale had asked. She was sitting on the fire escape of her room in Marigny, looking out over a sea of backyards: shrines, bicycles, vines, Christmas lights strung from rooftops.

"Sure I am," Bonnie said, before hanging up.

Vale finishes her coffee, puts the cup in the sink, and walks up the hill toward Deb's cabin.

They'd had dinner at Hazel's last night — a brief conversation, warm stew. Deb begged Vale to stay at her place in Danny's old room, but Vale declined. Said, "I like it where I am. All creeky."

"Can I borrow your truck?" Vale says now, standing in Deb's open doorway, her hands in her sweater pockets. Deb's cabin looks the same as it did eight years ago: the long porch running along one end, books and houseplants scattered everywhere, the yard one continuous tangle of garden. Deb stands in the kitchen with a cup of coffee in her hand. Her hair looks more gray in the morning light, her eyes more tired, but her face is still beautiful.

"The roads —"

"I don't care," Vale says. "I need to get there."

"Okay," Deb says, setting down her coffee

and reaching for the keys. "I'll go with you. I'll drive."

The damage is everywhere. They wind their way down back roads in Deb's rusted blue Toyota, the seats patched with duct tape, seeking a pathway. They turn around four times at washed-out culverts, try different routes.

Deb tries to make small talk, but Vale keeps her face turned to the window, mumbles her replies. "Let's try this way," Deb says quietly, pulling down yet another back road.

On every one they pass more destruction: new bends to old creeks, houses torn from their foundations, water carving new pathways through hillsides. Fluid — that's how the wrecked landscape looks to Vale. Not fixed, at all, as she had always presumed it to be. In New Orleans, sure. But here? She's always thought of this landscape as abhorrently stable.

It takes them an hour, but at last they find a way through.

Vale steadies her hand on the truck's door handle as they pull into the parking lot of Bonnie's apartment building.

Deb puts her hand on Vale's shoulder. "We're here. You all right?"

"Yes," Vale says, looking out the window at the torn-up river, at a house the color of mint ice cream across the street, at a woman turning from that house and walking toward a shed out back. Bent shoulders. A red coat. Not Bonnie.

Such pretty houses, Vale thinks. And inside so many of them: OxyContin, meth, heroin, fentanyl. Creeping into small towns like this one: a mill town, a hippie town. Winding its way up riverbanks. Anywhere poverty nestles. Where options and jobs are few.

Vale climbs the wooden, exterior staircase to that third-floor apartment — robin's-egg-blue Formica counters and a pink claw-foot tub, resting on rotting linoleum. She stops at the top of the stairs, closes her eyes, and breathes in. She wants her mother to open the door when she knocks. She wants Bonnie to put her arms around her and say, "Ha! And they thought I'd disappeared." She wants to see what her mother's eyes look like, lit up with her newfound love of Jesus. What might that love look like?

Deb puts her hand between Vale's shoulder blades. "You okay?"

"Vale," Dean says, opening the door. She hasn't seen him in eight years. He's worse for wear: arms shaking, jazzed pale-blue eyes. He opens the door wider, letting them in. "Long time no see. Come in. They'll find her. They will."

He's wearing gray sweatpants and a white tank top, has bruises threading up and down his thin arms.

Vale walks into the kitchen. Looks around. "You haven't seen her?"

He goes to the couch and lies down, sticks an unlit cigarette between his lips. "No. But she'll be back. She always comes back," he says quietly, closing his eyes.

Vale walks around the apartment slowly. Fast-food containers in the sink, pizza boxes in front of the TV, piles of clothes in corners. Vale settles in front of the windowsill where Bonnie's crystals are still lined up — dust-covered amethyst and quartz.

Beside them is a stack of tarot cards, a book on astrology, books on Native American mythology, and beside that, the Jesus stuff Vale's never seen before: a New Living Translation Holy Bible; a postcard of Mary holding the baby Jesus, his strangely thin limbs, small head, and adult features; a selection of brightly colored votive candles; a bowl full of rosaries.

Vale doesn't know what church her mother joined. Something within walking distance: Catholic, Baptist, evangelical. Vale notices how the rosaries, all shapes and colors and sizes — likely picked up at the thrift stores in town — make a bird's nest of sorts in the white bowl where they've been placed. Vale pockets a blue rosary.

Scrawled, with a black Sharpie on the wall next to the window, are the words: *Whoever drinks the water I give them will never thirst. — Matthew, 4:13.*

"She was high," Dean says from the couch, his eyes still closed.

Vale turns to look at him, her hands shaking in her pockets. "What?"

"She was high. She'd just shot up. Thought you'd want to know that."

Vale looks out the window: the creek and, on the far side, train tracks. "Goddamn you," she says, not looking at him.

He doesn't respond.

I'm cleaning up, baby. Getting clean, I swear! Bonnie said, the last time they spoke on the phone.

Vale goes to her mother's closet and sifts through the sweaters and T-shirts and jeans piled on the floor until she finds what she's looking for: the old peach-colored silk dress, full of holes, that her mother used to wear around the apartment when she was happy, gloriously drunk, at ease.

"This dress was my mother's," Bonnie

would say, slipping it over her shoulders. "The only thing I have of hers. Don't I look like a movie star in it? Glamorous like Rita Hayworth!" Rising and putting her arms around Vale's shoulders. Putting her cheek against Vale's cheek, making a kiss-face into the mirror.

Vale puts her nose into the dress: cigarette smoke, jasmine, sour sweat.

Deb touches Vale's arm. "You ready?"

Vale nods, heads toward the door.

"Don't worry," Dean calls out, grinning. "She'll come back. She always does."

Vale holds on tight to the stair railing on her way down.

Deb needs to go grocery shopping, but Vale wants to look around. "Pick me up here when you're done," she says, walking toward where the green bridge once stood. It hasn't yet been rebuilt; the street dead-ends in a gorge of broken concrete and twisted metal. For thirty feet downstream there's a tangle of branches, trees, boulders, rusted iron. The water has receded to its normal height. Water — so illusorily peaceful.

The air is cold, damp. A few raindrops slash against Vale's skin.

She lets out a slow breath, wraps her sweater around her shoulders.

"What on earth were you thinking?" Vale whispers, scrambling down the river's bank, pushing her way through and over downed branches and sumac. Tangled piles of rocks, river silt, trash. Plastic bottles. Metal cans. A sock — white and small. Vale bends and touches it. A child's sock. The heel threadbare. Vale sits down next to it. Closes her eyes.

Yesterday, reading the news on her phone, Vale saw a photo of a child in Somalia, where the droughts have been relentless: a boy sitting in a gray washtub, all bone. The victims will be plenty, Vale thinks. The victims are and will be everywhere.

Her mother is a fool, not a victim. One hundred pounds of skin and bones walking out into that torrential rain.

"Goddamn you, Bonnie," Vale whispers, rising.

They drive the twenty minutes home mostly in silence. Vale looks out the window at fields, a gray silo, a red barn, the bright streak of Silver Creek winking at them from between the trees. Every inch familiar, and in every shot something changed, upturned, carved anew. Living in New Orleans you get used to the shadow of storms, the earth's quiet yet undeniable sinking. You get used to recognizing the impermanence of the ground, the trees, the walls, your own skin.

But here? She isn't used to that temporality.

She thinks of glaciers melting, sea levels rising, widespread famine. Not one place is immune.

Deb pops a tape into the cassette player, and Etta James comes on singing "At Last." One of the many songs Bonnie loved — music for all those years her medicine and touchstone. Vale turns her eyes toward the trees flying by the windows and thinks of her mother's body, laughing and twirling, eyes closed, in peach silk. *At last.* Her mother will be found — she feels the fact of it in the cornfield passing by, in Etta's voice spooling: hope. Possibility. Redemption.

Back at the camper Vale pours herself a glass of gin. She picks up the silk dress, puts her face into it, and breathes in.

Vale pulls off her jeans and T-shirt and slips the dress over her shoulders. Strings the blue rosary over her neck. She charged her cell phone in Deb's truck: she turns it on now and blasts Missy's *Under Construction.* Looks at herself in the cracked and flyspecked mirror. She looks like her mother. She looks like Lena. She brings her glass to her lips, drinks; a breeze slips under the door, the air cool, damp, licking her ankles and shins.

DEB

June 14, 1974

There are seven of them who live there, sometimes more. There is Ginny (thick auburn hair, long-limbed, a laugh like a seal), there is Tim (skinny, acne, unbearably shy), Feather (quiet, pale) with her daughter, Opal, bearded Randy with a banjo, and a petite black woman named Bird.

"Bird?"

"Yes. Just Bird." She smiles at Deb, eyes gleaming.

Ginny, in a loose dress and red rain boots — braless breasts and jutting collarbones — gives her the lay of the land. There is the farmhouse, ancient, paint-flaking, on the hill, where they cook and rest and sleep and read. The walls are covered in artwork painted directly onto the plaster: a large, rough portrait of Emma Goldman with her arm around Martin Luther King, a picture of Woody Guthrie's guitar bearing the words *This guitar kills fascists,* various poems and sketches of mountains, forests, deer. Where there are not paintings on the walls there are bookshelves — pine boards resting on concrete blocks — filled to the brim and teetering in multiple directions.

Deb would like to spend all day looking at those bookshelves, but Ginny is leading her out the back door to the vegetable garden downhill of the house, a sea of green, which Deb assumes from where she stands is lettuce and spinach and peas but which, she finds out, once she's standing closer, is mostly weeds. The seedlings are in there, doing their best to surface and grow, but weeds and rocks, Deb discovers in the weeks to follow, always win.

There is the rusted school bus, resting on large stumps, where Opal was born, which now houses three ducks, twelve hens, and three roosters. "We couldn't bring ourselves to cut their heads off — yet," Ginny says, pointing to the three cocksure roosters, vying for their mothers' and sisters' love.

There is a barn where Ginny tells Deb they plan to someday have goats, sheep, cows, and pigs. "We want to make cheese — goat and cow's milk — and sell honey, too. Wool from the lambs," Ginny says. Her grin is radiant: spitfire.

Ginny takes one last look in the empty barn and lingers for a moment — tired perhaps, at the prospect of it all — and Deb decides she likes her. Her hair is pulled back in a ponytail that rains down her left shoulder. She is a realist, Deb thinks, despite her gazelle bones and cotton frock.

"And then there is the print shop," Ginny says, pointing the way.

The print shop is clearly where Ginny wants to be.

It's an old milking shed with a cluster of assorted tables gathered into its center. On one of the tables is a letterpress machine. On another is a printing press like the one in Deb's college art class.

"You're not messing around," Deb says.

"No," Ginny says.

There are stacks of papers everywhere, clotheslines running from one side of the room to the other, poems, etchings, and woodcuts pinned to them. There's a stack of flyers with a picture of Guthrie's guitar on it. "We hand those out in town," Ginny says, nodding toward them.

"Groovy," Deb says.

"Yes. It is," Ginny says, not smiling, but her green eyes warming. "We have to try and change the world, you know? Disrupt quiet New England any way we can."

"Yes," Deb says, fingering the flyer and thinking of her cousin Pierce, whose father bought his way out of Vietnam, thinking of her own half-assed activism and resistance. But she's here now. She has five $100 bills of her father's in her backpack, which she dreams of burning but doesn't dare.

"So," Ginny says, walking toward the door, and Deb follows. "You want to stay?"

They offer her the daybed on the porch and tell her the deal: you can stay for as long as you like, but you must work. Chip in. Do your part. If you don't, you will be politely asked to leave. It's Ginny who's talking, and Deb understands that Ginny is the wheel and the spoke around here. Both the feather boa and the center that holds. She also understands that if Ginny politely asks you to leave, you say thank you and leave.

In the farmhouse kitchen Bird flips potato cakes on the big wood stove. A Nina Simone record spins on a table in the living room. Deb offers to help, and Bird hands her a bowl of greens and nods toward the sink. Deb runs them under cool water but wonders what they are. They're nothing like her mother's iceberg lettuce.

"Dandelion. Sorrel. Plantain. Wild and

foraged," Bird says without looking up. Deb nods, pats them dry with an old dish towel, arranges them in the wooden bowl Bird hands her.

They eat at a big table in the living room, making space for their plates amid the books, canning jars full of flowers, and candles stuffed in the necks of empty wine bottles.

They laugh and tell stories that weave around one another. They talk about the Revolution, and Deb wonders what that word means for them. What is the revolution here in the woods? Bird quotes Frantz Fanon, whom Deb has never read (but she does, a few weeks later). "Each generation must discover its mission, fulfill it or betray it, in relative opacity," Bird says with tears in her eyes. She turns to them all: "And you, bitches. What will your mission be?"

Ginny lifts her glass of wine and toasts them all.

Randy says, "Fucking well. Fucking well is my mission," with a grin.

Ginny rolls her eyes. Bird says, "Asshole."

Feather gets up and puts on Dylan's *Blonde on Blonde,* and Randy and Ginny argue about whether goats are easier to milk than cows — teat size, milk production — and then Bird shouts, "Let's dance!" and

Ginny switches the Dylan to Ruth Brown and everyone gets up and starts dancing to "Lucky Lips." Drums. Horns. That irresistible Memphis swing.

Is she dreaming? Deb is bone tired. Unable to talk or keep up. After a second glass of wine she slips out the door to the screen porch. What will her mission be?

She takes off her pants and climbs under the heavy army-navy wool blankets, surprised by how cool it is already out here in the dark. There are peepers, stars, an occasional cluck or crow from the school bus. In the distance she can hear truck brakes from the highway, but that highway feels far away now. Moonlight falls on Deb's face through the battered screen, and at some point in the night she slips out from under the covers, opens the screen door, and steps out into that light. She's barefoot, barelegged, an old T-shirt slipping off her shoulders. She thinks: here I am. She thinks: have I ever been alive before now? Her legs and arms are covered in goose bumps. She squats to pee in the grass, and the piss hisses, then steams between her bare feet. The air smells like grass, like woods, like the heat from the chicken's coop. My life, she thinks. Is just beginning.

LENA

June 2, 1956

Woods,

Dawn. A blue jay screeches from the pines, a hermit thrush calls from behind a brush pile. My favorite songbird: it lurks in the understory, rarely seen, but sings the most beautiful of songs: spiraling flutelike melodies. Dangerously melancholy.

"Hermit thrush, Otie," I say. "Our state bird," walking downhill to milk the cows.

Four mornings a week I go to the barn at dawn to milk, clean the stalls, feed the newborn calves. My sister gives me cash at the start of every month. An envelope, thin with it.

"Thank you, Hazel," I say, hugging her. Her body retreats, but I hold on anyway. All bone and ropey muscle. Oh that they could become a cup — capable of holding, those bones! But she pulls away, my industrious, capable sister.

Lex does not work on the days I work; we take turns. But this morning there is a voice, tinged with brass, smoky like leather, from the back of the barn. Singing Elvis's "That's All Right." I gather a clean bucket hanging from the nail on the milk room wall and walk in the opposite direction of that singing.

I go toward Fran, a too-old Guernsey, pull up my stool, put my hands on her teats, and let the grass-rich milk spurt into the metal bucket. "Good girl," I whisper, putting my head against her side. I love these cows who keep on birthing, year after year. Every birth a loss. Milk sweetened with that grief.

I can hear him singing still. The barn plays tricks on sound, sends it in wrong directions.

The voice grows quiet. I think he's gone. But when I look up, Lex is standing above me, smiling in the morning light.

I duck my head, turn back to the bucket.

"Didn't realize it was your morning," he says quietly. "Must have lost track of the day."

"Or me," I say, rising, turning, heading for the milk room door.

"I don't mind the company," he says, following.

I pour the milk into the tank. Catch his eyes quickly. Leave by the back door and start walking.

Back at the cabin I pack a bag containing a knife and water, let Otie climb onto my shoulder.

We go west, over the top of the ridge, through the low-hanging arms of the tallest trees, up and over boulders.

Bear scat. Three-legged-coyote scat. Scrapings on beech bark from a bull moose, in heat and pining.

We cross Round Mountain to find Adele. She meets us on the porch, and I tell her I am afraid of my own body. Of what it wants. Adele puts a splash of rum into my smoky hemlock tea. Says, "Drink, Lena."

I do. She says, "It's hard to run away from oneself."

She steps off the porch and picks up her maul and starts splitting the ash logs piled up in the backyard.

I help her. I bring the unsplit logs to her, stack the pieces that shatter out from under the maul in neat piles near the door.

Otie watches us, clucking and hopping from log to log.

When the wood is stacked I lie back on the grass and spread my arms. My arms become the arms of a spider. My arms become a web. A yellow warbler calls out from the branches of a hemlock. A song sparrow from the other side of the road. I smile. Feel minuscule, evaporated.

"You're all right, Lena," Adele says, chuckling.

And then hunger strikes. "Climb on, Otie-O," I say to the bird, pointing to my shoulder, and he does, and we set off again, waving to Adele, walking over stone wall, over ledge, over stream and log, toward home.

DEB

September 8, 2011

Eleven days and no sign.

The main roads still shot. The power still out.

Deb cracks an egg into a pan, throws in some greens from the garden. It's the same twenty-four-inch-wide white propane stove — now rusted — Stephen put in thirty-seven years ago. Thirty-seven years. The number sounds like thunder in her head, somehow. Ridiculously heavy. Thirty-seven years of knife marks peppering the chopping block. Thirty-seven years of clutter everywhere she turns. Thirty-seven years of photographs tacked to her wall: Angela Davis, Simone de Beauvoir, Woody Guthrie, Nina Simone. Books of poetry scattered everywhere, too: Paley, Harjo, Neruda. Her wild-hearted late-life lovers, who somehow make joy out of their own suffering. Thoreau is still here, too, that dog-eared paperback she carried with her everywhere from age eighteen to twenty-two: *As you simplify your life, the laws of the universe will be simpler; solitude will not be solitude, poverty will not be poverty.* Solitude will not be solitude? Poverty not poverty?

Deb laughs out loud thinking of her young idealism. Of Thoreau's mother doing his laundry.

Deb still has a bucket under the sink. Her electricity still comes from a two-hundred-foot cord hooked up to Hazel's barn below — cuts in and out every time the wind blows. Her son, Danny, the one person she truly loves in the world, the one person she pines for — is living in a village in Guatemala. Ever restless. My God, she misses him.

If thirty-seven is thunder, fifty-nine is a freight train, Deb thinks, sipping her wine, bringing her eggs to the table. She turns on the radio, and there is a story about the number of natural disasters in the past two years. In January of last year: the earthquake in Haiti that killed 150,000. This March: the earthquake in Japan with its thirty-foot-high tsunami, Fukushima's leaked radiation, and 15,000 people dead. The ongoing droughts in East Africa that have killed an estimated 30,000 children. "Waking the beast," the reporter says.

"Shit," Deb says, turning off the radio. *Thirty thousand children.* She thinks: one town, hillside, island, coastal city, country, mountain at a time. Points on the map, scattered, until the points meld into one bright flame.

The storm up here on the hill had been so quiet. Deceptively so. At some point midmorning the power blinked, then went out, but no hurricane after all, Deb thought, slipping on a raincoat and boots and stepping out into the deluge.

A half mile downstream she discovered the damage — trees downed, power lines down, the roads washed out in all directions. She's never known a storm anything like this one. All that day: helicopters flying overhead — military and emergency crews — rescuing elders, dropping emergency supplies. And then the news of Bonnie.

Deb climbing in the rain, to the top of the field to call Vale: *Your mother.*

Yesterday Deb looked out her kitchen window and saw Vale walking across the field looking like a twentieth-century Tess of the D'Urbervilles: raven-dark hair in a tangled fray, brown eyes, crimson dress, a tattoo of an owl on her left shoulder. You never know who the victims will be, do you, Deb had thought in that moment, her heart in her knees.

It all leads to a near-crippling anxiety, which she deflects, most days, with her garden — raspberries, apples, peaches, pears, a quarter acre of vegetables, put up in jars — and her birds, one rooster and four hens. The rest of her time she fills with part-time and poorly paid jobs: housecleaning, gardening, elder care. All of it making her too eccentric, she knows, with her wine and books, her ceaseless solitude.

Deb pours herself another glass of the cheap but good Malbec from Argentina that smells of dirt and blackberries, the kind Deb combs these hillsides for throughout July and August. She bought a case of it in case they're stranded here for weeks. Deb is two-thirds through the bottle, her head dizzy, her thoughts soft the way she likes them.

"Fuckin'-A, Thoreau," she says out loud, lifting her glass of wine in the air and thinking of that berry of time when she was young and idealistic, how it had felt then like the perfect fruit — her life in the country — and how such a fruit can darken, age, ferment, become unfathomably complex.

Deb closes her eyes and sees Bonnie in a hard rain, Bonnie on a bridge, thin wrists, bruised bones. Will they find her? Helpless; that's what Deb is up here on this hillside. *Helpless,* she thinks, humming Stephen's favorite Neil Young song.

VALE

Vale borrows Deb's pickup truck and drives to town. The state highway is being worked on by crews from Virginia, Delaware, and Tennessee. A national disaster — that's what this one qualified as. FEMA funds to repair bridges, rebuild roads, compensate families for the houses that were washed away. Vale imagines those FEMA workers making their way downstream. Pictures some young kid, come north for the first time to repair roads, stumbling across Bonnie's body.

Vale gets her news updates from Deb at dinner. Each night Deb makes a thick stew out of dried beans and vegetables from her garden, brings it to Hazel's house, ladles it into bowls. Fresh warm bread and wine, too. Deb, wearing, as always, her blue jeans and flannel shirts. Vale thinking, *a face grown into this place.* Altered by it. Silver fox. Who is she? Vale never says much at dinner. Nods thank-you. Slips out the door.

This morning she drives slow around backstreets, eyeing the faces on porches, the faces in doorways. A girl, six or seven, sits on a porch in a puffy pink jacket, a cat rubbing up against her knees. There's a woman talking on the phone in an open doorway, her bare foot resting on her inner thigh. Vale thinks of Bonnie cleaning Motel 6 rooms. Bonnie working at the Sunoco. Bonnie cleaning up shit and vomit from toilets and shower stalls. No sick leave and late nights. When Vale was thirteen Bonnie tripped down the last third of the apartment stairs, broke her arm, was sent home with a never-ending prescription of little white pills for the pain.

Vale goes to the copy store and slips the photo of Bonnie at the river into the photocopier. She blocks her own face from the image, blows Bonnie's up to triple size. Writes: MISSING. PLEASE CALL IF SEEN, in thick letters, makes forty copies and posts them everywhere: grocery stores, gas stations, laundromats. Bonnie's face at the women's crisis center. Bonnie's face at the drop-in center. Bonnie's face tacked on the doors of various churches in town.

Which one was Bonnie's?

Most of the churches are locked, but the door of the Evangelical Baptist — a one-story concrete building at the edge of town — opens. Vale enters, sits in the back pew, and looks around. She can see why Bonnie might have come here: this large quiet room with so little inside. The church is mostly barren: blue carpet, wooden pews, a simple wooden cross affixed to the wall. The emptiness itself merciful. The heat must come from the people who show up here, Vale thinks.

She rises and steps closer to the nave. "Hello?" she calls out, her voice echoing.

"Welcome," a voice comes from a side room.

A tall man in his sixties approaches her. Kind eyes. Blue jeans.

"Do you know her?" Vale asks, handing him the photograph of Bonnie.

This man steps closer. He looks at the photo for a long moment. "Yeah," he says slowly. "I recognize her. She would come in occasionally."

Bonnie's church. This is the one. Vale feels a tingle at the back of her neck.

"Have you seen her lately?"

He looks Vale up and down slowly. "I don't think so," he says softly. "No. Not since the storm."

"Come back anytime," he calls out, as Vale turns. "You are welcome here! Jesus welcomes all through this door!" His voice rising.

Vale drives herself to a tattoo parlor, the one next to the 7-Eleven. It doesn't matter what kind of tattoo parlor; she isn't particular. She knows what she wants: to feel the burn of the needle, the slow release of red ink into skin.

It's an image of poppies, strewing, that she's had in her mind for years.

Poppies — that glorious flower. Wild in the deserts of Arizona and California. Cultivated in the gardens of New England. Propagated in Afghanistan, Turkey, Pakistan, and Colombia in farmers' dry and arid fields, so that those farmers can make a living, feed their children, send their sons to school. The opium sap cultivated, refined into morphine, further refined into heroin, shipped, on the black market, to New York, then driven upriver, through Springfield and north, under the seats of cars, and sold, in Nelson, for five or ten dollars a bag.

Cheap enough for Bonnie, addicted to her OxyContin. Cheap enough for half of Vale's old high-school friends.

Vale pulls up a photo on her phone and shows it to the woman inking: two red poppy flowers, the petals unloosing in the wind, on the arm opposite Vale's owl. One stalk. One set of roots. Two heads: Bonnie and Vale.

"Cool," the woman says, ink threading up and down both of her arms: snakes, vines, a pistol, a bear.

She smacks her gum loudly. Has a bright smile.

"What's it signify?"

"Nothing," Vale says, closing her eyes. Ten years of Bonnie injecting that poppy's serum, relief in ultrarefined form, into any vein she can find.

Vale picks up her phone and glances at the news headlines: a photo of a Somali refugee, a woman, carrying jerry cans of water from a tap at the Dagahaley camp in Dadaab.

The woman is beautiful: a gray headscarf and dark, resilient eyes. In the background — dead trees, a cow on its side, eddies of trash swirling around its gutted body.

The tattoo takes three hours and most of the cash Vale has left. The parking lot is dark by the time it's done. Vale drives through the streets of Nelson one last time before going home — past the Indian grocery, up and down backstreets, past the lit windows of apartments and houses where couples watch TV, babies sleep, kids do homework.

She drives slow, stares into every window.

How easy it would be to head back to that apartment in New Orleans where the magnolias and camellias bloom. To that city, braided in beautiful ways. Jack: slipping her shirt up over her head, taking a pen and drawing birds and vines across her breast, neck, shoulders.

But she can't, yet.

Dean: *She comes back. She always does.*

Bonnie, neck tipped back, laughing. Bonnie in a field of corn stubble, walking this way.

DEB

July 20, 1974

It's Tim she thinks she loves at first —
despite the field of acne — but it's Bird who
finds her. They are in the garden weeding
the tomatoes. The weeds are voracious, a
forest unto themselves, and they are there
for hours, pulling, plucking, under Amish
straw hats Tim brought back from a shop in
western Pennsylvania. They take off their
jeans and dresses, wear just their underwear
and cotton T-shirts, sleeves and necks cut
off to let in the air. Deb's back and shoulders are pink, raw, but the pain will come
later, will be soothed by creek water. For
now there are the weeds amid the tomatoes,
the rows upon rows ahead of them, brought
on by June rain. And there is Bird, before
her.

She doesn't know much about Bird. She's
from Atlanta, met Ginny at Yale. They came

north together in Bird's blue Saab 96, which her father, a banker, bought for her. Bird has all the best records: Ruth Brown, Nina Simone, Billie Holiday. When she dances in the living room, all eyes are on her.

She tells them stories about a grand-mother from Mexico City — *aristocratic* — and another grandmother — a goat farmer from the mountains of Greece. Tips her head back. Laughs. "I didn't inherit her love of the land."

Now, in the garden, Bird throws herself back onto the dirt and closes her eyes. "Goddamn manual labor," she whispers. "I'm parched. Why did we all come here again?"

Deb rubs the sweat out of her eyes, smear-ing dirt across her face. It's true. It's not at all how she thought, the day-in-and-day-out relentlessness of physical labor. Her back aches. Her legs ache. Her neck screams from sunburn. Bird rolls over and turns toward Deb. She puts her thin, dirt-caked hand on Deb's thigh. "Perhaps we should retire," she says, smiling.

Deb looks back, surprised. Her leg is cool where Bird's hand touches it.

"Perhaps," she says.

They go back to the house — its rooms refreshingly cool — and up the stairs to

Bird's room. Deb feels Ginny's eyes on them where she stands at the kitchen sink — suspect, or wounded, Deb can't tell. Deb follows Bird up the back stairway.

Her room is above the kitchen, an attic room with low ceilings and a bed on the floor. "Part of the Underground Railroad, I think, this room," Bird says. There are candles everywhere, a tapestry hanging as a curtain. She undresses Deb and Deb undresses her. Deb has never kissed a woman, never touched a nipple other than her own, never slipped a finger inside another woman's body. Never had a woman's hand draw constellations of the freckles on her sunburnt chest. She spends the evening and the night there, wrapped in Bird's arms, watching moonlight make its way across the rafters.

When she wakes, Bird is sitting in bed with a cigarette, listening to Gil Scott-Heron's "The Revolution Will Not Be Televised."

Bird grins at Deb; Deb flings her head back on the pillow, laughs. Lies there in the cotton sheets listening to the song and to the rooster below and to the crickets beyond them. She puts her hand on Bird's arm. Closes her eyes. *The revolution will be no re-*

run, brothers, Gil Scott-Heron sings. *The revolution will be live.*

VALE

September 18, 2011

It's 4 P.M. and there's an explosive rattle from the icebox below the counter. The lightbulb above the table blinks twice, then stays on.

Electricity.

Vale plugs in her phone, which has been dead for two days. There's a message from the police department — Vale's heart freezes for a moment as she listens. The officer who called says someone saw a person matching the description of Bonnie sleeping under the train bridge. That they will check it out, be in touch if they find anything.

Vale climbs out of bed where she's been for hours and puts on her sweater — she's suddenly chilled all over. She pours water from the plastic jug on the counter into the teakettle, strikes a match.

When the water's warm she wets a washcloth and cleans herself — her face and neck, under her arms, between her legs, rinses the washcloth and hangs it over the heater to dry.

She's been here for way too many days. They slip into one another. Lead nowhere.

But Bonnie under the train bridge: Vale pictures her hiding out there, near the water she's always loved, the storm her way of getting clean.

Vale checks the rest of the messages on her phone. Freddie at the bar: *WORRIED ABOUT YOU.* A couple from the club: *WHERE THE HELL.* One from Shante: *LOVE WHERE ARE YOU?* And one from Jack: *BABE!*

Vale makes a cup of instant coffee. Downs it.

She's been here for nearly three weeks. Too long. Too many days driving back roads and backstreets, hanging up more posters. Too many days of eating the stews and breads Deb brings to Hazel's house, drinking wine and leaving quietly.

Bonnie by the train bridge: Vale would drive there now, but she can see from here that Deb's pickup is gone.

Vale looks out her window at Hazel's house on the hill, the house where Bonnie lived for the first eighteen years of her life, and wonders what, if anything, is left of Bonnie there: bottles of nail polish, cassette tapes, clothes?

Vale puts on her jeans and boots, slips her phone into her pocket, and heads that way.

Passing the barn, Vale remembers a story Hazel once told her. Two slaves, a mother and daughter, uprooted from the barn and turned in. Is that story real? Vale wants to find the photos of those ancestors, look into their eyes and say, "Bastards." She wants to find a photo of her mother as a girl. Are there any?

"The power's back on," Vale says to Hazel.

"Oh yes," Hazel says. "Isn't that nice." She's sitting at the kitchen table, an empty teacup between her hands.

"A relief, huh?"

Hazel nods, turns toward the window.

"I was wondering if there are any family photographs?"

Hazel's eyes — pale blue, washed out with cataracts — are blank for a moment, then register, as if returning from someone or something far away.

"Photographs? Oh yes. I think there are some in the attic."

"Thanks," Vale says, heading toward the stairs.

There are dust bunnies collecting in the corners. It seems unlike the Hazel Vale once knew to let the dust collect like this. Vale can't remember a moment when Hazel was not cleaning in some way, keeping the wildness at bay with any tools at hand: broom, vacuum, sickle bar, scythe.

"I come from puritanical hard-asses," Bonnie saying. "They care only about the land and the dead. The land and the dead! As if this land was theirs to begin with! As if it wasn't stolen from Indians." Bonnie brushing Vale's hair. Parting it down the middle. Weaving it into a French braid.

Vale's pretty sure Bonnie slept in the small, east-facing room at the top of the stairs. She opens the door, steps in. There's an iron bed in the corner, a wool blanket pulled taut across it, faded yellow curtains. Vale looks in the closet — empty. Pulls open the dresser drawers — bare. She goes to the window and looks out at the view Bonnie had for her first eighteen years: Round Mountain, evergreens, Silver Creek. She puts her fingers on the windowsill and feels something scratched there, looks down: *Bonnie,* etched into the pine with the tip of a knife. The scraped wood is brown and faded — an old wound. Vale imagines sixteen-year-old Bonnie, that knife in her hand, desperate to get elsewhere. "You got free," Vale whispers, fingering the grooves.

The attic is a second-story low-gabled room above the kitchen: a single window at the far end, exposed rafters blackened with age. The floor is covered in old furniture, crates, chests, boxes. The detritus of two hundred years piled up, dust-covered, smelling of risen woodsmoke. There doesn't appear to be anything of Bonnie's. Just moth-eaten quilts and blankets, cracked dishes. Vale's ready to leave when she spies, on an upper shelf, a dark blue photo album. She reaches for it, wipes the dust off with her sleeve, flips open the cover. The first photo is of the entire family in front of this house. The wooded hillsides and open fields, a pair of oxen, boys in britches, girls in white cotton with furrowed brows, their lips straight lines and eyes hard as stones. Goddamn, Vale thinks. What stoicism. Where was the joy? At the bottom of the photo, scrawled in pencil, is the year 1901. Their names are scrawled there, too — Henry, Ezekial Jr., Faith and Helen, Willem, and on the far right side, Henry's young wife, Marie. Vale cannot take her eyes off Marie. She's pretty sure she's Hazel's grandmother — she recognizes the name — though she's never seen this photo before. Or any photo

of her. She has a wide face, dark almond-shaped eyes, two braids — thick and glossy — that fall down both shoulders. She looks Indian — Abenaki — Vale thinks. She touches the photo with her finger. Looks out the dust-hazed window toward the field beyond. Bonnie, years ago, tacking a dream catcher above Vale's bed: "You and me? We're Indian. Don't you think? I can feel it in my bones! Some native blood, somewhere. That's the wild streak in me. And in my mother. And in you, my darling!" Vale loved that theory for years, and then she learned about colonialism: their white ancestors stealing land from the Abenaki and calling it their own. Plagues. Massacres. And Bonnie's obsession made Vale cringe.

Vale looks through the rest of the pages, but there are no other pictures of Marie. Just the house becoming more worn down as the years pass.

No pictures of Bonnie either.

But Marie. Vale's great-great-grandmother.

Vale pulls the photo from the album, sticks it in her jacket pocket, and heads toward the door. At the threshold she pauses, something catching her eye. There's a hat resting on a pile of cardboard boxes. A dark green fedora, a feather tucked in its brim.

Lena's hat from the photo.

"Hell yes," Vale whispers, climbing over boxes to reach it. She picks it up, dusts it off, slips it on. The hat, miraculously, has not been eaten by moths. Fits Vale near perfectly.

Vale tacks the photo of Marie and the farmhouse to the camper wall next to the photos of Lena and Bonnie.

She checks her phone: a new message from the police.

Vale listens, her heart — stubborn — racing. They located the woman living below the train bridge, the officer says. It was a thirty-year-old woman. Not Bonnie.

Vale pours herself a tall glass of rum. Turns the light on — a strange novelty. Finds some Odetta on her phone.

She places Lena's hat on her head and eyes her reflection in the mirror tacked above the sink — she looks like Lena. The feather — Turkey? Owl? Eagle? Grouse?

And like — the almond shape of her eyes, the roundness of her cheeks — Marie, her great-great-grandmother. Those eyes, reluctant, half turning away.

She thinks of Jack, black-Creole, peppering the streets with his bird graffiti. She thinks of Shante playing old French folk

songs learned from her grandmother.

"Will you be my dance accompaniment?" Shante asked Vale not long ago. Vale had shrugged, spun around the apartment in purple lace and black leather. She made Shante cocktails, nasturtiums from the garden out back floating on the top. They went to the roof with a blanket and lay there in the hot sun.

"Who were you?" Vale asks Marie. The woman's eyes are not looking at the photographer but toward the field to her left, as if something is moving there — cat, creature, child. Vale takes a long sip of her rum. "Who are you?" Vale asks her own reflection in the mirror. She pulls some lipstick out of her bag and paints her lips bright red, dances to Odetta singing, "Don't Think Twice, It's All Right," in small circles around the room.

Hazel

September 19, 2011

A voice upstairs, calling. Bonnie? She goes that way. To the room at the top of the stairs, under the eaves, the room where her mother, Jessie, lay dying, and where, later, Bonnie slept.

She pushes the door open: drawn faded yellow curtains, a wool blanket the color of cream pulled tight across the bed. Hazel sits down on that blanket. She cleared out all of Bonnie's things — threw them into plastic bags and took them to the dump — years ago. Hazel smooths down the creases below her. She looks around. Smell of dust and mothballs. Smell of old lath and plaster. Didn't she hear a voice calling?

What was it Vale asked her yesterday afternoon?

"Hazel. What do you know about this

photo?" she had said, coming down the stairs.

Hazel was at the kitchen sink, staring out the window. She turned and looked at Vale for a long moment. She was wearing a green fedora, a turkey feather tucked into its brim. "Lena," Hazel said.

"What? No. I'm Vale. I'm Vale, wearing Lena's hat. I found it in the attic. See? Me. Vale," taking the hat off.

"Oh," Hazel said, blinking.

And then Vale showed Hazel the photo. This house with fresh white paint, the family in dark suits, pale wool and cotton, standing before it.

"Oh yes," Hazel said, a streak of warmth through her chest. "Look at that. Our people."

"And this? Who's this?"

"That's my grandmother. Marie. She died when I was eleven or twelve."

"Was she Abenaki?"

"What?" Hazel's eyes flicked upward at Vale. "Of course not. We're not Indian."

"Okay. I see."

And then Vale had left, taking the photo with her, and Hazel had returned her eyes to the field and its sunstruck view. Gypsy-nigger, her father called Buck, the man who lived back in the woods.

Hazel hasn't thought of him in years.

"Mother?" Hazel says quietly, turning back toward the bed. "Are you here?"

But of course there is no one.

The house used to be so quiet without electricity. Lena in the corner with her barn kittens. Lena: eight years younger than Hazel. Deathly shy. She wouldn't speak at school. Wouldn't speak to strangers. Made a fuss every time their mother, or later, Hazel, tried to brush her hair or scrub the dirt behind her ears. She refused to wear dresses, wanted to go naked, or wear blue jeans. It was animals she loved: barn cats in boxes in the kitchen. A pet baby squirrel, tucked into the front of her shirt. Once, after their mother died, Hazel found Lena in the cellar. She had cracked open every last jar of canned peaches. Those peaches: their mother's light — sweet and perfect — put up in jars, the top on every single one opened.

A quick slap across her face. Hazel had loved their mother, too. Had wanted to never touch those jars of summer, preserved.

Lena was nine when their mother died. Hazel was seventeen. Lena refused, after that, to go to school. Lena taking off into the woods. Truancy officers. A threat of her being taken away, and Hazel saying, with all her might: "No."

"Don't you think, Mother," Hazel says out loud, toward the bed, where her mother lies sleeping, face serene and beautiful, "that we should fill the hot water bottles?"

Her mother nods.

She did her best, didn't she? Their mother, for that year of darkness, breathing quietly in this room. These same yellow curtains. Lena would bring her jars of wildflowers, line them up on the bedside table, bright and faded and rotting in jars — Joe-Pye weed, buttercup, black-eyed Susan. Her father below: too quiet. Quiet footprints on soft pine.

Stop this. Hazel closes her eyes.

Hazel turns back to her mother, but she is not there. Empty sheets. The blanket pulled taut.

The taste of metal in the back of Hazel's mouth.

What is wrong with her? Hazel brought her mother soups as she was dying. Cups of tea. Cups of water. Breeze through the open window. Of course her mother is not here. Ninety years old and her mind is parchment, filament. Hazel lurches up from the bed and goes to the window. She looks out at the backside of the field and at the woods, sloping upward behind it.

"No, we are not Indian," Hazel says out loud. "Right, Mother?" Her mother's face moon-colored. Glowing from within. Hazel goes to her and kisses her brow. Her mother puts her hand on Hazel's shaking shoulder. Holds it there.

LENA

June 9, 1956

Dear Dusk,
   The cabin, this evening, smells like Otie's box in the corner, filled with moss and lichen and leaves. It smells like the pellets he throws up every day, full of fur and bones. I cover my mouth as I scrape the bottom of the box into a bucket, cleaning the putrid moss and leaves. Otie closes his eye and falls into a deep sleep. When I'm done I wash my hands with soap and collected rainwater. Pour more water into the teacup with a rose painted in its middle. Take a long drink. Look out at the darkening sky.
   I run my palms down my thighs, slip off my pants, pull the blood-soaked rag from between my legs. I wash it out in a pan of water warmed on the stove. The water runs red. More water. Rinse again. Hang it to dry on a nail above the wood stove. My

body pining for a child, Otie. The only thing I've ever wanted. A child! If I'm lucky, a girl, for reasons I don't know.

Otie wakes, hops around, sniffing, prowling, occasionally calling out. To some nearby lover? His one eye, his broken wing. What a match we are: our one-eye and our off-eye, my left one, drifting upward. "Unlovable, always," I say to Otie, putting a clean rag between my legs. Sitting back down at the table. "You and me."

I pull out my notebook, flip through the pages: drawings of beavers, moose, bear, mink, weasel, fisher, coyote.

I write: *Near the sickness also lies the cure* — something Adele told me. She knows the names and the purposes of all the roadside weeds.

For bleeding: bloodroot (strung around the neck), white pine for hemorrhage.

Colds and fever: balsam, hemlock, aspen, black spruce, white pine, cedar.

I think of my grandmother, Marie, who died when I was four, braiding my long, thick hair by the fire. Of her cups of fragrant, woods-rich tea.

Otie watches me draw, eye blinking. Owls mate for life, I read in my book. Does he think I am his partner? "I love you, too, Otie-O," I say, and he closes his eye, contented. I've been told an owl's memory of place is so keen, it can fly between branches of trees in total darkness.

"Shall we walk, Otie?"

At the bottom of the hill we hear music and circle the big house. The living room windows are open, and from them slips the voice of Buck Owens, crooning.

I slide against the clapboards of the house, stepping behind lilac and over periwinkle, holding my body close to the wall, and peer in.

Stephen is in the corner playing with a matchbox. His thin boy limbs. Shock of blond hair across his brow. Stephen! Beautiful child. Hazel is at the kitchen sink, blue dress and bent shoulders. I want to take those shoulders in my hands. Pull them back. Say: *There now.*

Lex sits in the chair next to the radio, a glass of bourbon in his hand, eyes closed, foot tapping. Long legs. Cheekbones. War-damaged. Song-strewn.

I turn from the window and put my back against the pine clapboard siding. White chips of paint flake off under my fingernails. I close my eyes. Feel Otie's ever-present talons on my collarbone. Feel the evening dew settle on my scalp and cheeks. Hold my body there — electric.

Down by the creek, the *yip-yip-yip!* of that three-legged coyote friend.

"Like you and me, Otie," I whisper, slipping away from the house, and walking back toward home. "Nocturnal. Pining."

VALE

Vale wakes at dawn. Puts on Lena's hat. Turns up the gas heater on the wall.

She is drinking too much. Losing track of reality. Is Bonnie back at the swamp, in some woodland cave somewhere, drinking hemlock tea over an open fire?

Last night Vale asked Deb if she has any books about Vermont's native peoples, and Deb returned from her cabin later with two: one about Abenaki history and a small book that fits in Vale's palm, called *No Word for Time.*

This morning Vale makes coffee and opens the books.

How is it she's lived here for most of her life, went to school here, and knows nothing of Vermont's native people? Some petroglyphs near the falls where she and Jimmy used to skinny-dip and get high. The place

109

in the river called Indian Love Call where her mother used to take her. Bonnie would make a hooting sound up toward the rock cliffs and when her echo came back, say, "See? Indian ghosts. Yours and mine!" Slip off her dress and leap — naked — into that cold water. Vale eyeing the woods around them, hoping no one was near.

Vale sits at the table, the lamp buzzing above her head, and flips through the books' pages. In the history book she reads about the Years of the Beaver: colonization, disease, genocide, with fewer than one thousand Abenaki remaining after the Revolutionary War. She reads about the early Years of the Fox — the late 1820s to mid-twentieth century — the time of Marie's photo — when many fled north into exile. Some chose to stay and merge with French Canadian neighbors. Others chose the Path of the Fox: heading for mountains and rivers, and others, to "pass" into English-American culture. The photo of Marie, according to the writing scrawled on its back, was taken in 1901, likely a few years before Lena's mother, Jessie, was born. Was Marie trying to pass?

Vale reads about something she's never known before. In the 1920s, the state's Commission on Country Life launched the

110

Vermont Eugenics Survey, whose explicit mission was to codify and perpetuate the state's lily-white reputation. The result: twenty years of institutionalizing Vermont's poor, uneducated, and people of color. Many of those targeted were the Abenaki. Many had their children taken from them. Many were sterilized. Others went into hiding — the woods, or camps by the river — or denied their native blood.

Vale closes the book. Pours herself another cup of coffee. Drinks it slowly. She looks at Marie's photo on the wall and thinks how that eugenics movement was still happening when Lena and Hazel were girls. Vale pictures Marie moving to this white house on the hill, unbraiding her dark hair, cinching an apron around her waist, unlearning her mother tongue. No longer going into the swamps to gather sweetgrass. Not telling her granddaughters much of anything, for their own protection, and hers.

Vale puts down the book and goes outside. It's cold. A bitter, balsam-scented wind rising up from the creek. She wraps her sweater around her, pulls Lena's hat low over her eyes and ears. Woodsmoke rises from Deb's cabin on the hill above her; sunlight reflects off Hazel's kitchen windows.

Vale pisses on the creek side of the

camper. The piss makes eddies through the dirt and grass. She rises. Lifts her arms above her head. Feels the sunlight on her face. "Jesus," she whispers, feeling the landscape unfolding in new ways.

Back inside Vale opens the pages of the smaller book, *No Word for Time.*

It's a book about the spirituality of the Algonquin people, of whom, Vale learns, the Abenaki are part.

The author, Pritchard, writes that for the Algonquin peoples, "to do damage to the earth does spiritual damage as well."

Vale feels that line in her chest. She sets the book down. Thinks of the earth's warming and the resulting storms. Thinks of oil spills, beach-wrecked birds, landfills full of plastic. She thinks of Bonnie's spiritual damage, those many books on her shelf — each an attempt to get found.

Vale laces her boots, buttons her sweater, and walks into the woods. They're ravaged still, the banks of the creek no longer mossy, fern-touched, Japanese-looking in their ancientness, but wrecked — upturned gravel, torn-up trees.

She walked up this part of the creek once with Danny, years ago. Leaping from stone to stone, balancing her way across fallen logs. "You're a natural-born ballerina, Vale!" he called out as she crossed the log, and she was — her body, in those moments, pure light. She was in love with him then. Danny, her cousin, nine years older than her, playing Leonard Cohen songs in the hayloft of the barn. Danny putting on the Rolling Stones in Deb's cabin up there on the hillside — turning the volume up, nodding his head, pouting his lips like Mick Jagger.

She wanted to be a dancer then: a ballerina in pink and white. Bruised toes and bobby pins. Not exactly how she'd describe her nights at the club, but not entirely different, either. Her body muscle and lightning. Fully capable. The last time she talked to Bonnie on the phone she told her that she was dancing — enough to pay her bills. She didn't tell her what kind. Bonnie's voice reeking pride — "Oh honey. That's so fine! I'm so proud of you! I always knew you were pure grace. Divine!" Then her voice drifting off into distraction, or exhaustion. Saying she had to go.

Vale continues along the bank, upstream. Farther back, where the creek turns to swamp, the damage lessens. Just fields of flattened bluestem, flattened ferns.

Eerily quiet. Eerily still.

Vale bends down and looks into the mud

at the edge of the open water: Deer tracks. Dog or coyote tracks.

No mother tracks.

This might be where I would come, Vale thinks, if the world were ending.

Is it ending? How high do the seas have to rise, how many storms, before the world as they know it is no more?

There are other tracks she doesn't recognize. Fisher? Weasel? Fox? Animals waking with the dawn and coming to water. I'll be like them in the apocalyptic near future, Vale thinks — eyes wild, ears pricked, head ever-turning. Living back here near the fertile swamp, relearning all those things that were forgotten.

Vale puts her palm into the murky, mud- and moss-flecked swamp water, and thinks of herself under bright lights at the strip club, undressing. The heat of the lights, sweat pouring out along her spine and under her arms. She thinks of the muscles in her legs, burning, and how she learned, up there, to make the greatest effort appear effortless — how to make the hardest work full of grace.

"We've got Gypsy souls," her mother saying, dancing around the living room in the apartment in an old T-shirt. "Gypsy souls! You and me. Screw the unbelievers who say otherwise. Indian souls! I can feel it in my *bones,* Vale-love."

Vale pulls her sweater around her neck, raises her face to the darkening clouds moving in fast from the west, to the drops of rain falling, just now, from those clouds.

"Are you here, Bonnie?" Vale says out loud.

Blue jay in the highest pine. Flash of far-off lightning.

Vale bends and puts her fingers into the print of that dog's or coyote's track, lifts her finger and smells it: heady scent of swamp water.

LENA

June 18, 1956

Birds,

I go to barn dances, because I love to dance. What God doesn't exist in that boot sole on pine floor, in that spinning? I don't go to church, despite my sister's urgent pleas. My mother died when I was nine years old; why would I go to church and pray to that cold God? My God is in the tree roots, in the creek song, in the smell of wild mushrooms and the potent scent of herbs. My God is in the face of Otie — God face — Owl face — Moon face — One-Eyed — and in the way he looks at me, silent, neck turning. His sharp talons. His forever hunger. Name that God to me and I will name my God to you.

My God is in the music, too — fiddle, bass, guitar, drum. My God is in the sweat and sway, the touch and the turning. And so I go to the dances.

I leave Otie in the cabin in his box against the wall. Two mice a day — that's what he needs. I have live traps set up all along the foundation and along the stone walls. I pull the mice out by their tails, whisper *thank you* in their ears, hand them to Otie, who lunges, devouring.

I ask Adele how to say thank you in her language, and she tells me it's *oliwni*. "*Oli-wni*," I whisper in the mouse's petrified ear.

I ask Adele the word for owl and she tells me it's *gohkohkhas*. "*Gohkohkhas*," I say to Otie, "take care of yourself, my friend. I would take you dancing if I could, but they would call me a loon." Otie blinks back, long and slow.

I slip out of my blue jeans and into an old dress of my sister's. Peach-colored silk, pearl buttons, a stain on the hip and a rip up the side I've mended with crude stitches.

Will you ever learn to sew? My sister has asked me for years. My quick answer, always with a smile: *no.*

I put my hair in two braids and don my wool hat.

I put my boots on and take a sip of whiskey and say, "How do I look?" to Otie, who blinks from his crate, serene and mum.

I walk down the hill and catch a ride with Hazel and Stephen. My sister brings a chicken pot pie, a Jell-O mold, and a carafe of coffee. She eyes me and my dress side-long: "You're wearing that?"

I smile. Touch the soft tip of my sister's nose. The cool line of it. She turns away, starts the car, drives.

I turn around to talk to Stephen. Six years old and moss-colored eyes like his dad's. He is grinning at me. I am grinning at him. He asks where Otie is, and I tell him I left him at home with the stars for company. That he would be terrified by the dancing — think we'd all gone mad. I touch Stephen's knee and ask if he will dance with me tonight. He shrugs. Smiles. Shakes his head.

I tell him that Adele told me, not long ago, a story about a woman who married an owl, and that I want to tell him the story some-time. That I think he will like it.

"The woman who married an owl?" He beams, showing off his crooked teeth, the new gaps there.

"Oh yes. And it might be me. It might just be a story about me!" I wink at him and turn back toward the open road. I roll my window down and take off my hat and put my head out and feel the wind in my face

and in my eyes and I call out in Otie's song
— *hoo, hoo, who-cooks-for-you*! — to the
dimming night air.

"Get your head back in here," my sister
says. I reach over and pinch her thigh. Turn
back to wink at Stephen, laughing in the
backseat.

Lex is the one who plays the fiddle. The one
with the fern-colored eyes, faint rims of
black. When he plays, it is like his body
becomes untied from this earth except for
one electric wire that runs from his left toe
to the top of his head. He spins around that
wire, rocking this way and that, shaking,
bending, flowing and flowering. Most of the
time his eyes are closed, but sometimes he
looks up at the dancers, and when he does
he grins, and that grin is like a lightbulb
exploding in that wooden room in which we
dance, in which the men are so taut and the
women so stiff, their faces contained, but in
that flashing bulb, for an instant, we all look
so beautiful, I think I might break open into
something I was not before — a hawk, an
ember, the petals of a beach rose, strewing.
Then he closes his eyes again, and the music
plays on, and I squeeze the arms of the man
who is holding me and let my whole body
surrender to his rhythm and his strength,

and we spin.

Oh, the way the music draws lines of alizarin, lines of crimson around that square room! The way you can follow those lines with your eyes closed and climb into the heart of another person, the maker of the music, drifting out in spirals amid the pine walls of a pine-floored room.

I'm nothing like the ladies in this town in my crudely stitched silk dress, my men's boots, my fedora. I'm nothing like the ladies with their Junior Ladies' Community Club, the ones who bake pies for good causes and dress in nice, freshly sewn flowered dresses. *Lena,* I can hear my dead mother say every time I step out the door, her voice echoed in my sister's. The tone of their voices make me pause: full of burnt molasses and smoke — a peculiar hunger.

But oh, how I love to dance! This dress I don so it can swing, soft silk that twirls up and over my boots and about my knees. I love to hold men and have them spin me around, their muscles tight around my arms and back, my braids whipping across both our faces. That spinning makes me laugh, and that laughing makes heads turn, but what do I care? I don't. What would caring be but a tether keeping us from the un- hinged future that is free, Otie?

STEPHEN

May 20, 1974

The clearing he makes is on the ridge above his mother's farm, an east-sloping bank at the top of the hill, accessible only by four-wheel drive or on foot. He's done being close to roads, done being connected by electrical or telephone wires, done being part of a system driven to killing, driven to war. Done being in a house with his mother and seventeen-year-old Bonnie. Their incessant bickering. David Bowie, War, the Bee Gees blasting from the radio in the upstairs bathroom, black nail polish, the toxic fumes of hairspray.

He cuts the hemlocks, the spruce, the birch, and the pines. The hard maples he leaves standing, for sap in spring, shade in summer, company come winter.

How to live one's life? Stephen's friends — more than half of them — went to Vietnam. When Stephen's card was drawn, two years ago, he walked into the woods with a jackknife and cut a half inch off the tip of his right-hand trigger finger. "Goddamnit!" he had screamed into the woods around him, wrapping the bleeding finger in the T-shirt he ripped off his shoulders. He wasn't planning to do it. But he couldn't go there. Do that. Kill. Or leave Bonnie, his cousin with the cracked heart, her body that looks like it might lift up from the ground and blow away. He drove himself directly to the draft office. "Sissy," Fred Cole had whispered. "Goddamn chicken-shit sissy." Breath like stale coffee. Breath like pennies. "That's what you are."

His mother had said more or less the same thing.

No matter how hard Stephen has worked since then, the words don't leave his mind. They have rooted there, and into his muscles. Seventy-two hundred Vermonters served. One hundred thirty-eight did not return. Stephen works harder.

He works at the sawmill during the day; in the afternoons and evenings he works on his cabin. He has made a small clearing with a chainsaw and an axe, felling the trees, cutting them into logs, and used his grandfather's adze, unearthed from the back of the barn, to shape the logs into rectangles. It's the way the barn below was built, and the old house, too — these wooden notches, wooden posts. The braces and beams he used to stare at for hours in his second-story bedroom, admiring the simple miracle of architecture.

Bonnie comes sometimes up the hill in the afternoons. She is failing school, screwing too many people in the backs of pickup trucks. Her eyes are magnetic, her fingers aflutter and on fire.

"Stephen-monkey!" she shouts. "Come smoke a joint with me."

He stops what he's doing. Joins her in the clearing next to his favorite maple, overlooking the farm below.

"Hazel's on a tirade today," Bonnie says, letting out a smoke ring and tipping her head back to face the clouds. "No way I'm going back there now."

Stephen nods, takes the joint, eyes his cousin: bell-bottom jeans and a skinny tank top. Motherless and coming of age in the post-Vietnam vacuum; inheriting all of the detritus of the 1960s without any of the hope, Stephen thinks. What is it people her age have to hope for?

And Stephen? What does he have? He passes the joint back to Bonnie, who takes it between her thumb and forefinger. There's not one of his childhood friends Stephen feels right with anymore. And so there is this house. This foundation: stone rooted up from old stone walls and dragged to this spot by hand.

"Stephen," Bonnie says, lying back in the grass, a smile across her thin lips. "Tell me about my mother."

Stephen has told her most everything he remembers — so little. About her barred owl, Otie, one-eyed, hit by a car and rescued from some roadside. When Stephen was young — five, six — he used to go and visit Lena and her owl at the old hunting camp on the hill overlooking the swamp. She'd laugh whenever she saw him. Serve him chunks of cheese with wild apples, say, "How goes your heart, Stevie?" She taught him how to feed Otie live mice from her traps, and how to hold him on his shoulder. He can still remember the feel of those talons digging into the thick denim shoulder of his coat and the lilt of Lena's voice in his ear saying, *Every bird is an omen, whether you know it or not.* He can still remember the smell of the bird in that cabin, too — shit and feathers and something entirely other.

He tells all this to Bonnie as he has told

her before, his eyes closed, the pot going to his head, and it's too late before he opens his eyes and sees she's rolled onto her side in the leaves, tears streaming down her cheeks.

He goes to her. Puts his hand on her shoulder. Holds it there. She squeezes his hand, stands, bows, and walks down the hill in the half dark that has somehow quickly descended, threading her way through the trees.

"Damn," Stephen whispers, watching.

When she's gone he remembers something else about Lena. Something he hasn't ever told Bonnie. One day Lena told him a story — Passamaquoddy, she said — about a woman who married an owl. She was leaning back on a rock, her eyes closed, a piece of grass between her lips.

In the story there was a beautiful girl who was too proud to marry. Her father promised to give her to any man who could make the embers of the fire blaze up by spitting on it. No suitor could, until a great horned owl, disguised as a handsome young man, showed up. He spit into the fire and the flames leapt into the night sky and the girl's father gave her to the owl-dressed-up-as-a-man, who took her home and slept with her that night. It wasn't until the morning that she saw his pointed ears and yellow eyes and true figure.

"Is this real?" Stephen had asked, eyes wide.

"Of course!" Lena replied, pinching his shoulder, laughing. She said she had heard the story from her friend Adele, who lived on the far side of the mountain. "But wait. There's more." The girl saw his true owl figure and fled. But he returned, again and again, in various disguises, until at last she accepted his devotion and his love, and, most enticing of all, Lena said, her eyes alight, "his alluring and bewitching song."

"So she married an owl?" Stephen asked.

"Yes," Lena said. "And they lived ever after in both worlds — human and creature." She sat up and grinned at him. "That's me, kiddo. Married to an owl." She put her lips against his hair and breathed in, then elbowed his ribs until he laughed out loud.

Stephen lies back in the leaves, his head spinning from the pot. He will have to tell Bonnie that story. He will have to tell Bonnie the next time she comes. *The woman who married an owl.* Is there an equivalent story, he wonders, for a man who does not quite belong in the human world?

He looks at the shadow of his cabin. There

are posts into soil. The clearing of darkness, the making of light. There is the plain old toil of it. Dedication of another kind — wood, light, this clearing, the trees he chooses to let branch here. *Here, here,* and, *a better world,* with every strike his adze makes, a world not of killing, or abandonment, but of self-reliance, of turning tall trees into the rectangular and sturdy and there-for-generations-to-come bones of a home.

When it grows too dark to see, Stephen sits down on the earth in front of the pile of logs and stones and feeds himself — cold cuts and a can of beans he picked up that day, beer. The world goes dark around him. Fills with the company of creatures — coyotes down by the creek, owls, brown bats flitting from one branch to another.

DEB

Deb's happy at the commune, happier than she's ever been, and yet. There's still something adrift about it; these characters too much like her, with their wingless ambition, their unhardened dreams. Tim has left. Ginny cannot bring herself to slaughter the chickens or slaughter the ducks; the ones that stop laying live on in the coop, and Deb has to drive to Nelson for expensive chicken grain every week. When she doesn't, the hens go hungry, cluck all day, watch her every move.

Bird leaves, taking her Nina Simone and Bessie Smith and Gil Scott-Heron records with her. The farmhouse does not seem the same without their singing. "Too fucking white here, my loves," she said on her way out the door, kissing their cheeks. "The snow and all of you. Who wants to be an anomaly?"

The roof of the farmhouse begins to leak, and they climb up there with tarps and scraps of tar paper, move out of the rooms where the water pools, where the plaster drips and the wallpaper peels.

Deb is broke. They are all broke. She knew she would be, and yet she's never felt it in her bones before. She borrows Randy's car, the only one they have, his grandmother's old Ford, to drive to town, but its brakes are shot and she keeps her hand on the emergency brake the whole time, heart racing, ready to pull.

She wanders the streets and the bright, nearly fluorescent aisles of the grocery store, eyeing the facets of the material world, wanting them all with a hunger that surprises her. She wants oranges. Grapefruits. Pretzels. Lemons! Red tomatoes.

The food they eat at the farm all starts to taste the same: potatoes and rice and beans. She craves meat, craves wine.

"We're too broke for wine," Ginny has announced, and so they are drinking the rotgut homemade cider that Randy and Feather have made in the basement. They pressed the apples in an antique Mast & Co. cider press that came with the barn, added sugar, added yeast, have let it sit all year in wooden barrels. It tastes like vinegar, makes Deb's stomach hurt, but it's all they have, so they drink it. With fervor.

Randy plays old folk songs he's learned from Woody Guthrie records. The girl, Opal, winds around his feet and laughs. It's Opal whom Deb eyes most often.

She's seven, beautiful, a string bean, her blond hair in tangles.

"Here, let me," Deb says, trying to brush it for her, but Opal screeches or laughs and runs away.

Opal carries chickens in her arms, paints on the farmhouse walls, pees her bed at night.

"Do you think she'll go to school?" Deb asks Feather, who says, "I don't know."

Opal crashes into the room; Opal spins. Opal cries out, "I'm hungry!" and Deb leaps up to fetch her an apple from the root cellar.

Winter is long. The roof continues to leak. Their road isn't plowed. They stay in and cook rice, cook beans, eat the potatoes and squashes and apples from the basement. The wood stove keeps them warm, if they stay inches from it; the records keep them sane: Dave Van Ronk, Aretha Franklin, *Sgt. Pepper's Lonely Hearts Club Band.*

Randy plays his plunky banjo.

"Do you know any other tunes?" Deb asks, staring at the wall.

Deb moves into Bird's empty room in the attic and wakes to frozen water in the jar beside her bed, wakes to limbs so cold she has to force herself out from underneath the covers. She never takes her long underwear off — top or bottom.

"Screw this," she whispers, running downstairs to warm her ass next to the wood stove. Her skin is slack, her hair thinning, she needs protein. And vitamin D. As does Opal.

Deb writes her mother telling her of her cold bones. She tells her about Opal, that apple from the cellar. She writes, "I think I underestimated the hardiness of pioneers." She thinks of her grandmother, Zina, in Russia, and what she might not have told her about life on a farm. The scarcity. The hard ropes of muscles in each of their arms. Deb walks the letter to the mailbox at the bottom of the road, and one week later a check for five hundred dollars arrives. Deb cries, she's so happy to see it. She cashes it and drives Randy's car straight to the grocery store, where she buys chicken and hamburger meat in bulk, the cheapest she can find. She fills a shopping cart with produce. She buys three jugs of sweet wine.

She brings it home and cooks a feast on the wood stove, which they devour, Feather and Randy and Ginny and Opal and Deb. "Thank you," Feather says, with tears in her eyes. "I'm so grateful." Opal eats the meat with her fingers, laughing, runs over to Deb and gives her a greasy, meat-drunk hug.

Deb sleeps that night in Bird's attic room above the kitchen, limbs at last warmed from red meat, limbs warmed from wine. She picks up her Thoreau book and reads it by candlelight: "Pursue some path, however narrow and crooked, in which you can walk with love and reverence."

Deb laughs, drifting into sleep, while snow piles up on the roof and water drips from the rafters.

DEB

September 28, 2011

"Morning, yous," she says quietly, opening the door and letting the birds out into the damp and heady tall grass. They are ferociously happy — clucking and eyeing her, there is no mistaking the look — with gratitude. She dumps yesterday's water, refills it with clean rainwater collected from a barrel out back. Fills the second bucket with grain. Throws the birds handfuls of scratch, which they come running for. "Thank you," Deb whispers to them, gathering four still-warm eggs. Thank God for these birds and her garden on the hillside outside her cabin, small but robust, teeming with tomatoes, beans, corn, potatoes, kale, fall raspberries, all undamaged by the heavy rain.

A Grace Paley line rings in her head: "Here I am in the garden laughing."

Isn't that her, after all these years? Deb goes to the garden, picks the day-ripened heirloom tomatoes, their purple and mottled skin, their bruised husks and tender bodies sweetened to perfection, and places them gently in the basket.

She laughs thinking of that year at the commune — candlelight and homemade rotgut cider, the basement full of acorn squash and soft apples. Their tomatoes that never ripened due to insufficient water, lack of fertilizer, insufficient sun. But look at her garden these days: enough to feed them for months! For half a winter. She'll fill the root cellar Stephen dug years ago with carrots, potatoes, cabbage. Fill the Deepfreeze out on the back porch with peas, tomatoes, zucchini, beans.

Deb brings the eggs and tomatoes inside, turns on the radio, though she hates to hear the news these days, can hardly stomach it at all since Bonnie's disappearance. Sure enough, it's more of the same: the pro-Assad army waging a cyber war in Syria; a family searching for respite in war-torn Somalia; a piece on the surprising number of extreme weather events in 2011: heat waves, Texas wildfires, earthquakes, dust storms, tornadoes, Irene. The director of the National Weather Service says he's never seen a year like the "deadly, destructive and relentless 2011."

Deb sits down at the table. Pours herself a cup of cold coffee.

She recalls Ginny quoting Yeats, drunk on that rank cider: "Things fall apart; the center cannot hold." Ginny laughing, holding her side, suddenly crying. Bird going to her, kissing the soft lobe of her ear. Opal dancing in the corner, a goopy-eyed newborn kitten in her hands, sick with worms and fleas. *The center cannot hold.* How had they known it, and Yeats, before them? These apocalyptic fevers seem to always come and go — but is it real this time?

Thank goodness for her Mason jars lined up on her shelf, full of beans, rice, lentils, quinoa. Raspberry jam. Plum jam. Apple butter. Self-reliant — is she? Those ten days with limited roads and no power she fed them all. But a year? Every day she makes a pot of soup — chili or lentil or white bean, full of tomatoes, potatoes, zucchini, summer squash, kale, sage, and thyme — a splash of pink sea salt from the Himalayas — and brings it, with a loaf of bread and a bottle of wine, to Hazel's kitchen. Hazel hardly eats anything at all. Vale eats ravenously.

"Thank you," Vale says after each meal.

"Thanks so much," her eyes on the pine floor, before turning and heading out the door.

Vale growing more distant by the day. Drinking too much wine.

Deb thinks how the storm and the opioid crisis here are, in some ways, symptoms of the same illness. Pharmaceuticals and crude oil. Hurricanes and heroin. Flooding and fentanyl. All of them making their way upstream.

"Goddamn money," Deb says, rising, dumping the rest of her coffee into the sink.

But there's action brewing, too, according to the next news story: protests happening in New York. Thousands of people camping out at Wall Street to protest big banks and corporate greed. The journalist describes a poster of a dancer atop Wall Street's charging bull. The words below it: BRING TENT.

The spirit of the Arab Spring protests taking root here, too, Deb thinks, feeling an old flicker. Does this next generation have it in them to fight unbridled greed?

Deb clicks off the radio. Goes outside to use the outhouse.

Thank God for this, too, she thinks, a couple hens trailing by her feet. She leaves the door open three seasons of the year, loves the view from the seat: mountain and mist and fog and rain and sunshine, cresting the farthest hill. She has papered the walls with *New Yorker* covers, keeps a stack of magazines to flip through. She never minds the cool shock of the seat in midwinter (except on the coldest days, when she swears like a sailor), is always grateful to head back inside and warm another cup of coffee. Is there a greater pleasure?

Deb stands on the porch — feels the sun wash over the pores of her face.

In the post-oil world, she thinks, I'll be heating the water on the wood stove. Canning tomatoes in ninety-degree August heat. Only I'll be dead by then, won't I? Here we are, coasting on resources — the wheat, the beans, the coffee, the wine, the salt, the propane for her gas stove. How rich we are without knowing it.

Deb turns to look at Hazel's house down the hill. The irony, she thinks — that Hazel is the only one who might still know how to survive that post-oil era but she'll be long gone by then.

The sky is apricot colored, luminous with the sun's rising. The birds come onto the porch and cluck by her feet, that familiar and comforting din. Undeniably changing, this world, but beautiful all the same, Deb thinks, tipping her head back. Songbirds still singing, stars still coming out each night, the earth still ripe with grass, leaves, dirt, apples. Isn't that the heart of it, this living? Death and beauty. Death and beauty. Pied, over and over again.

■ ■ ■ ■

PART II
WOODS

■ ■ ■ ■

LENA

July 6, 1956

River —

My sister Hazel does not dance. She sets up the tea and the coffee and makes sure there are fresh pies on the table and that the dishes are washed, and after the dance she sweeps the floor, gathers the tablecloths, nods to Lex and says, "I'll see you back at home." Most nights I go with her.

But not tonight. It's July and hot and the air is wonderfully thick and I have spun too much to get into my sister's car with six-year-old Stephen and drive back to our mountain. "I'll walk," I tell her, and she stares at me and shakes her head, climbs into her car and pulls away. I sit on the town hall step and watch the stars pop, listen to the musicians pack their things, to the crackling of car wheels on gravel as they pull away. One by one the musicians leave, all of them husbands, many of them farmers, and then it is just Lex and me outside that town hall, the lights off, the air still reverberant with music, the apple trees across the road lit up with fireflies.

He smiles and sits down next to me, pulls some cigarettes out of his pocket and lights one.

"I'd like one, too," I say, so Lex hands the pack to me and I pull one out and he lights it with the matches from his pocket.

"Lena," Lex says, breathing in, looking up at the stars above us.

"Lex," I say, and the sound of his name ricochets against my tongue.

"You want a ride home?"

"No," I say. "I don't want to go home."

Lex keeps looking up at those stars and takes another drag from his cigarette, and then he grins and says, "Me either." So we drive.

His truck is a '45 Chevy, and he turns the radio on and I crank it loud, so loud the music from *Harvey's Jubilee* fills the car so that there is no space between the music and our bodies and our minds. We go careening around back roads until we hit the pavement of Route 5, and then we are flying north faster than I've ever been, past cornfields and barns and motels and trees, the windows down and the night's breeze streaming through my hair. Once in a while we come to a spot where we can see the Connecticut River to our right and it is dark enough to reflect moonlight under those stars, and I can smell it through the open windows, its sand and moss-covered banks and languid sigh. New Hampshire winking at us from the other side, with its granite ledges and brick factories and hillside farms just like ours.

Lex fishes a bottle out from under his seat, pulls off the top, and hands it to me. I take a sip and my mouth turns crimson hot, then mellows to a golden glow.

"From Kentucky," Lex says, and I take another sip and feel its heat go all the way down to my toes.

I cackle. Screech out in that night. My teeth old bones the light gets through.

Lex swigs from the bottle, too, and laughs, then starts to sing along with the music. His voice is off-key and high and full of sorrow, singing along with Kitty Wells's "Making Believe." The dashboard lights up his face, and I can look at him now with the darkness hiding me, his long neck and pronounced Adam's apple and receding hair and high cheekbones and crooked nose. Full of a kind of joy I can see from here, while

Kitty sings about love and imagination.

Lex hands me the bottle again and I take a drink and feel my body grow sleepy with its golden glow and lower myself into the seat and close my eyes and then I feel the car slowing, and turning, and hear its wheels crunching over gravel, and then it rolls to a stop, and Lex turns the engine off and the air is suddenly alarmingly quiet.

I open my eyes and look up. We're on a high spot facing the river. It is so still and wide, that river, that you can see the stars reflected on its black surface. The water moves slow, making those reflected stars shimmer, and the crickets are suddenly loud through the open windows. Lex is leaning his head back on the seat with his eyes closed, his body emptied of sound, and in that silence his sorrow is as loud as anything else in that car. I reach over and touch his hand.

"Lex," I say.

"Yes." He doesn't open his eyes.

"This river is beautiful."

He smiles without opening his eyes. "Yes," he says. "It is."

"I want to go swimming."

He opens his eyes then, looks at me and holds that gaze. Fear tangled with sadness.

"Come," I say, and then I am climbing

out of the truck and clambering down the bank toward that cool, black water.

VALE

She finds a job at a small inn a few miles away. It's a place she can walk to — through the woods and along back roads. She makes the beds, washes the dishes, sets the tables for breakfast, makes ten dollars an hour.

She needs the job. It's been a month of driving around the roads of Nelson, re-pasting her mother's photo to every surface she can find. Why does she stay? Her legs won't walk her to the bus station. Her hands won't buy herself a ticket.

Her bank account is empty. She's lost five pounds. She forgets most mornings to brush her hair.

"Do you know my mother?" she asks strangers.

They turn away quickly, and Vale realizes, in those instants, how Bonnie felt walking these same streets: a person whose pain is

146

to be avoided.

She reads in *No Word for Time:* "There is no word for time in the Micmac language, nor in most Algonquin tongues . . . time is relative and elusive in nature, just as Einstein proved, and as quantum researchers are discovering."

No word for time. No Bonnie. No bus ticket.

And so the inn; the inn is her salvation.

The guests come from all over, say, "The damage around here is phenomenal."

Vale nods at them, these couples with their coiffed hair and bright eyes, sipping coffee and reading the *New York Times.* She considers sitting down and telling them about the Commission for Country Life with its institutionalizing, sterilizing, and corralling; its cutting up and clearing out what was unruly, nonwhite, native, wild, until it was just these white houses, these black and white cows, these sweet-smelling white pines these visitors have come for. But she does not.

They ask her why she's here as she pours their coffee. Vale says, "Back for a spell," turning.

They say: "So beautiful, despite the storm," and Vale says, "Yes," not mentioning Oxy, owls, bridges, heroin.

After work Vale walks the long way home — over Heart Spring Mountain, past the old Emerson cellar hole, the foundation sprouting ferns amid the shards of broken glass, chimney brick, and rusted metal. She kneels for a moment in a field of hay-scented ferns. Feels the cool ground below her body, the hot sun across her face.

She and Danny came here once. A week ago she got a postcard from him in Guatemala: "You've always been a star, Vale. I'm so very sorry. Sending you all my love. D."

He used to sing Leonard Cohen songs in the hayloft of the barn that summer he was seventeen and Vale was eight.

"Hear this one," he would say, a hand-rolled, unlit cigarette between his lips (*not going to catch the barn on fire*), a guitar in his hands, and she would close her eyes and listen, the words rushing over her, leaping into the dust-thick air. She liked the songs, yes, but also his voice — gravel and rust — and the sounds of the ticking of sunlight on the roof and of an airplane, somewhere, overhead. "Bird on the Wire," he sang. And "Suzanne."

"You like that one?" he asked, turning toward her, and she said, "Yes," and he said,

"Me, too. Here's another."

I'm in love, she thought then, at eight. Laughing. "Sisters of Mercy." "So Long, Marianne."

Vale rises from the ferns and grass and leaves. Keeps walking.

At the camper she pours herself a glass of gin. Downs it quickly. She wonders where Danny is now; pictures his sunburnt and dust-caked face in Guatemala. Vale pours herself another glass and steps outside. Imagines the dark-skinned or light-skinned, young or old woman he is with there.

"Danny," she whispers into the night. She is half-drunk. No one can hear her.

She wants to tell him about Marie, their great-great-grandmother.

A line from *No Word for Time* pops into her head, something she read earlier this morning: "Anywhere you stand should be sacred because the entire earth is sacred." Vale closes her eyes. Feels the solid and teeming ground below her feet, hears the soft rush of water over creek stones ringing in her ears.

STEPHEN

June 6, 1975

He picks her up hitchhiking by the side of
Route 100. Early June, that fluorescent
green blush in the trees. She wears men's
tight jeans and a flannel shirt, carries a
leather bag slung over her shoulder, filled
with groceries. As she climbs into the front
seat of Stephen's truck she tells him she's
looking for a ride to Farther Heaven, one of
the local communes.

Her dark hair is tied back with a piece of
twine; her wrists are pale, freckled, sturdy.

"You headed that way?" she asks, a slight
fever in her eyes.

"Yeah," he lies. "I was going that way."

"Dynamite," she says, closing the door.

She rolls down the window as he pulls out.
He turns the radio on to fill the silence. It's
the country station, playing Merle Haggard,
whose voice Stephen loves and whose poli-

tics he can't stand. She beats the toe of her boot to the rhythm of the music, taps her fingers on the door handle.

"You live on the commune?" he asks.

She turns toward him. "Yes. One year now."

He likes her. She is grounded. Wary. Unlike how he's imagined hippies to be, watching them from afar.

He asks her what it's like, and she warms, visibly. She tells him it's awful. Lovely. Complicated. Ridiculous at times. All those idealists, she says, crammed into one house, vying for authenticity and purpose, for meat and protein, but that she loves it, too. "More than I've loved anyplace before." She tips her head back and laughs — loudly. Without reserve. A loud bell. Overflowing. Then turns to Stephen. "Do you love it here, too?"

Does he love it here? What an absurd question. He's been a few other places — Boston, Montreal, New York once, where he got too drunk in a friend's apartment and wandered around the city that night, lost and terrified. He'd stopped for a spell halfway across the Brooklyn Bridge, wondering if and how he would ever make it home, and whether he wanted to. He could just keep going, he realized then, and never go back to that hillside where he was from. His mother and Bonnie. Be free. But he sobered up a little before dawn, found his friend's apartment, took the Greyhound back home. He'd never really considered living anywhere but here, other than that one moment. He'd never wondered why until this woman got into his truck. Her long limbs and dark hair and gray eyes and quick hands moving incessantly from her lap to the door handle and back again. Her absurdly simple question: "Do you love it here?"

Her eyes settle on the red, blunt tip of his right pointer finger, and she leans toward him, asks what happened.

Stephen winces. Turns toward the window — a barn, a silo, a wind-driven pine. But when he looks back toward her she's got her eyes straight on him and is holding steady there. So he tells her about his draft card and his knife. The blood in the oak leaves.

He has to force his eyes back to the road and the trees he was headed toward.

"You did the right thing," she says quietly.

"You think?" He still dreams of Vietnam. Images pulled from newspapers, come to life in his dreams.

She puts her thumb on that still-tender tip of his finger and holds it there for a moment, then pulls away and looks out the window. "You don't want to be part of that killing."

"No, I don't," Stephen says, keeping his eyes pinned on the road.

When he drops her off at the commune she looks straight at him before leaping out of the truck. "Come back sometime," she says, smiling.

Stephen nods but knows he won't. He isn't one of them — hippies. Dreamers. And they aren't one of him — tied. Beholden. To Bonnie. To Hazel. To the land. He fears entering a conversation he wouldn't know his way around in. Full of smoke and words that twine. "Okay then," he says, and nods.

Deb waves and walks up the hill toward the house. He doesn't want to stare but finds himself not wanting to leave, either, watching her strong legs moving up that hill — the determined stride of them.

He looks around, too. He hasn't been to any of the communes before but has always been curious. It's what he imagined it would look like — the old house surrounded by cars, a school bus, various buildings in various states of decay. A young guy dressed in rags sits on the farmhouse porch playing a banjo. South of the house two women are bent over weeding a vegetable garden in cutoffs and white tops. He can just see the blueish tint of their nipples through the thin cotton. He looks away, backs the truck up, and thinks of his mother's life, of the way her shoulders are bent now, the way her hips hurt when she walks. There is an ease to the way these people see the world — something he both admires and despises — like this landscape is a place they can own, buy, inhabit for a spell, love, and then leave, not a place they are indebted to, tied to like a tree's roots are tied to bedrock. What a thing, to see and know and inhabit the world like that, Stephen thinks, putting his truck into gear and pulling away.

LENA

July 6, 1956

Water —

I take off my boots and socks and then pull my sister's old dress up over my head. I don't wear anything underneath, and I know I am mostly obscured by the darkness of this moonless night, but I also know the darkness isn't complete. I hear Lex stumbling down the bank, and then I walk into the water. Its coolness shocks my shins, my thighs, my stomach, and then I leap in, my head fully submerged, and feel the current pulling me south and the pressure against my eyes and the pulse of the water inside my ears. When I pull my head up for air I can see Lex up to his waist in the river, looking my way.

"Whoo-hoo!" I call out. "Goddamn glorious!" My sister's husband's body is beautiful in this slivered light — slender, delicate,

155

full of grace. I think for a moment of her loving him, but the scene dissolves. He dives under the water and I put my head under, too, and feel myself drifting downstream and let go of all resistance to that pull, so that I am floating on my back under those stars, anchored by nothing.

Soon he is there next to me, reaching for my hand. "Lena! We have to swim up," he says. "Or we'll never make it back to the car."

I don't want to swim. I don't want to struggle against this current, but he is still holding on to my hand and he is paddling hard, so I join him. It's more work than I imagined. I kick and push my hands through that dark force, and when we finally make it back to the bank near the car I am exhausted. I climb onto that sandy stretch on my belly like a seal, and then I am laughing. Lex lies down next to me on the sand and smiles at my laughter. "We made it," he says, breathing hard.

"Yes," I say, still laughing. I don't know why. The air is warmer than the water, and it holds me. Then Lex reaches his hand over and runs his thumb down the bones of my spine.

"Lena," he says. His face is serious and full of that sorrow again, and he is staring into my eyes. I roll over onto my side to face him. His eyes drift down my body.

"Lena," he says again.

I often think I am the loneliest person alive. But that might not be true.

I take Lex's hand where it lies in the sand and bring it to my breast. His fingers bend around the small curve, his thumb touches my nipple. "Lena," he says again.

"Lex," I say. I have never been touched by a man. I never imagined it would feel so much like earth and like water. Like lightning.

His hand reaches up around my shoulders and neck, touches my face. He runs the back of his hand down my body between my breasts, over my belly, settles between my legs and a wave of heat rises and a sound escapes my lips.

"Lena," he says again, and it is a question and an apology and an expression all at once. I have been found in the dark.

"Lex," I say again, and then I pull him to me, and only much later do we drive home.

VALE

October 10, 2011

There's a man drinking at the inn's bar who
has recently returned from Iraq. Neko, dark-
eyed, a few years older than Vale. She
remembers him vaguely from years ago —
slender, a mother from Mexico, wheelies in
front of the post office.

He and Vale are the only ones there. It's
10 P.M. and Vale has just finished cleaning
the kitchen, setting the tables for breakfast.
The owners have gone to sleep, left Vale in
charge of locking up. She's come to love the
late walks home — back roads, her phone's
light illuminating the way.

'Tonight the old house creaks around
them. The inn's strange night music: toilets
flushing upstairs, the hum of the dishwasher.

Vale hasn't thought about Neko in years,
but here they are: Scotch and wine on the
counter before them, Gypsy jazz playing

quietly on the radio.

He tells Vale he's a photographer, that he's spent the last two years photographing the war in Iraq for Reuters, that he flew back from Baghdad a month ago for a break and to spend time with his mother.

He takes a sip. Tells Vale that his mother, Carmen, came here from Mexico when she was eighteen, married Neko's dad, and has sat huddled next to the wood stove, eyes on the TV, all winter long for thirty years. He spins the glass on the bar's counter. "A unique version of happiness, eh?"

Vale nods. "The winters can be long."

Neko takes a slow drink. "Yes. Long." He looks at Vale. "And you?"

Vale eyes his wrists, the blue veins that quiver there. Crooked teeth. One chipped one. Beautiful face. Beautiful cheekbones.

"Me," she says, turning from him and sipping her wine. "No story. Back home for a spell."

He nods, eyeing her.

"Isn't that," he says quietly, nodding toward the poster with Bonnie's face on it pinned to the wall near the door, "your mother?"

Vale doesn't look at the poster. Of course he knows. Everyone knows. She closes her eyes for a minute, imagines slamming her

159

glass against the bar counter, having it shatter into one thousand pieces. Little shards in the carpet — impossible to clean up. "Yes. That's Bonnie."

Neko nods. Takes another sip of his drink. "She's beautiful," he says, quietly.

"She is," Vale says, a sudden ache in her gut and thighs.

Neko takes another sip of his Scotch and tells her that he came back to be with his mother, yes, but that he also needed to be somewhere quiet for a while. "Away from the madness. And then Irene happened." He laughs into his drink. "The fire will find you anywhere, won't it?" he says.

"Yes, it will," Vale says, turning her wineglass in slow circles, making a mosaic of concentric rings on the bar's countertop.

This is how they begin sleeping together. They leave the bar and walk to his parents' house — a fifties mint-green cape a quarter mile down the road. They climb an external staircase to a room above the garage: a string of Christmas lights, a mattress on the floor, a wood stove in the corner. He puts a log on the fire, opens the damper, and the log bursts into flame, its birch bark crackling. Vale sits down on the futon. Neko pours Scotch into two cups. "Mademoiselle," he says, handing one to her. A smile she can't say no to.

Vale takes a sip. That glorious burn through her upper body. She leans her head back against the wall.

"What's war like?" she asks quietly.

Neko sits down on the floor across from her. He takes a sip from his cup. Closes his eyes. "It's unlike anything else, war," he says. "Humankind's dark underbelly."

Vale nods.

"But enough about that," Neko says, loosening his shoulders, opening his eyes again. Adept, she can tell, at partitioning his brain. "What is it you do, when you're not here, Vale?"

How will she respond to that question? Vale pictures herself undressing under golden and red lights, surrounded by the ogling bodies of sick and sad and lonely men and women, in order to pay her bills.

She thinks of the line from *No Word for Time: To do damage to the earth does spiritual damage as well.* "I tend bar. I make delicious drinks," Vale says.

"I believe it," Neko says, smiling. "I'd like to try those drinks someday."

Vale nods. "That can happen."

He is beautiful, Neko — dark skin, thin

bones, long fingers. Vale goes to him. Puts her lips against his lips. Slips his T-shirt up and over his shoulders. She knows nothing of war. Her pain has come from different wounds, but isn't all pain shaded the same color? Soft blue, plum. Running up and down our veins. Recognizable across the room.

STEPHEN

June 26, 1975

The second time he sees her is a few weeks later at the Stonewall. It's late June, the first truly warm night of summer. She raises her bare arm and motions him over to where she stands at the bar with some hippies: a tall striking woman who looks like a raven, a couple of soft-bellied, long-haired men.

"Stephen, right?" Deb says, smiling, as he walks toward her.

Stephen nods and tries not to look at the place where Deb's white cotton shirt — faint stains in the armpits, frayed at the edges — buttons closed at her chest.

"Hey, I owe you a drink," she says, butting her elbow into his ribs. "You gave me a ride."

Stephen refuses but orders himself another Miller and pays for her glass of jug wine.

"You live here?" one of the hippies with

stringy reddish long hair asks him.

"I guess you could call it that," Stephen says quietly.

"Stephen's a local," Deb says, hooking her finger into the belt loop of her jeans. They're the same tight blue jeans she wore the first time he saw her. She smells like cigarettes and some other scent he can't place — sweat, her sex. She asks about his summer and he asks about hers. On their second round of drinks she leans her mouth in toward Stephen's ear and tells him she'd like to see his place.

Stephen laughs. Nearly chokes on his beer. He is terrified of women always, but especially ones like this.

"I'm serious," she says. Those gray eyes. The space in the *V* of her shirt where he tries not to rest his gaze.

"My place isn't much," Stephen says. "I don't think you want to go there." But his blood is racing and warm from his scalp to his toes and he tries quickly to think of some other place they can go. The creek. A field. The front seat of his truck.

"No, I want to see your place," she says. "I really do."

They drive as far as they can in Stephen's truck up the steep track, then walk the rest of the way in the dark, breathing hard as they clamber up the old logging road. The night has not yet cooled, and by the time they reach the cabin they are both sweating. She leans in toward his body and looks around.

"It's beautiful," she says after a minute, tilting her head up toward the stars. All they can see in the quarter-moon light that filters through the pines is the outline of the half-built cabin, the roof of his mother's house below, and the lights of the town on the edge of the horizon ten miles away. Stephen offers her a Budweiser from the bucket where he keeps them cool, buried in a wet spot in the ground.

"Thank you. This is good," she says. They sit on a log, their legs spread out straight in front of them. She moves closer to him so their legs touch.

"It's something," Stephen says.

"More than that." She puts her hand on his thigh.

Stephen laughs. "Okay."

"Hey, Stephen."

"Yeah?"

"I want to live here with you." That clear resounding voice of hers — like a bell.

Stephen chokes on his beer. "You don't know me."

"I still want to live here with you."

"Why?"

"I like everything about it. Woods. The view. You. I just have a feeling." She's not smiling now. Her voice is serious. "Plus," she says. "I'm sick of the commune. This is far more real. Quieter. I like trees." Then she sets her beer down and reaches toward Stephen, puts her mouth against his mouth. He fumbles with the buttons of her blouse until she laughs and helps him.

"Here," she says, undoing the buttons herself and slipping the cotton off her shoulders. He doesn't have any rubbers that night, so he tries to pull out of her — Stephen's father isn't a man he wants to see reflected in himself, and he doesn't know his way in the world well enough to guide another — but she pulls him back inside her. "Don't worry," she whispers. "I won't."

"Won't what?"

"Get pregnant."

"Oh," Stephen says, not asking why, and then he lets himself loose inside her, a clean explosive sensation that leaves his insides feeling ripped apart and raw. They fall asleep like that, naked, their limbs wrapped around each other, his sleeping bag thrown over them to keep off June's midnight chill.

■ ■ ■ ■

She moves in with him that summer. They insulate the cabin walls with fiberglass, cover them with planed pine boards, fresh from the mill. Stephen cuts more trees to the east and south for the light, and turns the track that leads up the hill into a two-season road with three loads of gravel.

"I love it here," Deb says, often enough that it becomes a refrain. "Let's make everything we do right, Stephen. Everything. Down to the bone." She quotes the Nearings: "To take his life into his own hands and live it in the country, in a decent, simple, kindly way." Stephen withholds comment — thinks of his mother. The bitterness that can come from isolation.

But he likes her. She surprises him with her capacity to work, her willingness to learn new things, her ability to laugh out loud. Stephen borrows a neighbor's tractor, and they spend hours that summer transforming the once-forest into a small field. Deb follows behind the tractor, pulling rocks and roots out of the ground and piling them at the edge of the clearing in rows. She wears, every day, the same blue cotton eyelet top, cutoff blue jeans, and a straw hat she brought with her from the commune, and Stephen loves catching a glimpse of her behind him, small and strong, her feet and hands black with dirt, her limbs turning brown as tree bark.

All summer and fall they work like that, late, side by side, and on weekends after dark they drive down the long driveway to the store for cold beers and fast food.

"You're quiet," she says one night, sitting in the dirt outside the cabin, touching his leg with the back of her hand.

"I guess."

"I'm used to talking about how I feel. Blathering. Acting compulsive. You make me feel like a fool."

"No need to feel that way." Stephen smiles and runs a cold bottle up the length of Deb's browned thigh and feels happier than he has ever imagined he could.

In October she tells him she is pregnant. She says she doesn't know how it happened — that she must have gotten slack with the pill. She has cooked a dinner of ribs and green beans from the new garden. She opens a bottle of wine, rolls a joint, and sets the makeshift table — some boards laid across two sawhorses — with candles and a tablecloth. When Stephen comes in from splitting wood she meets him at the door and kisses him on the mouth. Her clean, still-damp dark hair smells like jasmine and lemon. A hint of woodsmoke.

"Guess what?" She closes her eyes and lifts her face up toward his.

Stephen sits down at the table and grins at her. He can't think what. A job? Money? "What?" he asks.

Deb sits down across from him and takes his hand in hers. She leans in close and squeezes his palm with her fingers. "You're going to be a father," she says.

In the future it will always hurt Stephen to remember that moment — how it affected his breath. What it had done to the strength in his legs. Deb stands and steps toward Stephen and grabs his hands and starts, there by the table, to dance. A single lightbulb hangs from the kitchen ceiling, and she moves directly underneath it, her body weaving in and out between shadow and light. He can smell her, the remains of her jasmine perfume overpowered by her particular scent of sweet, overripe fruit. He wants to reach out to her, grab her body, swaying in the light before him, but something catches near his heart, making his breathing quick. He thinks of his father's drinking, of his sad fiddle on the porch at night. Of him slamming the door, the reverberation of wood on wood. Of the day he disappeared and did not come back.

"You're unhappy," Deb says. She stops moving her body and looks up at him.

"No, no, I'm not. I'm happy," he says, and picks her up and carries her out of the house and onto the porch and sets her down in the rocking chair they have brought there and gently begins to rub her bare feet and legs.

"Thank you, Stephen," she says quietly, tipping her head back against the rocker, pointing her face up toward the stars.

VALE

October 15, 2011

Three nights a week she works late; three nights a week he meets her at the bar; three nights a week she sleeps in Neko's bed in the room above the garage. They find each other there between the sheets: lips on nipples, lips on ankles, lips on her inner thigh.

This night, afterward, they eat dinner at his table: a loaf of bread, chunks of cheese, a bottle of wine.

He tells her that he's been taking pictures of the wreckage here. That photographing the damage of Irene is a quieter job than documenting war, but painful all the same. "It's the connection that stings," he says. "These wars fought over oil. These storms caused by the burning of that same oil. I want to show the thread."

Vale nods, sips her wine. "Can I see them?

Your photos?"

Neko pulls out his camera and shows her: a white house by the river with a wrecked foundation, a Trans Am wedged ten feet up in the trees, the mustard-colored trailer Vale saw when she arrived tipped on its side, its pink curtain blowing through a broken window.

Vale takes another sip from her glass. The photos make it hard for her to breathe. The way they capture the startling stillness that follows storms seems too accurate: everything still and nothing the same.

"You're good at what you do," she says.

"Thank you," Neko says. "The challenge is to not make war or destruction too beautiful. Because they can be — aesthetic masterpieces."

He closes his eyes. Tells her that in August he pulled a girl — nine or ten years old — out of a bombed building. A yellow dress, covered in blood. That he doesn't know if she survived.

Vale looks out the window: orange trees, gray sky. Jesus. War: how little she knows of it. Her worst apocalyptic fears of the future, she realizes, are happening in many places in the world, right now. "I'm sorry," Vale says, laying her head on Neko's thigh.

■ ■ ■ ■

Later that night, Neko sleeping, Vale climbs out of bed, puts Lena's green fedora on, goes to the window and looks out. She feels the moonlight on her bare breasts, bare stomach, bare thighs.

She thinks how good Neko is at what he does. The necessity of his work. What is it she brings to the world?

Vale pictures herself dancing to Shante's music at a warehouse party. Shante singing, voice of liquid gold, ukulele strumming and the entire room lit by the heat of bodies, alcohol, rhythm. A circle parted around Vale as she danced in the center of them all. In that moment, sweat trickling down her spine, eyes all around her, she had felt powerful. As if she was doing what she was meant to do. Just for a moment — but that moment was there — amber-colored, the heat of it embedded in her bones and in her blood.

She wants to transport Neko to that room. Say: this is what I am. What I do.

She remembers a letter Danny wrote her years ago, quoting Faulkner: "How often have I lain beneath rain on a strange roof, thinking of home." Philadelphia, Pittsburgh,

New Orleans — those cities where she found herself but didn't find herself. Sleeping on couches and in closets and in windowless rooms the size of her camper. She missed the stars in those windowless rooms and in those cities. Stars in the Abenaki language, according to the book she checked out of the library: *alakws.* She missed the creek: *sibosis.* She missed the woods. She missed the fields and the creek and no — she did not miss her mother. She did not miss her mother.

Vale returns to the bed, picks up Neko's camera, lying on the floor. She turns it on and flips through more photos: the flooded contents of a downtown Indian import store — bright-colored saris and tapestries hanging from tree branches to dry. A woman standing in front of her house, a wash of gravel where her front yard used to be. An old barn Vale recognizes from town, collapsed, its timber bones scattered along the ground, its rafters and roof flipped on its side.

In the background of that photo: a street Vale recognizes, a metal shop, and standing at the edge of the photo, back to the camera, a small woman in white, orange hunting hat pulled low, dark hair pooled around her neck, a large gray jacket wrapped around her shoulders.

"Shit," Vale whispers. A shock of adrenaline in her chest.

She shakes Neko.

He opens his eyes, rolls toward her. "What?"

"Who is this?" Vale pulls on her underwear. Reaches for her bra. "Where did you take this photo?"

Neko sits up. Rubs his eyes. Glances at the camera.

"That one? In town. Cedar Street."

"When?"

"A week ago, maybe. Why?"

Vale reaches for her pants. She can't see the woman's face, but she is Bonnie-sized. Bonnie's thin shoulders. Bonnie's thin, dark hair.

Vale slips on her T-shirt and sweater. Her socks and boots.

"Talk to me, Vale," Neko says quietly, rising.

"I'll see you later," Vale says, lacing her boots, buttoning her sweater, heading toward the door.

"I'll give you a ride," Neko calls from the top of the stairs, slipping into blue jeans.

"No," Vale calls back. Walking. "Thank you." It's not definitely Bonnie, but it might be, Vale thinks, looking up: the sky full of stars, their fluorescent, punctured holes.

In the morning Vale wakes early. She downs a cup of instant coffee, puts her mother's blue rosary in her pocket. Rosaries and that evangelical church — you never got it right, Bonnie, Vale thinks, did you? Though maybe it's that she never once settled for a simple answer.

Vale puts Lena's green hat on and climbs the hill to Deb's cabin, asks if she can borrow her truck again.

"Of course," Deb says, eyeing Vale over her cup of dark coffee.

The pickup smells like mouse and sitting water; the Mexican blanket that lies across the bucket seat is ripped in various places.

Of course she's alive, Vale thinks, putting the truck into gear. My resilient-as-hell mother. That golden streak of laughter. Vale waking in Bonnie's arms for thirteen years in that sunlit bed above the river: morning breath, a smile. "You sleep in, baby. I'll make tea and coffee."

Vale drives to Cedar Street. The barn is easy to find — its timbers still scattered in all directions. She parks the truck and steps out into the damp and cold air, pulls her jacket collar around her neck, and walks the perimeter of the barn, looking for places one might make a temporary home — a nest amid the wreckage.

"Bonnie!" she calls out, shivering.

Vale walks toward the closed-up metal shop and around back.

At the far end there's a small section of barn, a tacked-on wing, still standing. Vale steps inside the open doorway and waits for her eyes to adjust — an earthen floor, dark pine walls, one window filled with cobwebs. The room is filled with old furniture, some rusting machinery, and in the far corner a cot, on top of which lies a pile of blankets and an old pillow. Vale takes a deep breath. Steps closer. The blankets are matted, contain the hollowed-out shape, Vale thinks, of a body sleeping.

"Bonnie?" Vale calls out again, quietly, her voice bouncing off the pine walls.

Vale bends closer, puts her face into those blankets, and breathes in: dank wool, dust, a hint of cat piss.

It doesn't smell like the Bonnie she knows, but what would Bonnie's smell be, after a month and a half of sleeping out of doors?

A broken windowpane has been covered with plastic; straw and T-shirts and scraps of wool are stuffed into the cracks in the walls. There's a postcard of California tacked above the flaking green paint dresser, a waterlogged Bible in the corner, a pen beside it. Vale rips out a blank page from the back of the Bible, picks up the pen, writes:

Bonnie? I am here. −V, with her phone number scratched below.

What does hope feel like in the body? Cool air moving through. An electric charge.

Vale drives slowly around backstreets for two hours, checks her phone every few minutes. In the early afternoon she drives to the supermarket for crackers and cheese, a bottle of red wine. She rips open the packaging there in the parking lot — breaks chunks of cheese off with her fingers. She unscrews the bottle of wine and takes a sip, looks out across the sea of mothers with their shopping carts, full to the brim, their small children tagging along after.

My mother is not gone, Vale thinks, heart rattling, taking another drink of wine. She's in a Shaw's parking lot drinking in broad daylight. She doesn't care. *My mother is not gone.*

DEB

October 17, 2011

In the early evening Deb turns on the radio and hears about landslides throughout Guatemala, El Salvador, and Nicaragua. Heavy rains and flooding. Eighty dead, according to the BBC. "Shit," Deb whispers, going to her computer to look for an e-mail from Danny. She hasn't heard from him for a month. She sends him a message. The BBC reporter says thousands of families have lost homes and crops. That the UN has classified Central America as one of the parts of the world most affected by climate change.

Deb turns off the radio, goes out to give her birds fresh water. She holds still in the late sunlight, the leaves on the trees around her outrageous colors — red, orange, yellow — and forces herself to breathe.

An hour later she gets a response: *Mamá. Ten villagers killed. Unbearable. Coming home for X-mas to see Hazel and Vale and you. Love — your Danny.*

Deb sinks into the chair on her porch. Leans her head back. Breathes deep, tears in her eyes.

He's alive, her boy.

It feels as if they need him on this hillside right now. Not as savior but as company.

Bonnie still missing. Vale: distant, quiet, refusing to crack.

And Hazel more and more off. Was it too much, Deb wonders, the shock of Bonnie's disappearance, for her aging mind? This morning Deb found Hazel in her nightgown in the middle of the living room, staring at a crack in the plaster wall.

"Where is Lena?" Hazel asked, turning toward Deb, her blue eyes strangely blank.

"Lena died many years ago," Deb said, going to Hazel and touching her arm.

Hazel pulled away quickly, then went to her chair by the window and looked out at the field. Snow flurries, the first, a dusting, across the old apple trees.

"Oh. I thought for a moment she was here."

"That happens," Deb said. "I'll get you some tea."

In the kitchen things were out of place —
clean dishes to the right of the sink instead
of in the dish rack. A half-eaten apple in the
cabinet next to the plates. The milk sitting,
warmed, in the cupboard next to the refrigerator. *Hazel,* Deb thought, heart sinking,
reaching for the apple and putting it into
the compost bucket near the door, pouring
the sour milk down the drain.

When she returned to the living room her
mother-in-law was asleep, head tipped back
on the blue armchair.

Deb spent the rest of the day cleaning
houses in town — a doctor's renovated
farmhouse, the apartment of a divorced
lawyer. She doesn't mind the work — she
takes strange comfort in the gratification of
a scrubbed floor and glistening countertops.
What a shock it would be if the people she
cleans for saw her own home, Deb thinks
— its spider webs and rough pine walls that
never get clean. The organism her home is,
separated from the woods around it by a
thin scrim only, and how she loves it that
way. She considers it a strange instinct so
many people have — the tireless struggle to
keep nature's chaos at bay.

From the porch where Deb sits now, the
relief of Danny's well-being settled into her
chest, she sees a light flick on in Vale's

camper. A Thoreau line rings in her head (how often they appear there): *The most I can do for my friend is simply be his friend.*

Of course. Be her friend.

"I brought us wine," Deb says, holding the bottle out, when Vale opens the camper door.

Vale smiles. "Nice. Thank you. Come in." The place is tiny, sparse, clean. Smells like coffee, and alcohol, and mildew, but there Vale is, reaching for two glasses, pulling over a chair.

She looks better than she has of late. Not quite so starved. Some color in her cheeks.

"I'm sorry I don't come more often," Deb says, lifting her glass to Vale's. "It's easy to grow solitary."

Vale shrugs. "I know. You want to take these outside?"

They take their glasses out to the field where they can hear the creek and watch the moon rise. It's unusually warm for this late in October. Freak dry spells, warm spells, cold spells: erratic, unpredictable, Deb thinks. Still, cool enough for a fire. Vale has made a simple fire pit out of a circle of river stones. She gathers sticks from the woods, crumples newspaper, lights a match. They sit in the damp grass, watching the flames swell, warming their hands. Deb tells Vale about Hazel's spottiness. About finding her in her nightgown in the middle of the room in the middle of the day, staring at a crack in the wall. About the apple on her shelf and the sour milk in the cupboard. "What do you suppose is going on?"

Vale shrugs. Takes a sip of her wine, stares into the fire. "Haunted by ghosts?"

Deb laughs. "Yes. Me, too. I suffer from the same disease. To our haunted hillside," Deb says, reaching her glass toward Vale's. Soft clink. Sparks from the fire.

"You know what I've been thinking these days?" Deb says, tipping her head back. "How hard it is to learn how to love within the span of one lifetime." She's thinking of Stephen and Hazel. Her own mother. Bonnie. Reverberations in creek water. "How easy to pass along our flaws — our anger, sorrow, reserve, withholding."

Vale nods, takes a sip of her drink.

"We deny them, so fiercely, our ancestors," Deb says. "But really they're written deep in our bones. Do you know about epigenetics? New research that says we carry the trauma — grief — joys — of past generations in our DNA." She tells Vale about her grandmother, Zina, growing up on the farm outside of Vitebsk. How she is the

183

reason Deb is here — the reason she came north on that highway thirty-five years ago.

"I didn't know any of that."

"There's a lot we don't know about everyone's story, isn't there?" Deb says, brushing a spark off her sweater. She thinks of Bonnie and Bonnie's motherlessness, that trauma without stories to accompany it, to make sense of it, to take that poison and turn it into medicine, as only stories can do. Create maps of the past, which become maps for the future.

"And Bonnie had — has — her epigenetic trauma, too," Deb says quietly.

"Yes," Vale says, rising and throwing another stick on the fire. Raking the coals inward with her boot. "Hey, Deb."

"Yeah?"

Vale stares into the fire and tells Deb about the photo of Marie tacked to her wall. Of what she has learned about the eugenics movement — the second wave of the destruction of a people and culture. The destruction of a way of living and knowing.

Deb hasn't ever heard about the eugenics movement in Vermont. The complexity of place, she thinks: how long it can take to peel back the layers.

"My mother always said we were Native American," Vale says. "I thought she was an appropriating asshole." Vale laughs, staring into the fire.

"That is a powerful thing to know. Or half know," Deb says. She closes her eyes and pictures Lena in her cabin. Pictures Stephen in his. If it's true, it makes sense, epigenetically. This calling back to the land. Being drawn to woods, creeks, swamps.

"You cold?" Vale asks, passing Deb a scarf, and Deb nods, grateful, and wraps it around her shoulders. She leans back in the wet grass and watches sparks rise into the dark sky. Marie possibly Abenaki. Did Stephen know? She turns again to look at Vale. She's gorgeous, this girl, lit by firelight, Deb thinks. As all girls are. If only they knew just how so.

Vale

October 31, 2011

Vale drives to the barn on Cedar Street every day. The note she left is gone. There are no messages on her phone. She checks the pillows and blankets for body heat, for strands of dark hair — there are none.

Vale rips another small piece of paper out of that water-damaged Bible. Draws a heart in its center. Writes: *Bonnie?*

She leaves the barn and goes to the river's edge. Lifts a large brick from the bank, hoists it above her head, and heaves it into the water. It crashes into a rock, splits in two.

The days bleed into one another. Lena and Marie's photos, pinned to the wall, keep her company on the nights she does not go to see Neko. The storms hit and you think the world is over, Vale thinks, and then the storm passes and the world is not over. The riverbanks heal. The houses that were destroyed are torn down. The people that disappeared are still missing. The people they left behind get by.

Vale brings more bedding from Hazel's attic. Obsessively scans news headlines on her phone. Drives the back roads and backstreets daily in Deb's truck.

How long does one stay in a place looking for a body that will not appear? *No Word for Time: Time is relative and elusive in nature.*

She asks again at the drop-in center. At the homeless shelter. At the police station, where the woman behind the desk turns, busying herself, when Vale walks in. When Vale asks if she's seen anything, the woman glances up quickly. Shakes her head. "No."

Vale goes to the town office and asks to see the marriage license of Henry and Marie Wood. The town clerk brings her into the vault, pulls out a thin sheet of paper, and hands it to Vale. Vale sits down at a small table and reads it. Married: 1901, the year the photograph was taken. Marie's DOB: 1885. Place of birth: Mallets Bay, three hours north, along Lake Champlain. Her father's name: Pierre. Her mother's name: Louise. In faint pencil, along the edge of the page, barely legible: *INDIAN.*

"Holy," Vale whispers, there by herself in the back room vault. A cool sensation along her spine.

At the camper Vale puts on her coat and Lena's hat and tucks a bottle of wine into her jacket pocket.

"Indian," Vale says to Marie's photograph, and Lena's, grinning, on her way out the door.

She walks across the field and toward the woods.

She wants to find Lena's cabin, that one-room shack at the top of the hill, overlooking the swamp, no doubt falling in by now. Vale hasn't seen it for years, and even back then it wasn't much — moss-covered, broken windows, the door swinging open in the wind. She hadn't gone inside — Danny had been with her, had turned at the sight of it, said: "Hell no."

Vale turns north and uphill along an old logging road. It might have been passable by truck or car forty years ago in good weather, but now it's grown up in blackberries and hemlock saplings, is crisscrossed with fallen pines.

Maybe this is where I'll go for the next great storm, Vale thinks, heading uphill, swiping the thick and low-hanging branches out of her face.

And then there it is. A roof at the top of the hill, nestled between the tall trunks of maples and birches and pines, overlooking the swamp.

I love the rain. I fucking love the rain! Bonnie calling out, standing in the middle of the river, rain dripping down her hair and shirt and legs. *Vale, baby, come get wet with me!*

Always courting the water's edge.

Bonnie used to call Lena's cabin "Stephen's spot," also refusing to go near it.

It looks like a body or a creature, there tucked into the hillside, rising out of the afternoon sunlight. One room, three windows, and one door. Asphalt roof shingles, green with moss. A few of the windowpanes cracked or missing.

Vale walks closer, thinks of that photo tacked to her wall — Lena standing here in her fedora, Otie on her shoulder.

The wooden door, green paint flaking, has blown open in the wind. She walks toward it and looks in. The floor is covered in leaves, pine needles, the abandoned homes of mice, squirrels, skunks, porcupines — who knows what other creatures.

Vale steps inside and takes a deep breath.

The room smells like decay — a den, a lair, a part of the woods. But the light in here is lovely — slant light through the spider-web- and dust-covered windows. There are things on the windowsills. Vale steps closer to look. A glass jar full of feathers — turkey and owl. A parade of animal bones Vale can't name. A collection of river stones — round and smooth, shades of cream, slate and iron, covered in cobwebs and dust. Vale picks up a round stone, polishes it with her sleeve, holds it in the palm of her hand. Takes a deep breath.

Lena's things. All this time. Her grand-mother — Bonnie's mother — has been up here on the mountain, within these walls.

Vale looks to her left. There are some photos, cut out of magazines, tacked to the pine wall to the right of the window. Curled, mildewed, but the images still legible: a mountain lion in a stricken clearing, a Na-tive American woman seated on a stump outside of a wigwam, a hawk on her knees. Vale touches the woman's face with her fingers. Whispers, "Hello."

There's a single bed in the corner — the mattress full of mouse nests and holes. There's a small, hand-built table with two chairs. A potbellied stove. A counter made of rough-cut pine. Above the counter are two china teacups hanging from two bent nails. Vale slips one off its nail and holds it in the palm of her hand — a dust-red rose in its center. Vale cleans it with the hem of her dress, sits down at the table, pulls the bottle of wine out of her pocket, and fills the teacup to the brim.

She holds the cup out in front of her.

"Lena," Vale says out loud, her hands shaking slightly, toasting the other cup still hanging on the wall.

Her voice sounds strange within the empty walls. "Who are you?" Vale says. There's a crow call from outside. The racket of Deb's rooster down the hill. "I'd love to goddamn know."

Vale sips her wine, looks around at Lena's things. The cabin still. Eerily quiet. Dust lacing the sunstruck air.

LENA

July 18, 1956

Coyote —
Adele shows me jars full of herbs she's gathered: juniper, pokeweed, black cohosh. She tells me a little more about them every time I come, teaches me how she dries them, stores them, adds a splash of this and a drop of that depending on the cure.

She leans toward me, winces.

"You smell like your body, Lena." Smiles. Hands me a cup of steaming tea.

It's sex I smell like, between my legs, but I don't tell her that.

I pull my notebook out of my pocket. Write down the names of the herbs she tells me.

"Why you writing this stuff down?" she asks, piercing me with her dark eyes.

"Bad memory," I say. "Is this okay?"

"Of course," Adele says, rolling some tobacco.

I think of my grandmother, Marie, who died when I was four, a low and sweet-voiced singing. What were those songs?

I ask Adele if she knew Marie. She shakes her head, says, "No."

I tell her I miss my grandmother and the sound of those songs. She smiles. Lights a cigarette. Walks out the door.

Late that night we walk down to the creek, Otie and I. I slip off my pants, my shirt, my boots. I splash my armpits, my crotch, my nipples, with the ice-cold water. It smells like earth, like decaying animal, like ferns. Otie watches me from the bank, winking.

I call out toward him. "Come in with me, you loon bird you!"

He merely winks and turns away.

Another memory: my grandmother, in a field, me and Hazel by her side, pointing up at the stars above us. Words spilling from her mouth that sounded like they were underwater.

I'm about to climb up onto the bank when I see eyes at the edge of the woods. Umber. Earth-colored. I feel them before I see them. I think: Lex Starkweather, and close my eyes, grin. A musky heat there. But when

I open them again it is that coyote. Sly, feral, brute, three-legged. It catches my eyes for a long moment. Our breath like invisible water, traversing between here and there. Otie flaps his one good wing, hops toward that dog, squawking. The coyote wheels, turns, disappears into the hemlocks and pines.

"It's all right, Otie," I say, rising from the water and slipping back into layers of thick wool. "It's all right. Nothing to fear." My whole body shaking. "Let's go home."

I shiver the whole way back.

The kerosene lantern on the table flickers; the night air sends goose bumps up my spine, up my ankles and shins to the top of my knees.

Otie hops from the bed to the chair to the floor. He pecks at the water-stained curtains, hanging from the windows. Torn. Fly-speckled. He begins to shred them. Furiously. I let him. He is building a nest. An ancient instinct — this craving for a mate. My mother used to say owls were a sign of the death of something old and the start of something new. Hear that? The death of something old and the start of something new, Otie, my friend.

■ ■ ■ ■

PART III
FIELDS

■ ■ ■ ■

STEPHEN

December 14, 1986

Stephen sits in the dark on the hill above his parents' farmhouse in the clearing he and Deb have made together, a quart of Jim Beam between his knees. It's December and the air is cold, five degrees — colder? Dropping. The ground is covered in a couple inches of snow, a few stubborn leaves cling to the oaks and beech, the smell of woodsmoke drifts uphill from the cabin where Deb and Danny sit near the fire. Deb will be drinking wine now, and Danny — ten years old — will no doubt be bent over a Tintin, lost on some desert island. They fought, Stephen and Deb. "Goddamn you," Deb yelled. "Why don't you talk to me?"

The words caught in his chest, unformable. His silence ice castles in the air. And so he left, with his coat and this bottle. The woods his solace, always.

When Stephen built this place he had wanted it to be different: higher ground, above the valley where clouds hung half the day in summer and the sun didn't settle for more than an hour in winter. A place apart from the unfit world. A place apart from war. But Reagan is back in office and British scientists have discovered an enormous hole in the earth's ozone layer above Antarctica. Is this place he built on the hill — adze, log, nail, timber — immune from it all? He doesn't think so anymore.

Where had they gone wrong? He thinks of that night, ten years ago, when she told him she was pregnant — barefoot on fresh pine, dancing around the kitchen table. Her warm laugh. The way his heart had stopped just then, stepped backward into the woods — hard maples, twisted beech, soft pine.

Stephen walks uphill, leaves and ice crackling under his feet. The snow coming down harder now. He thinks of his son, Danny, and what he has, and has not, been able to give him. He thinks of Bonnie, living in town now with her baby, Vale. Of the part-time, low-paying jobs she works. He brings her money occasionally. Groceries. Venison stew. Still — a mother, alone? It's the exhaustion in her eyes he cannot quell.

Deb's unhappiness, either. At what point

does a cabin — its aging pine and dim lights, its mineral-rich outhouse and trickling off-colored spring water — no longer suffice? "I'm sick of this hole we're in, Stephen," she said to him earlier. "It's dark, we're poor, we're miles from anyone other than your mother; our cars don't fucking run when we need them to. It's a hole, Stephen. A hole! And you?" She'd put her hand on his chest, full of the tenderness he'd long denied, and said, eyes brimming, "You're an asshole."

He had remained quiet, watching the shapes rage made out of her face. Watching her tears. Standing and putting on his coat and boots. Before stepping out the door he had turned to her. "I didn't ask you to come," he said, finally. Its cruelty bitter on his tongue. Its truth bitter, too.

A few snowflakes fall, heavy and large, on Stephen's face. The first snowstorm of the year: it always feels like a blessing. A way to start over. Stephen puts the bottle in his pocket and hikes farther up the hill. He always heads for the higher ridge, the spot where Lena's cabin sits. The place they have let rot, corrode, fall back into the earth since Lena lived there. Porcupine-eaten holes in the floors, broken windows, a door that won't close, the rusted potbellied wood stove. Stephen goes there sometimes. Some of Lena's things remain — some pictures tacked to the wall, feathers, bones. A coffeepot on the old two-burner stove. He likes to feel Lena's presence there. The woman who married an owl. *Every bird is an omen,* she used to say. *Every one.*

The hike up the hill doesn't take long, but the night is cold. He should have brought paper, matches, kindling. Stephen takes a long sip from the bottle, stops at the door of the cabin and looks out at the dark hillsides around him. From this height he can see the edges of the barn below lit in moonlight. It looks alive like the coals of a fire or Christmas tree lights or the neon flickering of a TV. He watches the lights go out in his own cabin below. He can imagine Danny asleep in his loft, Deb climbing the ladder, undressing, slipping into the cotton nightgown full of holes she sleeps in. He wants to go to her, lift that nightgown, put his face against the warm, soft skin of her stomach, the skin still softened from when Danny was inside her, put his lips against her ear and say, *sorry.* She's still beautiful. The most beautiful woman he may have ever seen, her face now shadowed by sun lines, smile lines, worry lines, like a well-loved world. Everything looks better to Stephen when it's older — barn siding, floor-boards, leather — and Deb is no exception. But he can't bring himself to go back down there. Can't bring himself to say those two syllables: *sor-ry.* He'll wait until he's sure she's sleeping. Until he can climb into bed unnoticed, lie there unseen, studying the contours of her face in moonlight. For now he'll stay here at this wind-loved cabin at the top of the hill, Lena's haunt, watching it snow. Snow: such permission for silence! A world where he doesn't have to speak, where he never had to speak: the strange groaning of the oak and the sweet-wintry scent of the pines and the air so brisk it stings his skin, turns his breath to icicles on his beard.

He goes inside, sits on the floor with his back against the wall, takes a long swig. His grandfather built this as a hunting shack. A place to go and drink, be alone. A place that stank of animal blood and whiskey. And then Lena made it into something other — light-flecked, feathered, warm. Stephen takes another sip from his bottle, then another, and feels the noise of his thoughts recede, feels his limbs strengthen, feels himself brave and deep and wise, feels himself capable of love and fatherhood and the tenderness required of a husband. The woman who married an owl. The man who married an owl. Is Deb one? He takes another sip. Lies down on the hard floor. He should get up and make a fire, but is there paper? Kindling? Wood?

Lena. He used to visit her when he was a kid. Loved her laughter, her touch of wild. "Here," he'd say, handing her some treasure he'd found, and she would get down on her knees and look closely. Put it to her nose and breathe in — that fox skull, that hawk feather, that quartz stone. Rub it in her fingers. Ask him where he'd found it. Imagine the life it had before it found them.

"Because things find us, not the other way around," she'd said, touching her forehead to his forehead. "Like you to me, and me to you — we needed each other, and so we both went looking."

They found each other, Stephen thinks, his body slipping into sleep. He shouldn't sleep here, he knows it, but the whiskey has warmed him, the bottle now empty. He just needs a short doze. A quick one. *And so we both went looking.*

VALE

November 10, 2011

The trees go bare. The earth grays.

Vale drives to all the places her mother loved — Indian Love Call, the fireworks warehouses in New Hampshire, the ruins of a burnt mansion on the backside of Mount Wantastiquet across the river. Wantastiquet — an Abenaki word, Vale realizes for the first time. She thinks about a news story she heard on the radio a few days ago: an uprising of Bolivian indigenous peoples that led to a 375-mile march demanding compensation for the effects of global warming. It's all connected, Vale thinks, listening to the description of an eight-year-old girl walking with her mother to La Paz, a city neither of them had ever seen before. The tides are rising. All of them.

The burnt mansion is named Madame Sherri's after the eccentric New Yorker who built it in the twenties. Her story has echoed around these parts for years: a convertible, lovers, boas, gay strippers. Legendarily subversive for this town. The mansion burnt to the ground in the thirties, but the ruins are still there, home to generations of high school parties: the stone arches of the windows, some burnt piers, and a grand staircase, also made of stone, curving and reaching thirty feet up toward the sky.

Vale looks around: broken glass, trash, the rocks peppered with graffiti. TZ + NB. GUNS RULE. SCREW YOU CAPITAL-ISM. Below the latter, in thick black ink: *Find me.*

A thin cold rain starts to fall. Vale closes her eyes and pictures Bonnie here, writing those words with her black Sharpie: *Find me.*

She is so tired of these clues that go nowhere. By the Bonnie who never appears, despite them all.

Vale goes to the staircase and starts to climb. It's a stupid thing to do, reckless — the rocks loose beneath her feet, slick now in the rain that is falling and freezing to the stones. Black ice. She's amazed they haven't gated this place off or torn it down. How many beloved teenage haunts actually survive?

But Vale makes it to the top, a spit of stone barely wide enough for her two feet. She stands upright, looks around. The clearing is surrounded by trees, boulders, the faint reflection of a pond in the distance. The rain falls harder on Vale's face and limbs. *Find me,* she thinks, taking off her hat and throwing it to the ground. She takes off her sweater. Lets it fall. Takes off her shirt, flings it over her head. Raises her arms, slowly, into the cold rain. All those eyes that watched her do this at the club, gazes unflinching, did any one of them see her? Vale reaches behind her back, unclasps her bra, pulls it off, lets it drop to the ground below. She closes her eyes. Her nipples raw in that cold air. Her old tricks, with no one to see. A line she read in *No Word for Time* yesterday: "In this world we are largely defined by the sum total of our relationships, to nature and to each other." Vale hears Jake brakes on the highway. The shiver of wind in pines. *The sum total of our relationships.* Vale closes her eyes. Calls out, "Find me!" Guttural. Loud. She has spent her entire adult life learning how to be alone.

Vale lifts her leg, spinning once: a slow-motion pirouette on a funeral pyre.

She drives to Neko's. "Find me," she says,

going to him.

Neko takes off her wet coat. Wet sweater. Wet hat. Leads her to the bed. Unties her boots. Brings her a towel. She's shaking, every inch of her stiff with cold. Neko pulls off her wet pants, covers her with warm blankets. He brings her tea in a fluorescent green mug, lies down beside her. Vale tells him about Lena's cabin. About the marriage license, that barely legible word: *Indian*. She tells him about Madame Sherri's, the words written on that rock. "You'll tell me if you ever see anyone like that again, yes?" she says, her teeth still chattering. "You'll go to her, and talk to her, and tell her I'm here, yes?"

"Of course," Neko says, putting his warm hands on her cold chest.

"But you haven't?" Vale asks. Her body warming. The chills subsiding.

"No," Neko says, kissing her left rib. Kissing under her arm. Looking into Vale's eyes. "But I'm always looking. I swear."

Vale nods. Takes off his clothes. Pulls him inside her. She doesn't want to wait. That streak of heat that runs from her head to her toes. Reverberates everywhere.

LENA

August 6, 1956

Baby Bird —

It's the hour before dawn I love best; rooster, crow, birdsong, the sky ink blue. I step outside and the grass is dew-wet, the world's waking face foggy with mist. Lex is here sometimes beside me, his body golden amid the tangled sheets, his sleeping face shadowed with dreams. Hawks? Wars? Beloved, what rages in there?

Sinners we are. Black with night. Black coffee, sweetened beans. I bring the cup to his lips, the meat to his sleeping fingers. I say, "Home, love. 'Tis best you go home." Oh what pools of guilt, those moss-green eyes! I take my finger and run it down his face, down the edge of his stubbled jaw. I say, shhh, and slip my finger between his lips. Beautiful face. Crow face. The punctured lives of men and women. Otie eyeing us from the corner.

Once Lex is gone, the morning becomes all mine — mist rising, the field alive with grasshoppers. This cabin is a hamlet, this cabin is a cave. Swing low, sweet chariot. I put bread crumbs out on the wooden table in the yard, and my friends the birds come — robins, chickadees, sparrows, jays. Chirrup, chirrup, cheep cheep. The black coffee cools and tastes even better. A sluice along the tongue. The blood wakens, fully alive to the world.

And then that sweet child. Stephen! Coming up the hill. Long-legged, towheaded, barefooted.

To the room that still smells like his father, though he doesn't know that.

"Look!" he exclaims, a skull of some kind in his outstretched hands. I throw my arms to the air, throw my arms around him. "Oh, Stephen," I say, "It's a bona fide treasure! Muskrat? Otter?" He says he found it near the creek, its hue sun-washed, spotted with green mildew.

We wash it in cool water. We find a spot on my wooden shelf for it to sit.

"Come back and visit it anytime, Stevie-o. It's your animal spirit," I say. "You muskrat, you otter." He turns and runs back down the path, singing at the top of his two-pint lungs.

I go to Adele, tell her I am deathly afraid. That love has come over me like a sickness. She gives me herbs — turtlehead and black ash, dark and bitter. "Make a tea," she says, "and drink every morning." It works: a week later my blood comes pouring. I kiss this woman's dark and wrinkled hands that smell of Dawn soap and herbs and tobacco. I bring her a bottle of whiskey, a six-pack of Coke.

Adele tells me a story about M-ska-gwe-demoos, a swamp-dwelling woman, dressed in moss with moss for hair, who cries alone in the forest and is considered dangerous.

"Don't be M-ska-gwe-demoos," Adele says, laughing, shaking her head, cracking open one of the bottles. She says, "Love is risky stuff."

"Have you ever been in love?" I ask.

The minute I say it I want to pull the words back in. But they have wings — a flock of red-winged blackbirds — making their way over the roof of the house, over the hoods of the tallest pines. Adele grows still beside me. Drinks her Coke slowly. Tells me that when the roundups happened she was sixteen.

She grips the counter's edge, drinks her

Coke empty, tells me that she was taken to a hospital and cannot have babies. "Ha," she says, a near howl in her laugh. "Just like that."

She goes to the stove, brings me another cup of dark, steaming tea that smells like trees and dirt and earth.

I bow my head to her knee. Say, "I am so very sorry."

"Mmm," she says. Her eyes are cold. Dark stones under river water. "Lena." She touches my wool-coated arm, lays her warm and callused hand there for a long minute. "Don't mess around."

STEPHEN

How long has he been here, in the cabin?
The snow falling in deep drifts around him.
The cold, bone deep.

He can make out, on the moonlit windowsill, an animal skull, the size of his fist, and
a blue jar full of feathers.

One day when he was a kid — six? Seven?
— he walked up here, skipping, ready to
find Lena, and heard voices. Laughter. He
knelt by a tree ten feet away, not breathing.
Who could Lena have here?

And then, from within these walls, these
very walls, a familiar whistle. His father's.

He'd recognize it anywhere.

Lena's laughter again. Then silence. Just
squirrel, wind, distant highway.

Stephen stood up, crept to the window,
looked in, and saw the naked body of Lena,
rising, her breasts loosened, nipple, waist,

211

long hair, and from below, heard his father's laughter.

A beast, Lena looked like. A terrifying half human, her eyes turned inward in a way he had never seen before.

Stephen tiptoed away and ran down the hill. He ran into the barn, climbed up the ladder to the hayloft and made a bed there, amid the bales. Lay there for hours, filling his fists with hay.

He's never told a soul.

Not Hazel. Not Deb. Not Bonnie. Not Danny. The holding of that secret is part of what makes him, he is sure, a good father, a good partner. The not-burdening of others.

This cabin — where Lena and his father lay. The woman who married an owl. Christ, he is cold. He should go home, but his legs won't move. So cold. He should go back to Deb and Danny.

His family. When he thinks of them, asleep now in the loft of the cabin below, he feels proud, generous, and thinks how tomorrow morning he will wake before Deb and get the fire going early, make her coffee and bring it to her, like he used to do, and when he does he will bend down and kiss the soft skin of her forehead. Maybe, if Danny's still sleeping, they will even make love. He would like that. He would not be afraid to make love in the daylight. He will not be afraid to let her undress him, like she used to do. And he wants to undress her, too. Slip that nightgown up and over her shoulders. Kiss the soft skin between her breasts. Hold them in his hands. Be still there. Put his breath into her ear. Say something. What would he say? *I love your body. I love your arms and your hands and your neck and your hair. I'm so glad you are here.* He will do it. In the morning he will say the words, and then, if she wants, they could make love, and he would wait for her to come, wait for that tender and quiet release that he loved to feel, that ripple below his body, and then he would come inside her, too.

DEB

December 15, 1986

Deb can't sleep. She lies in bed with the lights off waiting to hear the click of the door latch, the creak of Stephen's boots across the kitchen floor, the sound of their bedroom door opening. At four she drifts off, but when she wakes an hour later he still isn't there. At six, just when it's starting to get light, she wakes Danny and tells him they are going for a hike. A hike! She adds that touch of false enthusiasm to her voice. The cabin is cold, a mess, last night's dinner dishes piled up in the sink. Danny's Tintins and Legos scattered across the floor.

It reminds her of the commune on winter mornings — that frozen water in Bird's attic room, the frozen pipes in the kitchen, the sea of dirty dishes that arose around them.

They set out following Stephen's footsteps

through the snow — barely visible shadows.

"Look, your dad's footprints!" she says, her body nauseous, her arms and legs shaking. She wants to smell woodsmoke from that shack at the top of the hill, wants to believe that he has made himself a winter camp up in the woods, in the trees, where he is always happiest.

"What is it you do up there?" she had asked him just last week.

He had shrugged.

"Don't you miss us?"

"Of course," he had muttered, but it wasn't the tone she needed to hear. She wanted him to reach toward her, put his arms around her, cup his palm against the small of her back and hold her.

Hold me, she says more often than she wants to. Sometimes he does, a loose-limbed, nervous hold, and sometimes he turns away from her and does not.

Why doesn't she leave? Deb thinks, pausing to wait for Danny. The snow is deep. Surprisingly so. It's what her mother has asked her for years. *I have no idea why you're raising that boy in such squalor.*

Squalor. Is that what this is? Is that what her grandmother's village in Russia was? Outhouse, wood stove, dark pine whose corners never get entirely clean. They have water from a spring but no plumbing — the gray water still collects into a bucket in the sink, which she empties two times a day. Her twenty-year-old Datsun will only turn on when the radio's playing — will only turn off when she clicks the radio back off. "What the fuck is that about?" she said to Stephen, who grinned, shrugged, walked away.

"Where are we going?" Danny says, pausing in the snow behind her. "I'm cold."

"I know, hon," Deb says. Hiding the terror in her voice. "It's an adventure!"

What she has no way of describing to her mother are all the other gifts of this life she has chosen. The way it feels to wake in the dark, climb down the ladder stairs, and light a fire in the wood stove. The way it feels to make a pot of coffee and sit in the dim light with it cupped between her hands, a thick blanket wrapped around her neck and shoulders, and watch the day come. The way she has come to know the hillside with its cellar holes and springs and creek and wildflowers so that it feels like an extension of her own living body. The way the seasons create a rhythm to her days, and her years. The sensation of having made a world for yourself with your own hands. Of belonging somewhere. Yes, she is frustrated, and sometimes lonely, and poor. But still.

Where is he? The boot tracks faintly rising. Deb scans the treetops for woodsmoke, hoping, but sees none. "Shit," she mutters under her breath. "C'mon, Danny. Hurry."

And Stephen: How can she describe to her mother her reasons for staying with him? The mornings when he used to go downstairs before her and bring her coffee in bed, brush the hair back from her face and wake her. The way he looked at her then — surprised, each time. The way he smells — of wood and earthy sweat and salt. The way, when they have sex — less and less often these days — he cries out at the last minute, a ripple of pain and joy and love into the dark loft of the cabin. How afterward he burrows his face into the folds of her body, strokes her bare skin, and whispers *thank you.* How can she tell her mother these things? How the hazy blue sorrow in his eyes is not something she feels like escaping but something that draws her closer. How when Danny was a baby Stephen would go to him in the night and pick him up, and rock and soothe him, so that Deb could keep sleeping. The way he has given her this world — this cabin, this hillside, this child, this chance at something other.

They're closer now. Neither of them speaks. Deb reaches out and takes Danny's ten-year-old hand in hers, and he accepts it, and they continue up the hill that way, side by side, mittened hand inside mittened hand. Sunlight glistens on the crackling snow. The air is clear, cold, dry. They reach, at last, the small hunting cabin at the top of the ridge. No woodsmoke. No goddamn woodsmoke. The door is closed. Deb pauses and feels her bowels swirl. The taste of nails floods her mouth. A blue jay screeches from the trees above them, and its cry riddles through her limbs until it stings the bottoms of her feet. She turns to Danny and takes his other hand in hers. "You stay here, okay, love?"

He doesn't blink, just looks into her eyes and nods.

She goes to the door of the cabin and opens it. The room is dark; her eyes haven't adjusted. But she can make out a shadow. A body across the floor. He lies on his side, an empty quart bottle beside him, piss soaking the pine beneath him. His eyes are closed and her first thought is how peaceful they look. How peaceful he looks. Those cheeks those arms those shoulders. Stephen. She steps into the cabin and picks up his heavy arm, his leaden hand, peels back his sweater, and feels his wrist, as cold as snow, no pulse beating, and then she opens her mouth and a sound comes out, a deep and anguished howl. And then she stands, and leaves the cabin, and starts down the path to where Danny waits, shaking in the deep snow. She kneels down in the snow before him and puts her arms around him, buries her face into his neck, says, "Come, Danny. Let's go home. We're going to build a fire."

VALE

November 15, 2011

Vale lies in bed in the morning flipping through news stories on her phone.

There are flash floods across Europe. A story about a Filipino-born woman, Cecilia de Jesus, a hospice worker, who drowned in her basement flat on Parnell Road in Dublin. A blurry photo taken months ago of beautiful Cecilia, in her blue scrubs, a smile across her lips.

The victims will be many, Vale thinks, staring into Cecilia's dark eyes.

She drives to town again, stops at the Shell station for gas, walks the fluorescent aisles gathering crackers, peanuts, sparkling water.

A swallow is trapped inside the shed behind the barn — it crashes against the one window, panicked by Vale's presence.

"I'm sorry," Vale says, ducking, the swallow crashing again against the glass window-pane before darting out the door past Vale's shoulder.

The bird has shaken her. She can't get the name, *Cecilia de Jesus,* out of her head. Vale goes to the bed and sits down, checks the pillow, finds: a thin gray hair, three inches long.

Vale picks up that hair and holds it in her hand.

Is Bonnie's hair gray now? It's possible. The waterlogged Bible still sits in the corner where Vale left it. Nothing else seems changed.

Vale drops the hair onto the floor, walks outside and looks around on the ground. She finds a gray stone, the size of her fist, riddled with quartz. Inside she lays the stone on the pillow, rips another scrap from the back of the Bible, writes down her phone number, and slips out the door.

On the car ride home she hears about ten thousand protestors surrounding the White House two weeks ago to protest the XL pipeline. Good and evil, Vale thinks. Duking it out. Everywhere.

Vale fills her backpack with water, wine, crackers, candles, matches, and kindling, and walks to Lena's cabin. She sits at the little pine table, room for two. One seat for her. One for Bonnie. Time seems to have no grasp there in the cabin — the shadows lengthen. She thinks how if the world goes to hell, this would be a good place to camp out. A wine-loving prepper in the backwoods. She lights a fire in the old potbellied stove, adds sticks from outside, lies down on Lena's mouse-chewed bed, and falls asleep. Her dream is a collage: Jack, Neko, Bonnie — young, body streaking with joy — stripping off her clothes and stepping into the river. River sleek and smiling. She calls out to seven-year-old Vale, sitting on the bank. "Join me, honey-pie!"

The Vale in the dream wears thick wool pants, a thick wool jacket, boots and mittens made of soft deer hide. Her clothes are wildly inappropriate for the weather: all protection. She rises. In her right hand is something small and warm. She opens her fingers to see what it is — a bird, dead, its left wing bleeding.

Vale wakes, heart pounding. She's cold, her hair tangled with stray horsehair from the bedding, pine needles, leaves. That bird: the sparrow who was in the barn earlier.

"Goddamnit, Bonnie," Vale says out loud, rising. "I'm so tired of this."

Vale pulls the leaves out of her hair,

brushes them off the sleeves of her sweater. As she stands up she glances upward and notices a box, tucked between the rafters, that she hasn't seen before. Dark wood, two feet square. She climbs up onto the bed to reach it. Pulls it down and opens the lid. Vale takes a deep breath. There are books inside: *A Field Guide to the Birds, A Field Guide to Ferns, A Field Guide to Mammals.* And underneath them: a small notebook, black, leather-bound.

The edges of the pages are dust-speckled, rippled from water damage. The paper has that particular old-book smell, mingled with the smell of mouse and woodsmoke. She opens the book and finds, rivered through-out the pages, drawings made with pencil and black ink. Drawings of bobcats, coyotes, moose, bears. Drawings of birds. Drawings of plants — ferns and trees and wildflowers. Drawings of Otie from every angle. There are words scattered here and there as well, a loose and sprawling script: *The smell of leaves . . . what kind of bird? . . . the broken saddled rib of leaves!*

"Lena," Vale whispers.

Outside it starts to rain.

Vale sits down and reads: *Sunday, dawn, mist rising. Bird shit on stone step out door. Crow? Jay?*

Vale flips the page.

Adele says: near the sickness also lies the cure. Under the words: drawings of grasses, roots, leaves, their names scrawled below them: *purslane, bloodroot, burdock.*

Who is Adele?

Vale closes her eyes and breathes in.

She thinks of Lena with her long braid and fedora. Mother to Bonnie for one week and one day. She opens her eyes and turns the page again: a sketch of a three-legged coyote, looking out from behind some pines. Eyes wild, feral, curious. In the margins, in Lena's hand — *Three-legged-friend! Eyes: Kerosene. Meteorite.*

Vale thinks — vodka. Heroin. Are they that different? A desire for what lingers near the edge?

Vale puts the book down. Feels a flush across her neck and back and spine. She shuts down the stove, closes the book, and stuffs it into the pocket of her coat. It's late, cold, wet out there, the woods shadows — no watch, *no word for time,* Vale thinks, walking downhill, skimming past dark trees.

HAZEL

On the far side of the lake there is a canoe, rowing toward the shore. Two bodies, familiar yet strange, upright, bare-shouldered, bare-armed. Four arms, rowing. A man and a woman. The body in the bow stops for a moment and drops a wrist into cool, dark water.

Hazel is by the lake with Stephen. It is afternoon and too late — she should be getting back to make dinner. Stephen is six years old, half-naked, brown-limbed. She doesn't know where Lex is — he's gone so often these days.

"Time to go, Stephen!" she calls out to where he is swimming, diving, but he doesn't come.

The couple in the canoe paddle to the far side, pull the canoe up onto the shore. Strip off their clothes. Hazel cannot make out

225

their faces or their ages from here, just the birch-white blanch of bare skin.

Leaping. They are leaping into the lake water, avoiding the muck and slime of the shore. They are swimming in loops, silently. They orbit each other, not speaking.

A sudden ache in Hazel's chest. That silence. That swimming.

"Mother!" Stephen calls out, running toward her, lifting his fist up to her face. He opens his fingers, calling out, "Salamander!" and one squirms out of his fist and into her lap, crawls up her legs, near the hem of her dress, and then there is her hard palm across his cheek.

"Don't," she says, unable to stop her hand in time. "Put it back in the water."

His eyes retreat. That stormy green, his cheek blossoming.

Oh, what treason, Hazel thinks, stomach sinking: a mother's rage.

She wants to say she's sorry, but her boy is walking back to the water, the salamander cupped once again in his hands.

The couple, swimming, launch themselves onto the bank, dry themselves off with their clothes, slip them back over their shoulders and hips and legs.

They climb back into the canoe. Push off. Drifting and paddling back toward where they came from, the far side of the lake she cannot see.

Hazel thinks of them, swimming in concentric circles. Thinks of Lex, no longer touching her. Rarely sleeping in her bed.

"Stephen," she calls out, gently this time. "It's time to go home. Get your things ready." That wrist into dark water, those blanched bodies, birch white, unashamed of bare skin. And then her boy, her small child, running in her direction, gathering his things, walking beside her toward the car.

LENA

September 19, 1956

Plum —

Two months into this madness, this forest fire we can't put out. Lex comes every day. I hear his footsteps in leaves, in grass. That particular hesitant, rhythmic breath, then: "Lena? You here?" Beautiful cheek. Beautiful sunburnt neck. Beautiful moss-green eyes. Songster. Trickster. Coyote.

We don't talk about Hazel. We don't talk about the future. I make black coffee on the stove, fill the teacups for him and for me. We sit at the table, facing the window, facing the pines, talking, breathing, looking, sipping the black earth of coffee, full of grounds. He tells me about the Battle of Taejon, the Twenty-Fourth Infantry Division, 3,602 dead and wounded. He tells me about stumbling, early one morning, across a ditch full of dead civilians in Yongsan —

women and children. Flies in their wounds, flies in their still eyes.

He says, "I've never told anyone."

I put my head against the pine table. Take both his hands in mine. Hold them there a long time.

I tell him about the animals I've seen of late: my friend the three-legged coyote. Its night song down by the creek.

Lex sings me his favorite songs: Elvis's "Love Me Tender." Little Richard's "Long Tall Sally." Kitty Wells's "Making Believe." He closes his eyes, taps his feet on the cabin floor.

Sometimes I go to him, put my palm on the back of his neck, and he pulls my body to him, holds his face in the shallow hollow between my breasts. Sometimes we do not touch. Sometimes I say, "Here, look at this," and show him something I have drawn — a mountain lion, a deer's antler, an owl. Otie watches us, blinks, calls out when we do.

"You're genuine, Lena-love," Lex says, with a thin smile and sparking eyes.

Sometimes we walk: stone walls, cellar holes, the swamp at the back of the woods, where the trees part and open into marsh grass and open sky. The bank is covered in coyote trails, paw marks litter the damp mud.

"Treasures," Lex says, fingering the ribs and hollows and gouges of the bones on my windowsill with his callused fingers and wide thumbs.

And then, a desperate hunger in his eyes, "Lena?"

We make our way to the bed. Undress each other. My sister's face is at every window. Her eyes in every knothole in every board of pine. But we don't stop. "Don't stop," I say, before he disappears back down the hill, "coming here."

He kisses my forehead, where the hair meets the skin.

"Lena," he says, helpless eyes, leaning his body into mine.

Stephen comes, too; young legs, pounding, the knock on my door, his voice calling out: "Lena!"

We hike to our favorite spot in the woods — an outcrop of ledge overlooking the house, the fields, the creek below. The rock surrounded by wood ferns, yellow dock, feverfew. "Lay your head back, Lena, and you can move with the clouds!"

I do. And I can! We float to the sky side by side, traveling over treetops. Stephen is laughing, his little body in blue jeans and flannel, his shorn hair and freckled nose and

230

green-flecked eyes, like his dad's. And then Stephen is quiet. "Lena," he says. "Are you ever scared?"

I touch his hand. "Of course I am."

"I don't want to die."

"Everybody dies. And then we turn to light."

He is quiet. We are quiet. We listen to the leaves quiver above our heads; we listen to a far-off tractor, to a bird in the branches above us.

"Common yellowthroat," I say.

Stephen nods and puts his small, nail-chewed, callused hand in mine.

"But if I do die, Lena, I will turn into a butterfly. And it will be okay because I will fly around you and you will say, 'Hey, who is this beautiful butterfly?'"

"Yes, I will," I say. I take his hand and bring it to my chest.

"And I will be a magic butterfly. So I can talk to you."

"I would love that, Stephen."

"And I will be the most beautiful butterfly, covered in leaves and kings."

"Yes, you will, Stephen."

"And you can keep me with you everywhere you go."

"Yes. I will. I would love that. I will keep you with me everywhere I go."

And then he rolls toward me, puts his head and hair on my chest, and I kiss his beautiful boy brow.

VALE

November 16, 2011

She climbs the hill to Deb's cabin, Lena's notebook tucked in her pocket, and knocks on the door. Through the window she can see Deb rising from the table where she sits, a glass of wine and an open book in front of her.

Deb's face softens when she sees Vale. "Come into my lair," she says, moving a pile of books off a chair. "Tea? Water? Wine?"

"Water would be good," Vale says, sitting.

"I was just reading Grace Paley," Deb says, bringing Vale a glass, plopping down on the couch. She tucks her legs beneath her, takes a sip of her wine. "My radical poet hero. She keeps me company when the nights are long. Do you know her work?"

"No," Vale says.

"Ah, you should! Writer of poetry and

stories. War resister. Antinuclear activist. She moved to a farmhouse in Vermont in the 1970s and lived a life of poverty. Wrote beautiful things. She valorizes all of this," Deb says, laughing, nodding toward her books and walls, the bucket under the sink. "Me and my hovel."

Vale smiles. Pulls Lena's notebook out of her pocket and hands it to Deb. "I found this. At Lena's place up the hill."

Deb takes the journal. Flips through the pages.

"My God. This is spectacular," she says, fingering the drawings.

"Yes. I had to show someone."

Deb turns the pages slowly. Takes a deep breath. "Your mother would love to see this, yes?"

"She would," Vale says, emptying her glass. She stands up, goes to the wall where Deb has posted photographs of artists, writers, musicians. A kaleidoscope of voices keeping her company on this hill through the long haul.

"You know you can always stay here, Vale," Deb says. "In Danny's old room."

"I know. Thank you," Vale says, looking at a photo of Frida, a bouquet of pink roses atop her head. A photo of Marilyn Monroe in a straw hat and dark leather. "I'm happy where I am."

Vale stays for dinner — beans and rice, a salad of kale and other late-garden greens — and a movie.

Deb pulls a fourteen-inch TV and a VCR out of the closet. "I still live in the dark ages," she says, showing Vale the VHS. "The tapes are so cheap to buy online." She puts in Agnès Varda's *Vagabond,* one she says she's never seen before, and brings over two full glasses of wine. The film starts with slow pans over barren winter fields. Men and distant fires in the French vineyards. String quartet, cello, and suddenly — the discovery of a woman, frozen to death in the roadside drainage ditch.

"Shit, I'm sorry," Deb whispers. "Just what we don't need. Do you want to turn it off?"

"No," Vale whispers. She feels gutted. Bonnie in a ditch, tits up. She can't pull her eyes away: wine stains in the frozen grass beside Mona. Mona's hair tangled.

The film wanders back in time: Mona quits her job in Paris in order to wander. Along the way she meets a slew of other vagabonds — a Tunisian vineyard worker, a family of goat herders, a professor researching trees. These people who live at the quiet thresholds.

Vale feels remarkably less alone, watching this film. Its refusal to ignore pain or solitude. The screen's cool light bouncing off the cabin's dark walls. Mona with the goat herders. Mona with the maid. Mona on the road again, alone.

The cuts are elliptical — the moments strung together without smooth transitions. You have to do the work yourself — piece together this life of Mona. Smoking fields, goatherds, grapevines. The loose strings of violin threading through the room.

When the film ends, Vale can hardly move.

"I'm sorry. That was inappropriate," Deb says.

"It was beautiful," Vale say, her stomach in tangles. Her limbs frozen. Mona as Bonnie. Bonnie as Mona. The cabin suddenly too dark and quiet around them.

"Too relevant," Deb says quietly, "for both of us."

Vale rarely thinks of Stephen's death, but she thinks of it now. What it must have been like for Deb, living here, alone, for all these years.

"Our lives are pitiful," Vale says.

Deb laughs. "Yes. Remarkably so."

"We need to dance, Deb. Otherwise I think we might die," Vale says.

Deb smiles. Goes to the wall, slips a record out of a sleeve. "Georges Brassens — my favorite dead French songwriter," she calls out, setting the needle down.

Vale rises off the couch, closes her eyes, moves her arms in slow motion.

Dancing, she thinks: an occupation of the spirit.

A refusal to give up joy.

"Georges Brassens — the sexy father I never had!" Vale says, opening her eyes again, moving her toes and fingers and arms.

Deb laughs. Closes her eyes. Moves her hips slowly. An old heat there, Vale thinks, watching.

HAZEL

December 15, 1986

The sound of boots on the front porch, the scraping of snow, and then her front door opening. "Stephen?" she calls out. She's at the table with coffee, next to the blazing Stanley, and is sure it is him. Her son. Long-limbed. Handsome. Kind. It was well below zero last night, the first real cold night of winter, and the Stanley this morning needed three logs going good before the kitchen warmed. "Stephen?" she calls out again.

But it isn't Stephen. It's Deb, with Danny behind her, their mittened hands wrapped together. Deb is still in her nightgown with jeans and Sorels on underneath, her hair a mess. Always the floozy.

"Hazel," Deb says. Her face paler than Hazel has ever seen it, and she isn't breathing right. The room suddenly smells strange, and then Hazel looks at Danny's eyes. They are dark and small, two deep holes that seem to disappear too far back into his body. He's shaking. His lower lip trembling and blue.

"What is it?" Hazel says, her throat dry.

"Stephen," Deb says, not blinking, or moving, or looking away. "It's Stephen."

Goddamn you, Hazel thinks later that day, after the body has been carried down the mountain by two neighbors, after the police have come, and Bonnie with her baby. At last it is just Danny and Deb and Hazel and Bonnie (Vale sleeping on the couch), sitting in Hazel's kitchen at the table, the only spot warmed by the fire, watching the sky give up its light for the grays and blues of dusk.

They are sitting eating the pea soup Hazel has warmed up on the stove, when Hazel says it out loud.

"Goddamn you," she says, looking at the woman who turned her son's life into who knows what. The woman who never seemed to work a lick in her whole life, who spent money on wine and records and had never wanted Stephen, or Danny, for that matter, to have anything to do with cows or the land. She wanted to take this place and Hazel's son in her slender fist and turn it into some kind of fantasy, walk the hillsides

239

in a poetic reverie. But what did she really know about any of it? Of who made those beautiful, now crumbling walls, of the blood and sweat and work that went into these now overgrowing fields. She was sure Deb had never loved her son like she should have. Was too demanding — needing him like a child needs a mother. And Danny. Danny sits next to his mother eating the soup, his eyes wide and still full of that too-deep look that made Hazel nearly gasp and turn away. In her mind: a flash of her own boy at that age streaking across a field, laughing. My son was perfect, she thinks, loving him as deeply as she has ever loved anyone.

Hazel turns toward Deb. "The boy can sleep here," she says, coolly. Her daughter-in-law's eyes have dried, and they look at her then with a look so cold it frightens Hazel.

"No," Deb says. A cold laugh of disbelief. Standing and reaching for Danny. "Come. Let's go home."

And then they are gone, the door closed quietly behind them, and it is just Hazel and Bonnie and Bonnie's baby, Vale, and soon they leave, too, and then it is just her there in her kitchen, alone again, alone as she has been, it seems, for years, and it isn't until all the lights are off, and she is nestled deep under the wool blankets of her four-post bed, that she feels the pain streaking from her legs up into her back and neck and shoulders. An unbearable pain, which will not subside.

VALE

November 20, 2011

Vale buys a Sharpie and writes notes in the places Bonnie might go: in gas station bathrooms, on lampposts, on the stone pilings beneath the railroad bridge: BONNIE COME HOME. THE MOTHER IS THE LOVE FACTORY. MY BONNIE LIES OVER THE OCEAN.

She pictures Bonnie hitchhiking to California. She pictures Bonnie in a cave somewhere, living off roadkill and scavenged nuts and herbs. She pictures Bonnie, mercurial, nocturnal, good at going unseen, making her way through the backstreets of town.

There's another gray hair on the bed at the back of the barn. The rock moved. The note gone. Bodily smells. Cat piss. Swallow shit.

Vale writes on the wall: MY BONNIE.

Neko picks her up at the end of the driveway in his mother's car.

"Do you ever break into houses?" he asks, opening the passenger side door for her.

"No," Vale says, eyeing him suspiciously, sliding in.

Neko pulls out onto the gravel road. Accelerates too quickly.

"What's up, Neko?" Vale asks.

"Nothing. I want to take you dancing," he says, smiling.

"Okay then," Vale says, reaching for his hand. She loves his hand: its heat, its thick fingers.

It's a short drive — ten minutes or so.

A one-story house up a long driveway, made of wood and light — built in the sixties, large panes of glass, no cars in the driveway. "Summer house," Neko says.

He checks the windows until he finds one, in the basement, that slides open.

"Señorita?" he says to Vale, pointing the way through. The strange ways we find solace and joy, Vale thinks, hoisting herself inside.

They find the stairs to the first floor. Neko turns on a handful of lights. The house is all straight lines, dark wood, bookshelves. New Yorkers, Vale guesses: clean, spare, simple sophistication, dripping money. Though she's discovering that money is relative — that the people her mother called "rich assholes" her whole childhood — academics and artists — are both rich and not rich, in the strange twist of inequity, at once.

Neko flips the kitchen track lights on, pours Vale a glass of wine from a bottle on the counter. Catalunya, the bottle says. Garnacha. Vale runs her fingers across the label, breathes in — smells the earth of those mountains in northern Spain. Dry and ancient — she can feel it on her tongue. She closes her eyes and pictures herself in some Spanish city, cobblestones beneath her feet.

Neko smiles. "Beautiful here, no?" He looks around the room. Then steps toward Vale and touches the rim of his glass to hers. "Dance with me," he says, holding his arms out to her.

"Why not," Vale says, smiling, and they dance, to no music, around that room. They tango. They salsa. They crash into a bookshelf, spill wine on an Oriental rug. "Shit!" Neko says, wiping it with the sleeve of his sweater.

"Talk to me in Spanish," Vale says. "It turns me on." And he does: *Te quiero. Bonita. Quitate la ropa. Huir conmigo.*

Vale laughs. Neko kisses her throat, pulls

her to him, spins her in tight circles. Tiny kisses, from the hollow between her breasts to the tip of her chin. Whispers into her ear: *Me hace feliz verte reír.*

Vale smiles. "You have to translate."

Neko puts his lips against Vale's ear: "It makes me happy to see you laugh."

Vale pulls Neko's body to hers, collapses onto the couch.

He finds her there. Puts his face into her stomach. Whispers, "Have me."

Later his eyes are clouded, on another continent. He tells her that he will go back. Needs to. That it feels imperative: documenting the true terror that is war.

Vale rolls away from him. Eyes the dark mahogany of the ceiling.

There is a grand piano in the corner, books scattered all around. Vale nods toward the piano. "Play for me."

"Of course," Neko says, standing, going to a pile of records. He scans the labels, pulls one out, slips it onto the record player.

The needle touches down, that high, rotating hiss, and then solo piano rises into the air. "Bach's Piano Concerto no. 5," Neko shouts from across the room.

He sits down at the piano with his back to her, moves his hands back and forth a

quarter inch above the keys. Vale smiles.
Closes her eyes.

The music escalates, trembles, stops
abruptly and suddenly in places, midair.
Then resumes, slowly, bringing her back to
solid ground. She's never listened closely to
Bach before. Never listened to it with eyes
closed like this — letting it wash over her
body. It's beautiful. The humor of Neko's
motions fades and something else enters.
Vale sees mist rising. Smoke. The air punctured with bullets, with stars. An unbearable grief settles in her chest, brought in by
that piano: Neko's bent shoulders. Neko's
Iraq, and Vale's mother. War, heroin, hurricanes: all symptoms of the same illness,
Vale thinks. Corporatization, militarization,
greed.

Neko stops moving his fingers. Bends over
the cream-colored body of the piano. Rests
his arms and head there. After a few minutes
Vale sees he is sleeping, eyes twitching in a
dream.

She pulls on her jeans and sweater, puts
Lena's hat on her head. Unlocks the front
door, slips through, and starts walking. She
doesn't want him to leave her. She doesn't
want to have to beg him to stay. She doesn't
want him to look up from that piano and
into her eyes and see whatever lies there.

It takes her an hour to walk, the flashlight of her phone leading the way: back roads, fields, Silver Creek.

She's shivering. The night colder than she expected. The walk longer. But she's grateful for it: the sting of cold, the ache of muscles.

A branch breaks above her, followed by a whipping sound, and Vale looks up to see the wings of a large bird taking flight overhead. Owl. Lena's owl, Vale thinks, her breath catching, her eyes following its wings into the ink-blue sky.

"Hello, Barred," she says, shivers up and down her spine.

She read a few days ago that they inhabit dense forests, swamps, and streamsides. Of course they are here, Vale thinks, standing in the cold, the sound of that bird's wings still ricocheting in her ears. Along this creek bank, tucked amid tree branches, seeing me long before I see them.

HAZEL

November 20, 2011

She lies in her bed, the radiator ticking near her feet, and watches the leaves, lit by pale moonlight, fall from the maple outside her window. It's late evening, a cold draft leaking from the cracks around the single-pane windows. She doesn't know what year it is. Time, impossibly tangled. The house suddenly feels thin-walled: all bone. Stephen has moved out, she thinks, and it is just Bonnie and Hazel here in the old house at the back of the field.

"Bonnie," she calls out. But there is no answer.

Bonnie: thin dark hair, thin brown limbs. That god-awful music leaking from under the door of her room too many hours of the day. Bonnie asking a day ago, or was it two, where and who her father is, and Hazel saying, "You have no father. Get ready for

248

school."

The slam of pine door on pinewood frame.

A lifetime spent taking care of others, Hazel thinks. And now this moonlight, and this bed, and this house, too cold even with the radiators on. Hazel pulls the sheets off, restless, and looks down at her threadbare nightgown, her pale legs, her wide feet, in this first-floor bedroom she slept in as a child, and as a married wife, and since then, alone. She should draw the covers up. Close her eyes. Sleep. Instead she stands and undoes the buttons of her gown, slips it off her shoulders. She goes to the wall, feels for the light switch and flicks it on.

There she is. Bathed in light in the mirror above her dresser. Her ninety-year-old face. An apple doll, ravaged and dried, her hair white flames around it. The sagging fruits of her breasts, barely filling the loose polyester of her bra.

The first time Lex loved her it was August. A dance at the town hall. Not the man her father would have chosen for her: a fiddle player, quiet, aloof, magnetic, from a poor family on the edge of town. Not a farmer. Startling green eyes.

It was Hazel who asked him to dance, not the other way around.

He turned, grinned, eyes glinting with

curiosity, and said, "Sure."

Why him? She has wondered for fifty years
now. The dance floor was his place, his river,
his whole body shifting in and out of light.
And then her own body suddenly spinning,
head thrown back, hands gripped tightly to
his shoulders, his chest against her chest.
Why him? She could have chosen so many
others.

She reaches behind her back and unclasps
the bra. Lets it fall to the floor. A few
snowflakes falling outside her window. Her
small breasts hanging there.

He loved them in that field. Held them.
Kissed them. Treated them like they were
some kind of jewel, some unfathomable
treasure.

She closes her eyes. Lex Starkweather.
Fields. Frost-burnt grapes. Hazel brings her
hands to those breasts of hers.

Reaches her left hand lower. And there it
is. That old sharp burn.

When was I ever really loved? she thinks.
When was I ever really loved.

VALE

The owl is still crashing through tree branches in Vale's mind as she walks the last stretch of woods home; she feels its wings beating at the edge of her skin, feels its presence behind every tree.

She feels spooked — surprisingly so.

When she reaches Hazel's field she stops. There's a light on in Hazel's bedroom, unusually late. It's out of her way, but Vale walks in that direction, up to the old farmhouse, and peers in the window just to be sure everything is fine.

It takes her a moment to understand what she's seeing.

Hazel in front of her bedroom mirror, unclasping her bra, bringing her sun-spotted hands to her breasts.

Hazel reaching her left hand down her body, down her stomach, to the crease

251

between her legs.

Jesus, Vale thinks, ducking below the window frame.

An explosive silent laugh rises from her chest.

But the laugh ends. Vale crawls away from the window and walks back through the field, feeling the earth's faint curvature beneath her feet. A living body, the earth: a woman's spine, those stones she nearly trips over. Shit, she thinks. The unbearable loneliness.

And also: good for you, Hazel, you old lady. Seeking pleasure. Finding it.

DEB

We all grieve differently, Deb thinks, walking up that snow-covered path, Danny's
hand in hers, but inside she wants to break
something. She wants to scream. She wants
to give up — toss herself over the bridge
and float downstream. At the cabin she
turns on every light and settles Danny on
the couch with all the blankets she can find
wrapped around him. She starts a fire with
newspaper and, because she can't find any
kindling, takes a kitchen chair and slams it
onto the living room floor so hard that it
shatters, then picks up the pieces, lays them
on top of the newspaper, and covers them
with hardwood until a fire is blazing. She
goes to the gas stove, puts milk into a pan,
dumps cocoa and sugar in, stirs until the
milk is dark and thick, then brings two
steaming cups to where Danny sits next to

the fire. What can she say to him? She's been trying all day, but the words, for the first time, seem lodged. She hands him the hot cocoa and he takes it. She puts her free arm around him and holds him close to her body.

There were times when he was a baby (so many) when she felt her body was all she had to offer: her breast, her arms, her lap. Times when she had been too tired or overwhelmed to sing to him or play with trucks on the floor and so she had simply laid herself down on the bed and brought him to her and let him suck on her breasts and find what comfort and warmth he could while she closed her eyes and let her mind drift elsewhere. In those moments she had escaped, thought of the places she had loved before she came here: her childhood bedroom with its white muslin curtains. A lover by the Monongahela River in high school. That bed on the porch at Farther Heaven, waking alone in the mornings to crickets, roosters, crows. She had always felt half-guilty in those breastfeeding escapist moments, but should she have? Isn't the body sometimes as much a comfort as anything else?

Finally he turns to her. He doesn't say anything but reaches around her waist and puts his hand up under her shirt to the soft skin of her belly and holds it there. When he finishes his cocoa he hands her the cup and leans across her body and puts his face into her stomach and Deb strokes his hair and ears and neck and shoulders until she feels his body become heavy with exhaustion, and then she feels the small shudder that lets her know he has slipped into sleep, and she stays that way all night, by that fire, holding her son's body, until the hillside blushes pink with dawn.

She wonders, for a week or two, if they will go somewhere else, move back to her mother's house outside of Pittsburgh, take Danny across the country in her rusted Datsun, find some cheap apartment in the desert somewhere, but she and Danny stay there, in the cabin, on their own. She clears most of Stephen's things out of the closets and begins wearing the things she keeps; his too-long jeans, which she crops at the ankles, his wool shirts and sweaters. On a Tuesday in January she drives to the library in Nelson and asks if they are hiring, says maybe she can help out for free for a while until a position opens up, and the green-eyed woman at the desk looks at her for a moment, an all-knowing and pitying look, then glances down at the book in front of her and says, "Sure."

Small towns, Deb thinks. They are a bitch this way.

Other people have died, she reminds herself while splitting and stacking firewood. Other husbands. Other fathers and sons, she tells herself while washing dishes at the kitchen sink, while reshelving books on Tuesdays and Thursdays. Other people have suffered and lived on beyond the window of their loved one's lives. In small towns, even. She knows a woman whose husband killed a man, shot him in the head in broad daylight, and that woman lives here still. Visits her husband, whom she manages to still love, once a month in the prison north of Rutland. That woman has come to love, she once told Deb, while checking out a book at the library, living alone. She told her that solitude is the only thing that brings any comfort anymore. But that it does — in abundance: geese on lakes; herons on ponds; boots on leaves in cold weather.

Eventually the library hires her and Deb makes enough money to buy their food and firewood. Her mother sends her money sometimes, and Deb doesn't turn it down. She empties the stinking water under the sink. Takes her old car to town to get it fixed. Their lives become quieter, hers and Danny's, more rhythmic, in many ways more peaceful: no longer reaching out for Stephen's love. No longer trying to touch his sadness or assuage his anger. In the evenings they read books, play board games. Deb drinks wine, too much of it, she is sure, but enough so that she can fall asleep early beside Danny's body and sleep deeply. She listens to Stephen's favorite records — John Prine, Townes Van Zandt — and her own — Ruth Brown, the Nina Simone album Bird sent her in the mail, Georges Brassens — and sometimes she and Danny dance around the cabin. Shuffling and laughing by candlelight. Sometimes they laugh so hard, they both end up in tears.

He is a boy lost at sea, her son, and she his only anchor. "Come," she says, pulling him toward her, his face the same contours as Stephen's, his hands the same, his legs the same. She holds him, and sings him the songs she sang to him as a baby, and ten years old or no, he lets her.

LENA

October 19, 1956

Plum, bird, sarsaparilla —
Adele opens the door and goes to the
stove to put on water for tea. Herbs from
the woods she's gathered — hemlock, yar-
row, burdock — followed by instant coffee.
We drink it outside on the porch, no matter
the season. Her thick boots, her mangled
hands. She says we drink outside so that we
don't forget to hear what the birds have to
say on the matter.

She says, her voice soft this time, "Loving
another woman's husband. Tsk. Dangerous."

She says, "You better be careful. Love can
be more powerful than herbs."

I tell her, "Never!" and laugh, but I stop
bleeding; my body grows thicker around the
waist. In the morning I leave the cabin
where the smell of Otie is everywhere, lean

against my favorite oak, and retch into the leaves.

Adele says, "There's only one way now, and that is forward." She gives me hemlock and yellow lady's slipper.

I don't tell Lex when he shows up at my door that night. I grab his hands and pull him to me. His green eyes glint in the western light, shafting through the window. He says, "If only we had music, Lena-belle," and I say, "Oh we do, Lex-icon. We do," whistling the entire tune of "Saint Anne's Reel."

He pulls me to the floor. He lifts my shirt off of my shoulders, puts his lip against my nipple, twines there.

I am laughing. I am cooing.

I say, "Lex, you coon you," and then there is the music we find there — starlight, murk, flicker — and then crawling toward the bed, where he sleeps wrapped around me until dawn.

We wake early. He has lost his joy in the nighttime — he wakes with his brow furrowed. He is shaking, which always means he is back at that war and its eternal battlefield. I climb out of bed, throw a sweater on, and make us coffee. He joins me at the table. Puts his face into the steam and breathes in. "Lena," he says, eyes desperate. "What are we doing?"

I take a sip of my coffee. Look up to face Otie, who is blinking from the corner. I say, "We are animals." Outside: jay, crow, chipmunk.

He touches my finger with his thumb. Rubs it there. "Stephen," he says, his voice a hoarse whisper.

"Stephen," I say. I don't say: I am with child. I look out the window: red leaves falling from the maples, beech leaves rattling.

"I've done so much wrong," he says, and I don't deny it. I don't deny either of us our wrongdoing in our quest to be loved.

I kiss him on the lips — bristle, moist, coffee-dank — before he walks down the trail to the house below, where his wife is already up, cleaning the stalls, milking.

HAZEL

November 25, 2011

Thanksgiving was yesterday: Deb brought a
small turkey, green beans, mashed potatoes.
Vale came. Not all that different than any
other day. Was it once? When they were girls?

Hazel looks out the window and sees a
girl in a gray sweater walking into the mist-
filled woods. Lena?

Once, that summer their mother died,
Hazel found Lena knee-deep in the creek,
naked, her dress in the leaves beside her.

Hazel wrapped her own sweater around
her sister's naked shoulders and said,
"Come."

But Lena just smiled. Her body cold.
Shivering. "The leaves, they look like rubies,
don't they?" Face lit up, glowing. Leaves
and sticks tangled in her hair.

"Yes, they do, Lena. Time to come home,"
Hazel said, taking her sister's arm and lift-

ing her up, gathering her dress, walking her home across that field.

Is this Lena now, headed toward the woods? Hazel puts on her jacket and walks out to the porch. "Lena," she calls out, but the girl doesn't turn around.

Hazel pulls her collar up around her neck. A cold morning. Brutally so. A fierce wind. The girl turns and waves and grins and keeps walking, and so Hazel follows.

She hasn't been into the woods for so long. The mess of it surprises her: its many roots, fallen branches, and blackberry canes near impossible to pass over. She's never liked the woods — has always preferred the clean order of fields. But she continues, following the girl, stumbling over a fallen tree and catching herself, standing upright. When her breath returns, the girl is gone. Hazel braces herself against a pine tree and closes her eyes. She's dizzy, spinning uncontrollably, her head throbbing.

It's five in the morning and she's young again. She wakes at the crack of dawn to the rooster's crow and the sky's slow blueing. She rolls over to wake Lex, to say "milk" into his ear, but the bed is empty.

It's not the first time. Those sheets vacant beside her. Hazel rises, pulls her nightgown up and over her head, looks down at her body, caught in this early morning light. She is thirty-five years old and still young. Flat stomach, full breasts, strong legs.

She gets dressed and turns to look out the window: Lex's truck in the driveway. No lights from the kitchen windows, no lights on in the barn.

Outside it's cool, already the mornings so dark here on the hill, just a pale moon setting over the trees on the west side of the pasture.

"Lex," she calls out at the door of the barn, but there's no answer, just the cows' restless shuffling, the low storm of their voices rising.

Hazel goes to the woodshed, but the woodshed is empty. She goes to the edge of the field, but it is empty, too.

She heads up the old logging road to the camp where Lena lives, not sure why she's going that way.

The cabin is quiet, all stillness, woodsmoke rising from its thin tin chimney. There's something near the door, a familiar shape.

She steps closer. Takes a deep breath. Her husband's boots. Cracked leather she's oiled many times.

Hazel stands still, twenty feet away, her

hands by her sides, breathing in the cold air.

Goddamn, she whispers to the pines on her way back down the hill. *Goddamn* to the grass and leaves and ferns underfoot, to the sunshine that touches her brow. To the mountain, to the spring, to the house, to the barn, to the boy, in that second-story bedroom, sleeping: *Goddamn.*

Hazel turns and a spruce branch whips across her cheek, drawing blood. What on earth is she doing out here in the woods? Her stomach is in knots. There is no girl. You fool, there is no girl. Her arms and limbs and face are cold. Swamp water pools around her feet, soaking through her shoes.

She turns to make her way back to the clearing, just visible through the trees. Not far, she tells herself, her body shaking, her socks soaked through.

She's almost back to the house when she stumbles. Falls, there behind the barn. There's a cracking sound, and an unbearable pounding in her head. A streak of pain shoots up from her left side, and she feels a pool of wet leak from between her legs. *Jesus no,* she thinks. Lying still. Trying to breathe. Will I be found? Also: the unbearable indignity.

DEB

November 25, 2011

Deb is at the kitchen sink, a John Prine record spinning, a bottle of wine beside her. What a sad old bird I've become, she thinks. She should be drinking with Vale. She should be drinking with Ginny, her old radical pal. They should be at a movie, or out listening to jazz (who cares how long a drive). Put on their old dresses or tightest jeans — show off their sixty-year-old asses, fight this diminished sense of verve.

She finishes her second glass of wine and glances down the hill at Hazel's house. It's an old habit, this referential checking.

But tonight there's no light on. Deb looks at the clock next to her sink — 8:47. Deb knows, from years of watching, that every night between six and nine Hazel watches TV in the living room, but tonight that first-story window is dark. No blue flicker.

265

Deb takes the shortcut through the woods, the early moon bright enough to see by. No snow yet, but cold — fifteen and dropping.

Deb's on the porch when she hears the sound: an animal cry from the far side of the barn.

"Shit," she whispers, running that way.

Hazel smells like piss; her whole body is shaking. "It's okay, Hazel," Deb says, looking into her mother-in-law's terrified eyes. "It's okay. I'm here now. I'll be right back," she says, going to the house to call 911, returning with a couch pillow and an armload of blankets. "It's all right, Hazel, an ambulance will be here soon," she says, a half-truth — it will take twenty minutes or more. She places the pillow beneath Hazel's head, covers her body in blankets, takes her hand in her own and then sings any songs she can think of as the stars come out above them.

There aren't that many she knows the words to. What an absurd thing to discover in the moments that matter. It's the lullabies that come out, the ones she sang to Danny when he was young — Woody Guthrie's "Hobo's Lullaby" and "Silent Night," of all things. But the singing seems necessary. Anything to keep Hazel awake. Voice and warmth under that cold sky. And then the sound of a siren, and the strobe of flashing lights, and the paramedics arriving.

Creutzfeldt-Jakob. That is the disease the doctors tell them Hazel has. A broken rib, yes, but also this rare and swift dementia. One in a million — the proteins of the brain consuming themselves, causing rapid mental deterioration, the part of the brain that delineates space and time the first to go. Rapid physical deterioration, too — breathing, heart rate, motor skills. Hazel spends four days in the hospital for testing, and Deb is shocked at the change she witnesses in that time alone — Hazel suddenly unable to walk, her appetite gone, her mind growing more and more wily. This is, the palliative doctor comes to tell her, terminal. How long, depends: a few weeks to a few months. He says it's hospice care at this point. In a center or at home.

Deb turns to Hazel, eyes closed on the bed next to her, and asks where she wants to be, and Hazel's eyes flash open, and she says, her voice alarmingly clear: "Home." And so home it is.

Vale and Deb set up the bed near the window in Hazel's living room. A hospice nurse will come two times a day to help them change the bedding, check their supplies of painkillers, empty the catheter.

"What is happening?" Hazel says, her voice thin, cracked, her blue eyes terrified, and so Deb tells her mother-in-law about the disease she has. That it is terminal. She's never before had to tell someone they are dying. Hazel looks to the window, nods. It's hard to know if she understands.

The hospice nurse brings a vial of oral morphine and teaches Deb how to manage the pain, which seems to be significant since her fall. The nurse has light-blue eyes. Kind ones. "Your job is to make her as comfortable as possible. You understand?"

Deb nods.

The synchronicity is not lost on her — Bonnie easing a needle, filled with a related narcotic, into her arm four months ago and walking out into the storm. Deb wonders what storm Hazel is walking out into now, and what she'll find there.

Darkness or light? That is the question. Millions of years of queries, and that is still the everlasting one.

She thinks: how little I knew when I was nineteen on those back roads hitchhiking, as she brings a cup of water and a straw to Hazel's lips, as she checks the catheter bag.

VALE

November 28, 2011

She is at the big house with Deb, sitting by Hazel's bedside, when she gets the call. It's nine in the morning; the police officer says they've found some footage a neighbor brought in months ago. Vale takes the phone out onto the porch.

"I'm sorry," the officer says. "It somehow got lost in the shuffle here. Do you want to come in to see?"

"Motherfuckers," Vale whispers, pulling the phone away from her face. She looks out across the field at her small blue camper, the line of trees above it. Her heart rattles in her chest. How can they be that incompetent?

"Sure," Vale says. "I'll come see."

She hangs up and stares out at the bare trees, at the overcast sky, at crows on the horizon.

269

Does Vale want to come in to see? Vale hasn't seen Bonnie for eight years. What kind of a mother does she want to remember? In the last month Bonnie has become something other in Vale's mind. Has transformed into the mother in the photograph plastered all over town: thick hair, laughter — her cheek on Vale's cheek. Does Vale want to see the one who put a needle packed with heroin and fentanyl in her arm and walked out into a hurricane?

Vale stands still for a long time before climbing into Hazel's fifteen-year-old maroon Ford Taurus, the car Hazel will never drive again. "It's yours," Deb said yesterday, waving her hand in the air. "All yours. Take it. Be free."

It's been a long time since Vale has had a car of her own to drive. She could drive it to New Orleans. She could drive it to New York and join the protests. She could start driving west with Neko, lock the doors and not stop until they run out of gas somewhere, start anew in some abandoned farmhouse in North Dakota. Burn his credit cards, passport, camera. She hasn't called him or seen him since slipping out that night. He hasn't called her, either.

Vale pictures cracking open that farmhouse door. Flicker of swallows. And standing in the center of the kitchen in a blue housedress: Bonnie.

"I don't want to be here," Vale says, slamming her fist into the steering wheel as she pulls into the police station parking lot.

She looks the woman working at the front desk in the eye: "I've heard there is some footage."

The video is grainy, blown up on the computer screen. The sound: rain and howling wind. The screen covered in droplets that smear and stretch like veins. The woman who held the phone was standing on her rooftop, filming the creek and the rising water, a plastic toy, car tires, crashing by.

Bonnie appears in the left-hand side of the screen. A drift of white — white sweatshirt, white shoes — stepping off the back stairs of the apartment building, standing still for a moment, looking upward, crossing the street. She's tiny in the footage — Vale can't make out the details of her face, just the outline of her body: bent shoulders, too thin. She walks with a spring in her step. The phone shakes and the woman holding it calls out, "Careful! Dangerous!" and the Bonnie in the screen, small as a child, getting soaked by rain, turns and waves — ghost-face, a blank patch of white — turns again and continues walking toward the bridge. She walks onto the center of it, lifts her arms, holds them out on either side of her, head tipped back — her body shaking — laughter? — and then the screen turns to black.

Vale can't breathe.

"Do you want to keep the footage?" the policeman standing behind her asks.

Does she want the footage? Her mother, a ghost woman, walking into the rain?

"No. Thank you," Vale says, heading for the door.

Vale drives until it's nearly dark. She drives to the river. At the cornfields, an entrance spot to that deep pool in the river where that photo was taken nearly twenty years ago, Vale hits the brakes and pulls over onto the gravel edge.

She gets out of the car and walks across the stubbled field, cornstalks ankle high. She stands in the middle of that clearing, facing the river on the far side. She gets down on her knees. She digs her fingers into the damp and cold earth between the frozen stalks. She opens her mouth to scream, but no sound comes out. Headlights from cars on the highway shoot past on the bridge overhead. "Damn you, Bonnie!" Vale says, her voice coming out at last. Choosing that drug over Vale. Choosing Dean over Vale. "Damn you," Vale whispers, putting her head against the damp earth.

"Oh, honey," her mother says in her ear.

Vale is seven years old. She is in this field with Bonnie, leaping across green corn plants, thigh high. The air crackling with heat — July or August. "Come!" Bonnie yells, in cutoff shorts and blue cotton, running toward the water. Vale races to keep up. When she does, at the river's bank, she reaches out for her mother's hand and her mother reaches back. She pulls Bonnie's hand to her face and holds it there. Squints up into the sun. Her hand smells like cigarettes and lemon. Someone takes a photograph. Someone sends that photograph to Bonnie — she tacks it to the wall. Vale takes that photo with her when she leaves: her mother's hand, her mother's laugh: spikes of gold. And then Bonnie pulls away, throws off her clothes, and leaps into the cold water.

LENA

April 28, 1957

B —

My belly is big. Absurdly so. With you, B!
With you. A girl, I'm sure. B for Bonnie. B
for the bonnie month of May.

Stephen comes and we walk. Late April's
sweet, warm woods — coltsfoot, trout lily,
trillium. We are walking to see Adele, whom
Stephen's never met before, Otie on my
shoulder. Then Otie on Stephen's shoulder.
"Really, me?" he says, laughing as Otie's
talons dig in. Otie finds the bones there,
holds on tight. Stephen grimaces. Sets his
jaw. Is brave.

I tell Stephen, as we walk, about my
grandmother Marie. Two braids down her
shoulders. Dark eyes. Warm laughter. Of the
ways I would go to her when I was young
and we would sit, shelling peas, while she
told me stories. About moons and animals

and monsters and how the earth was made.

"Though I was four when she died," I say, winking. "So maybe my mind is telling lies."

"Indian?" Stephen says, eyes lit up, grinning, a boy in love with books about them, and I shrug, grin back, say, "You never know!"

Who does know? Not me. Not Adele. Maybe my mother, Jessie, but she's gone, too.

The woods are damp, the shadows cool and deep, the earth springing. Stephen hums as he walks, melodies learned from his father's fiddle — "Saint Anne's Reel" and "Bill Hopkin's Colt." Otie starts clucking, and I take him back from Stephen, who runs ahead. Circles back. His legs and limbs bounding. Like a dog. Like a colt! Like a mountain lion.

"Stephen! How dare you make me feel so old?" I grab him by the shoulders and squeeze him hard. He laughs. Frees himself. Skips ahead.

Adele's mouth peels wide at the sight of him. "A child, Lena. You brought me a child! God's holy creatures."

She brings us tea. Cracks open a package of cookies.

We help Adele light a fire in the pit outside

— throw pieces of fresh venison on, salt the rest thoroughly and put it in plastic bags on the shady north side of the house. Adele tells us she'll smoke it later, hands us steaming, smoky ribs from the fire that taste like earth and nuts and beech leaves and spring.

We devour the meat, this boy and I. Ravenous, we are! In love. We wipe our meat-greasy hands in the dirt and leaves.

On the way home Stephen is quiet, taken with moss, stones, swamp pools, the bark of trees.

"Lena," he says, his voice soft.

"Yeah?"

"I like the woods."

I take his tiny hand in mine. Tiny hand, tiny bones. "Me, too," I say.

Stephen smiles and looks up at me. His green eyes that beautiful and bountiful — never-ending — color of moss and leaves. "Run?"

DEB

March 20, 1987

Deb goes to Ginny's farm to borrow her TV and VCR. It's been three months since Stephen died and she wants to show Danny there is a world larger and more capacious than the one they are living in. She wants to show him how art — poetry, film, visuals — can make meaning out of suffering, carve a pathway through one's grief.

It's been a long time since she's been back to Farther Heaven. Ginny's the only one of the originals left there — she pays the mortgage with a slim inheritance; paints the walls with birds and vines and stingrays and bees.

Ginny greets her at the door, leans toward Deb with a long hug, which Deb accepts. "Oh baby," Ginny says. "I'm so sorry." Old friends.

They drink coffee in Ginny's rambling

kitchen and joke about Randy and his banjo. About that cold winter. About Deb fucking Bird in the attic at the top of the stairs.

Ginny spits wine as she laughs. "Jesus. We're growing old, Deb."

"Eccentric."

"Wild," Ginny shouts out, cooing. "And broken," she adds, her voice quieter.

Burnt sienna, Deb thinks, perusing the artwork in Ginny's studio. A horse's body and a woman's head. A woman's body and a horse's head. Oil on pine boards. Grays and blues and blacks — the color of smoke, the color of November.

"I love these," Deb says, brushing her finger along the dried ridges of the paint.

So nonpolitical, these muted landscapes of white birches and rust-colored leaves. These conversations between darkness and light, color and space. Or maybe just quietly political. A way of saying: *here.*

No matter, she loves them, gets lost in them — the texture of far-off ferns, the graceful necks of birches. The way light moves, radiates, reflects, dances. Cadmium yellow, alizarin crimson, sinopia, rose. A way to be less lonely amid the trees. A way of talking back to them. Beauty: she grows fonder of it every day. Keats: *Beauty is truth,*

truth beauty, — that is all / Ye know on earth, and all ye need to know. How wrong she thought he was when she was twenty-two! How right she now thinks he might be.

Ginny shrugs. "They're something. A reflection of light."

Deb nods. What is she doing to make her way through the days? Danny. She has given her life to Danny, her child, and to the house where they live. She splits kindling to get the stove going every morning, pores over seed catalogs, feeds and tends to her birds, works at the library. In the late afternoon she starts making dinner, does laundry, washes the dishes. She recalls reading Simone de Beauvoir in her college dorm room, a cigarette perched between her lips, furiously underlining: *Few tasks are more like the torture of Sisyphus than housework, with its endless repetition.*

Is her life now radical in any way? Widowhood. Mothering and housewifery. No different from Hazel's life down the hill. Not all that different from her mother's, after all. She'd like to ask Helen Nearing: But what about feminism? How do you reckon with that, amid all your loaves of bread?

Standing in Ginny's studio she thinks maybe she should have stayed here, in the commune on the hill, and grown old with

Ginny — artists in their refuge — yoga in the mornings and wine in the early afternoon. A diffused feminism. Art a way to at least feel engaged with the conversations of the world.

But Danny. Her son. No way to regret the life that brought him to her: green eyes, long limbs, his blood and hers. And Stephen, too — the way when he walked in the door she wanted to go to him, every time, draw his body, in a thin T-shirt or thick wool, toward her. Put her nose in the crook of his neck and breathe in.

On her way back from Ginny's she goes to the video store and scours the racks for something decent. Some Fellini, Godard, Bergman, or Tarkovsky; the directors she loved in college. A part of her that's been shut down for too long. At last, in a far corner, she finds Fellini's *8 1/2*.

She sets the TV and VCR up in the living room of the cabin. She makes popcorn, opens a bottle of red wine she's picked up at the store, pops the movie in.

Blue light projecting onto those dark pine walls. It will be the first movie Danny sees, and she can't remember if it's at all appropriate. She saw it in college sometime and has had Anouk Aimée's face etched in her mind ever since, accompanied by Nino Rota's buoyant and emotive score.

The images light up the screen: Guido the tortured artist in dark-framed glasses, a cigarette drooping from his lips. Deb smiles at the pleasure of a good image. Drinks her wine, pours herself more.

They watch Sandra Milo fling off her towel: "Guido, do you love me?"

The sex scene turns to dream: his dead mother in the room. A steady stream of flashbacks and dreams interwoven with present time. "Is that you, Mama?" Guido the boy-child asks.

"So many tears, my son," she answers.

Deb glances at Danny. He's staring, transfixed. She puts her hand on his arm.

The Italian actresses are glamorous and elegantly coy — coiffed hair and dark eyeliner.

Look at me now, Deb thinks, nearly laughing out loud, glancing down at her legs and feet. Stephen's old blue jeans and the plaid shirt — also once his — full of holes. Her hair, shoulder-length, which she cuts herself in front of the cracked mirror in the upstairs hallway. A form of feminism, yes. But does it bring her joy? Does one need to be desired in order to feel beautiful? Deb wonders, watching Anouk walk though a crowd of admiring men. De Beauvoir: *One is not born, but rather becomes, a woman.*

So many sex scenes! She should have known. Danny sits beside her not moving, not looking at Deb.

"Don't worry, kiddo, it's just the movies," Deb says quietly, and it is, just the movies. Nothing like real life. All of the unknowns that live between the sheets no matter how well you know each other.

Sometimes when she was having sex with Stephen she would close her eyes and think of Bird. Not because she didn't love Stephen's body but because she was desperate, occasionally, for something other. For another life lived. To live out all the possibilities she has shut out in the night, in the dark, with his body beside her.

Of course she never told him that.

And who did he imagine while he was making love to her? She'll never know that, either. That's the thing about marriage, she thinks — all those dark places, untouched and unknown. How you share the laundry, and your dinners, and the bed you sleep in, and the child you make, and yet there can still be so many facts or secrets, shameful or mundane, left in shadow.

Nino Rota plays on — spikes of humor, constant motion.

The credits roll, and Danny rises, smiles at Deb briefly, climbs up the ladder to his room.

"Night, love!" she calls out, overly cheerful, a half-drunk creature, and he nods and closes the door behind him.

Deb sits in the dark and finishes her bottle of wine for a good hour or more. Her head is buzzing with images of Rome. Of bordellos and leather and quick one-night stands. Of the woman she might have been if she was elsewhere, if she had not married the man she married. A bear. The woman who married a bear. If she were to make a film about her life, that would be the title.

Deb laughs. The woman who married a bear who watched Fellini films during the winter, got perversely drunk on red wine in the dark alone.

What a film that would be! Choking on her wine. What a sad film that would be.

That night, like many others, she wakes at three in the morning, cold, and finds herself reaching across the bed for Stephen's warm body. After a while she becomes sure that 3 A.M. is the hour he froze to death, that her waking is some kind of spirit vigilance. Maybe even that his spirit is hovering. Her dead unhappy king of the woods. She hasn't ever believed in spirits before, no matter what Hazel thinks of her. She wasn't and isn't that kind of hippie. But when she wakes in the night she feels closer to Stephen than she does any other time. Sometimes she cries, and sometimes she whispers things to him. *Our son . . .* , she says, quietly, toward the rafters and the window above their bed. Or, *my life without you . . .* And sometimes, and this she would never tell a soul, he answers back. He places his callused, warm hand on the small of her back. He rubs it, gently, says quietly: *Hello in there. Hello.*

DEB

November 29, 2011

The darkest time of year. Isn't some kind of
light in order?

Deb puts the TV and VCR in the back of
her truck and brings them down the hill to
Hazel's kitchen. She's rented *The Unbearable Lightness of Being,* a film she hasn't
seen in twenty years. She and Vale need
something transporting, something sexy; she
wants to go back in time and be Sabina with
her artistic broodiness, bohemian and
solitary by choice. She wants to watch films
about hard times and remember the ways
that people go on living in the face of
tragedy. Art as blueprint.

"You ever seen this before?" she asks when
Vale arrives.

Vale shakes her head.

Deb dumps olives into bowls. Pours them
each a glass of French wine.

285

Vale picks up her glass. Sniffs it. Smiles. "Enlighten me."

They sit at the kitchen table to watch it, not wanting to wake Hazel. It's set during the communist takeover of Prague in 1968. Sex and politics and people finding one another in the dark. Across the screen: Lena Olin as Sabina with her hat, undressing. A young Juliette Binoche snapping photographs of the occupation. 1968: Deb misses, in so many ways, the immediacy of that year. The way her purpose and direction felt so clear. The way the resistance — to war, to racism — brought her generation together in art, in academia, in action.

The quiet beauty of the ending guts Deb now just like it did when she watched it the first time — the way Daniel Day-Lewis and Juliette Binoche found light in each other. Happiness!

Just before their car crashed on that rain-slick back road at night.

"Harrowing," Deb says, when the movie ends.

Vale leans her head back. Closes her eyes. "I don't want the dream to end," she whispers.

Deb smiles. "Me either. The return from that transportation is unbearable."

And not just transportation, Deb thinks;

the film makes the stark wood of the kitchen cinematic, Vale's autumnal beauty magnified, Hazel's dying a harbinger of something greater.

"I've met someone," Vale says quietly, her eyes closed.

Deb looks at her, eyebrows raised. "You have?"

"Yes," Vale says, eyes still closed. "Neko. A photographer."

"No shit." Deb grins. "I'm happy for you, Vale." She takes a sip of her wine. "And jealous."

"It's terrifying," Vale says. She stands and puts on her sweater. Her hat. Slips into her boots.

"Yes," Deb says. "I remember."

Vale stands in the doorway for a moment. "Is it worth it?"

Deb laughs — her old-lady laugh. Half-crow. "Hell yes."

Vale smiles, tips her hat, steps out into the dark and wind.

Vale

November 30, 2011

Vale drives to the fallen barn on Cedar Street.

She walks toward the back shed. There are noises from within: plastic rustling, a clank: something more than swallows.

"Hello?" Vale calls from the door, her breath quickening, uneven. That old familiar feeling of hope that Vale has come to dread.

A man's low voice: "What is it?"

Vale steps through the doorway. There's a homeless man she's seen around town these last few months — gray beard, gray hair tied back in a ponytail — sitting on the bed, knees pulled up in front of him, his back against the wall.

"Sorry," Vale says, stepping back.

"You looking for someone?" he says, eyeing her. Rheumy eyes. A large army-green backpack on the floor.

How does he know? Vale wonders. But in his world, maybe people are always looking for someone.

Vale reaches into her back pocket, pulls out the folded flyer with Bonnie's face on it. "Have you seen her?"

The man takes the photo. Looks at it for a long time.

"Sure," he says quietly.

Vale look into his eyes — pale blue, sur- rounded by a sea of wrinkles. "You have?"

"Months ago," he says. "But since the storm? No. Just your posters."

Vale nods. Thinks of Bonnie in that foot- age. Idiotic. Sick. Complicit.

"I'm persistent," she says.

"She looks like she was wonderful," the man says.

Vale takes a deep breath. "She was," she says. "She loved dancing. She loved to swim."

The man nods. Reaches into his pocket for a cigarette. Offers one to Vale. She takes it, even though she hasn't smoked in years. "Thank you."

He lights it for her. Lights his own. "Bru- tal," he says, letting out a slow-moving rib- bon of smoke from between cracked lips.

"Yes," Vale says, coughing. *Why the fuck did you walk out onto that bridge, Bonnie?*

"And surprising," he says, lying down, turning his back to Vale.

"Yes," Vale says. She looks at her words on the wall: MY BONNIE.

"Thank you," Vale says, turning and heading out the door.

She stands outside for a moment sucking on that cigarette. Her lungs burn. Her eyes sting, take in: the railroad tracks, the ice-edged river, pigeons on the rooftop of the sheet-metal shop, their plump iridescent bodies backlit.

She drives to Neko's. She knocks on the door above the barn, opens it.

"Fuck you," Vale says, entering.

He eyes her for a long minute from the table. Stands up and walks toward her.

"Screw you, Neko," Vale says, going toward him. "You have no clue. No clue what it's like to have a mother like mine!" She pushes his body against the wall, slams her fists into his chest. "You know where she was on my sixteenth birthday? No. You do not. In the bathtub with a needle in her arm."

Vale slams her fists into Neko's chest again. "In the bathtub with a needle in her arm!" she yells, collapsing onto the floor.

"I'm sorry," he says, quietly.

"No clue," Vale says, looking up at him. She's crying. Tears and snot dripping down her face. She wipes her face with her sleeve.

"I know I don't," Neko says, standing still. "I'm so sorry."

"Neko," Vale says, looking up.

"Yeah?"

"I'm so tired. So goddamn tired. You know what I want? I want to find her body. I want to find my mother's dead body." Vale takes a deep breath. Collapses over her knees. Turns her head to look out the window. Gray sky. Gray trees.

Neko bends down. He unties the laces of her boots. Pulls them off her feet. Puts his hands on her shins and looks into her eyes. "I'm so sorry, Vale," he says.

"When do you leave?" Vale asks, meeting his.

"I'm not sure yet. Sometime after Christmas."

Vale nods. Curls into a ball on the floor. Stills her body. Slows her breath. Holds still there.

PART IV
HOUSE

LENA

Baby B —

A girl-child. That's what slips from between my legs. Slips — how quickly we use
that word! How easily it slides off our
tongues. And you do — slip — after eight
hours on my hands and knees, of mouth to
the moist armpit of the earth — moss,
leaves, ash, dirt — beside the outhouse and
north of the trash pit. I don't have time to
run down the hill. No way to call for help. I
say, *Here baby.* A car slamming into my
abdomen, time and time again. Ripping my
dress off my shoulders. Weeping. Sweating.
Swearing like a sailor. *You goddamn bloody
cunt of a god,* and also, *Here baby. Here
baby. Here baby, come.*

Otie hopping around in the leaves, frantic,
warbling his throat-call of danger. The radio
playing quietly in the cabin: Patti Page,

ridiculously jaunty. Me thinking of all those heifers in the barn I'd seen, their arching backs and quaking legs. Their low bellows. Thinking, sure, we were born for this, but I've seen too many stillborns to count. Plenty of heifers who didn't survive: bled to death or gave up on the trying. Thinking, *goddamn cunt of a god.* Thinking, *Lex, goddamn you, this is what it costs me. Not you. Costs you nothing but pleasure. Your live dick and quaking back, but this — this — this! Goddamnit — is what it costs me and women everywhere.*

And then another wave, and I'm on the ground, cheek pressed to dank earth, teeth clenching, arms shaking, spit rising from deep in my throat, thinking, *Breathe, breathe, open, breathe,* and *Come baby, oh god, dear baby, come. Otie — hello. I'm okay. Oh, god.*

And then he finds me.

Lex.

"Lena," he whispers, putting his hand on my back, saying into my ear, eyes wide, "Hold on. I'll be right back, with help." Turning and running, and then my sister, strong and loyal-as-an-ox sister, Hazel, who has done this before, who has helped hundreds of times with the cows in the barn, is beside me. Those strong, capable hands.

Breathe. She commands. Body smelling of flour, of butter, of barn. She says: *Lex. Truck. Soon.* But there is no soon. There is my back, rising, arcing. There is a sound escaping my lips. And my sister's astonished gasp, a gush of water and gush of blood, and my hand reaching down and *oh, there,* the wet soft bulge of a skull, and then you are in my arms, there in the dirt, blue-green-eyed, blood-smeared, blue-limbed, breathing.

And I am breathing, too. Good Lord. I am alive. And I am breathing. And you are breathing, too.

"Bring her to your breast," my sister commands, and I do. You leaf-flecked squalling thing. My sister takes off her sweater and rubs down your bloody face and limbs, covers you. Brings a blanket and covers me. A girl. A daughter. "Hold her there, until she gets it," my sister says, and I do, this bird mouth, open wide, reaching, craven, baby bird eyes, brown or blue or green, I can't tell, and then you're there, latched, sucking.

Otie watches us from a nearby tree. Heartbeat in your little neck. Heartbeat in your bare blue shoulder. Heartbeat to the right of your visible eye. Translucent skin. Sucking. Oh, B. We are alive! Tears on my cheeks. Blood and shit on my thigh. We are alive. You and me. And you are fine: leaf-flecked, blood-speckled, perfect. I put my face against your girl scalp, still bloodied and blue and unbearably tender. "Bonnie," I whisper. Bonnie for beautiful, for the Bonnie month of May, for the tune my mother sang: *my Bonnie lies over the ocean.* "Bonnie May Starkweather," I say out loud, baby girl I bring to my chest again when you lose your latch, pulling my blood-smeared shirt away from your face, my whole body shaking, your little body against mine.

LENA

May 21, 1957

There is blood. Lots of it. Too much of it. There is a truck, bullying its way up the old logging road to the cabin, bullying its way back down. They bring Lena and the baby to Hazel's house. Lex carries her to an upstairs bedroom full of bright-painted pine and curtainless windows. "It's okay," he whispers, his body smelling like fear — animal. She holds on, puts her face against his chest, holds still in that familiar wool, the well-loved pocket below his clavicle.

Somehow there is her girl-child, suckling, and then Hazel takes her from Lena's arms, and her girl-child is gone.

Hazel says, "Sleep, Lena. You need the rest."

The house she left so many years ago. The house that called its Abenaki neighbors niggers and Gypsies. The house that scoured

299

Lena's dresses and forever tried to tame the tangles in her hair.

But she cannot sleep without Bonnie. "My child," she says into that white room, those white walls, but Hazel does not come. Lex does not come. Lena tries to rise out of the bed, but her body will not move. Streaks of shooting pain between her thighs. Breasts that leak and spurt and weep.

HAZEL

December 6, 2011

The room spins — blue-green ships, pale
lemons.

They bring her down to the house, set her
and the baby up in a bed upstairs, but
Lena's not well enough to care for the child.
She has a fever, an infection somewhere. Is
weak, has lost too much blood. Hazel has
done this for years with cows in the barn;
brought them warm water and rubbed
down their teats. Helped them heal. Hazel
takes the baby from Lena. The baby
screeches and Hazel fills a bottle with
formula, the stuff the doctor delivered, puts
it between Bonnie's lips until she stills.

Lena weeps, rages, in her room at the top
of the stairs. "Bring me my child!" she calls
out, her voice weak, cracking.

"Shh," Hazel says to her sister. "You're
not well. What you need is rest." Hazel

brings the baby to Lena every morning but does not let her nurse.

"Let me," Lena implores, crying, but Hazel pulls the child away. Lena's breasts swell, engorge, grow hot to the touch.

"Squeeze them with your fingers," Hazel says. "They'll dry up."

The doctor, on the telephone, says *best not to nurse.* He says: *hot water compresses. Aspirin.*

Lena's brow grows beads of sweat. Her fever rises. Her shirts are soaked from spurting milk, her breasts red, rock-hard, burning.

Hazel brings the baby to her crib. Gives her the bottle. Wraps her in thick cotton. Puts her on her stomach and slips out the door.

"I'm sorry, Lena," Hazel whispers, looking around frantically. Reaching her arm out into the room. But no, she's confused again. This is not Lena, walking toward her.

This is Deb. Handing her a cup of something too sweet. A straw. Placing it between Hazel's lips.

She closes her eyes. Sucks in.

A disease of the brain. That's what Deb tells her she has. And now she's in the living room in a hospital bed, and Deb is here all the time. Sometimes a woman she doesn't know. Sometimes Vale.

She closes her eyes. It makes the breathing easier and eases the pain, which seems to be from nowhere and yet everywhere. What is the name of the disease they tell her she has? All she remembers is one in a million.

One in a million. She and Lena are girls, picking wild blackberries on a hillside. They are singing. The church songs they knew then. Lena in a pale-blue gingham dress, covered in stains, a hole by her left knee. That knee covered in scabs. Those legs running out ahead: a ball of fire, or sun-stricken light, wild hair in flames, that hair Hazel tried to brush that morning. Lena throws her arms into the air and runs and does not stop running.

"Lena!" Hazel calls out, but it's no use.

Hazel saw her giving birth. Lex tearing down the path like something was after him, face ghost pale. And then Hazel was running, too. Hazel thought then: dead. My sister will be dead. Just like all those heifers. And then Lena reared up, like a horse, like a lion, and made her hands into fists and raised her neck and bared her teeth, and it was girl-Lena again, that feral child, swearing, spitting, and then the head of a baby.

Crowning. The wet, bloody orb of a child's head, coming into this world.

Hazel wiped the baby down, brought her to Lena, there in the dirt, saying, "Let her drink."

And she did. Lips to her rising breast. Bare cheek against bare skin. There in the dappled light. Her sister's fingers on the girl's crusted skull, and then the next wave of contractions, as she pushed the placenta out: magenta, still half-alive, that pulsing thing in the dirt and leaves.

"Lena," she calls out now. "Take the baby."

But it's Deb leaning closer, brushing her hair back from her face. "Hazel? Are you okay? Do you need anything?"

"Where am I?"

"Your living room. Here. I made some soup. Full of fall vegetables."

She brings a spoon to Hazel's lips. Warm soup. Cool hands. It slides down Hazel's throat and settles in her stomach. Vegetables — tomatoes, potatoes, squash. Just like when she was a girl, a young woman, a wife, a mother. Vegetables from the garden, always.

VALE

December 12, 2011

Hazel is sleeping. So often sleeping these days.

Vale sits in the chair on the far side of the room under a lamp, *No Word for Time* in her hands. She reads: "The essential poetics of the Algonquin might be called 'poetry in motion,' or becoming one's own medium of expression." Poetry in motion: Vale looks at her leather boots, her red dress from the thrift store, the poppies on her right arm. All these material things: clothes, Lena's green hat, the green mottled chair on which she sits now, the texture of the plaster walls — they speak to her, affect the way she breathes, affect her ability to feel at peace in the world. "Everything that really matters is enacted," Pritchard writes, and Vale thinks of Lena's life up there on the hill — the simplicity of it, the bottles stuffed with feathers, the skulls on her windowsill, the philosophical statement of her living. A physical turning away from power lines and the machinery of want. A turning toward: trees, woods, animals, stars.

What are Vale's poetics saying? And Bonnie's? Crystals. Patti Smith. Bowl full of rosaries. Vale reaches into her sweater pocket and pulls out the blue rosary that's lived there since her trip to her mother's apartment. She slips it over her neck. Fingers the beads, one by one.

She looks out the window and sees it has started to rain. A December rain, bringing down the last of the oak leaves, streaming down the fields and ditches where there should be snow.

There are footsteps on the porch, the front door opening, and Deb's freckled, sun-weathered face entering. "Hey there," she says, grinning and peeling off her raincoat, pulling a bottle of tequila out from under her sweater.

Vale nods toward the bottle. "You're not messing around."

"No, I'm not," Deb says, glancing at Hazel in the living room. "Are you?"

"No," Vale says, rising from her chair, going to the cupboard for cups.

There are no shot glasses in this house — they pour the Patrón into half-pint canning jars. For how many years did Hazel fill them with raspberry, blackberry, blueberry jam? And how many years now since she has? The garden moved, at some invisible point, from the farmhouse to the hippie cabin on the hill. What a strange cultural transformation, Vale thinks, bringing the cups to the table.

"To winter," Deb says, raising her glass.

"To would-be winter," Vale says, raising hers.

Deb sits down at the table. "Tell me about the book you're reading."

And so Vale tells Deb about *No Word for Time* and embodiment. About the slippery nature of time — past and present. About how, according to Pritchard, the past is in the present and the future, too. Vale tells Deb she can't stop thinking about Marie, her great-great-grandmother. Of what was not passed down — how to braid sweet-grass, the medicine that exists outside our back door, a way of belonging to the world.

"Shadow stories, these ancestors of ours," Deb says. "Blueprints for how to be in the world."

Vale nods, taking a sip of her tequila. "Yes. But what happens when we lose those

stories? When the story lines are severed?"
She pictures Bonnie's face at that river,
holding Vale's chubby body against hers,
laughing. Bonnie — who never held Lena's
notebooks. Never saw Marie's photo. How
might her life have been different if she
knew what Vale knows? How might it not
have been any different at all?

Deb reaches across the table and puts her
hand on Vale's. "Vale, you are one tough
motherfucker."

Vale smiles. "Thank you. Hey, Deb." A
warm heat in her chest from the tequila.

"Yeah?"

"Tell me stories from the commune."

Deb tips her head back and moans. "Farther Heaven! How long ago that life seems!"
She tells Vale about Ginny hanging artwork
from the rafters of the barn, about the girl
Opal, hungry all winter, her thin bones,
about Bird and her radicalism, the rafters in
her attic room, its candles and frozen jars of
water. She tells her of the time Randy,
drunk on home brew, dragged a keg and a
chainsaw up into a pine tree, then cut off
the branches below him. Of the time Ginny
leapt over a bonfire, catching her dress on
fire. Of the snow-pissing contests they held
in the dead of winter. "Easy for men to write
their names in the snow. Harder for us

women."

Vale smiles. Pours some more tequila for them both, looks up at the rough-hewn rafters. "Sounds like the punk anarchists of Pittsburgh and New Orleans, only more hopeful. Not a bad way to come of age."

"Hopeful, yes," Deb says. "But we were also on the tail end of a god-awful war. No radical change comes during good times."

Vale nods. "To change," she says, lifting her glass for a second time. Downing it. That fabulous sting. She closes her eyes and wonders if her generation has it in them to try and shift the world, here at this new crossroads. Not just war but honeybees, and drinking water, and oceans, and super-storms, and widespread famine. When will the hearts of her generation rise up in one communal scream? She thinks of Occupy, 350's Keystone XL, the indigenous protes-tors trying to protect forests and rivers in Bolivia. Dots connecting across the globe.

Deb takes a sip from her jar. "All of that earnest hard work and love we put into that land, but we failed terribly. My God, we stank." Deb guffaws. "Everyone left but Ginny. But you know" — she nods toward the window, the fields Hazel's tended so fiercely — "sometimes not upping and leav-ing is the hardest thing to do, but it's the real work, too."

Vale nods and looks down at her hands, twirls the blue rosary.

"Oh, what an ass I am," Deb says. "I'm sorry. Everyone is free. To stay. Or go. To own your past or shed it. You can do anything you want, you know, Vale. You don't have to stay here."

Vale looks into the living room where Hazel lies, her limbs curled inward. She imagines upping and leaving tomorrow — joining the protestors in New Orleans, New York, San Francisco. How easy it would be. She thinks of Neko's wrists. Neko's lips. Neko's collarbones. She raises her empty glass to Deb's. Thinks: *We are the sum total of our relationships.* Thinks: *Near the sickness also lies the cure.*

She enters Neko's room in the early morning. Climbs into his bed. Wraps her cold arms around his warm body.

"Hello," he says, turning, rising onto his elbows. "You're here."

"I'm here."

"I'm glad," he says, putting his arms around her.

Vale puts her face against his chest. "Hey, Neko."

"Yeah?"

"Can I bring you to my place?"

He climbs into the passenger seat, and Vale takes a circuitous route, not talking, sunshine beaming in through the windshield, the car passing River Road and Hogback Mountain, the boarded-up general store, Silver Creek and Sunset Lake, ice glistening across its surface. She winds her way back to the farm, crosses the bridge, and parks halfway up the driveway. She nods toward her camper sitting at the edge of the field.

"Home sweet home," Neko says, squinting at it across the field. Vale nods.

She hasn't brought anyone but Deb to this camper since she was sixteen. She feels strangely naked having him here: Lena's hat perched on a hook by the door, her mother's silk dress hanging from a nail on the wall, the owls she collected when she was sixteen, the pictures of Bonnie and Lena and Marie.

Neko takes his time looking around. He stares for a long time at the photographs.

"Coffee?" Vale asks, putting water on.

"Please," Neko says, fingering the silk dress, the crude stitches running up its side.

Neko sits down in one of the two chairs and looks up at Vale. "You're in here," he says, smiling. "In this camper. In all these things. You."

Vale nods, pours the boiling water into their mugs, bring them to the table. "Sorry. No cream. No sugar."

Neko holds the cup to his lips. "Perfect."

He opens *No Word for Time,* skims through the pages.

"What a cultural vacuum we live in, eh?" he says after a few minutes. "We each have to go looking. Make sense of the world on our own. What a lot of work it turns out to be."

Vale nods, thinks of her mother's crystals, tarot cards, Native American mythology, newfound love of Jesus. All those years of looking in order to fill the hole of Eve's banishment from the garden, she thinks. A culture based on division rather than interconnection. Isolation rather than belonging.

"How badly I want Marie to be Abenaki because of the ways in which that would make me feel I belong here," Vale says. "That I have a right to these woods. You know?"

Neko nods. "Yes. But no need to be so hard on yourself. Or them. The ones who came and carved homes out of this hillside? They were poor, desperate, hungry, too. Survivors. Most of us do our best with what we have, no?"

His eyes are distant. Vale thinks: Iraq. The

312

girl he pulled from the wreckage — Vale pictures her slender arms, her still, dark eyes.

Vale brings her head to Neko's head. Rests it there. "Can I show you someplace else?"

They walk uphill, across the field and along the old logging road to Lena's cabin. She doesn't know why she's bringing him here exactly. She wants to show him the way the cabin has grown into the hillside and land around it, burrowed, half-swallowed, yet still containing light. She's been coming here often — near daily, before or after work. She has stocked the cabin with armloads of kindling, newspaper, matches, candles.

She lights a fire in the potbellied stove. They sit, huddled in front of it, while the newspaper bursts into flame and the kindling slowly catches.

Neko is quiet. Warms his hands by the fire. Watches Vale, a gleam in his eyes.

"She's here," Vale says, after a few moments, holding her hands over the iron of the stove.

"Lena?"

"No. Bonnie."

Neko raises his eyebrows. "Yeah? Tell me."

Vale shrugs. "I don't know. I just feel it. But enough of that," Vale says, smiling.

She rises and pushes Neko backward onto Lena's bed. She climbs onto it and stands over him. Takes off her hat. Takes off her jacket and her scarf and stands there, breathing.

It's then that she sees the drawing. On the underside of a beam above the bed, a spot she's never seen before. It's a rough sketch, cartoonish, of a man and a woman. Vale leans closer.

The naked man holds a fiddle. The naked woman has thick long braids, is laughing. Next to them are the initials: LW + LS.

LW and LS. Vale's mind is spinning. Lena Wood. Her grandmother. A sudden heat in Vale's chest. Lena was not alone. And who is LS? LS. Lex. Starkweather. Hazel's husband. Stephen's father. Lena Wood and Lex Starkweather. The fiddle player. Vale takes a deep breath. She looks down at Neko. "Jesus Christ," she whispers, stepping off the bed, picking up her sweater and wrapping it around her shoulders.

Vale knows exactly what it's like to not know who your father is. She's spent her whole life eyeing the face of every man she passes, looking for one with bone structure and eyes matching her own. *Who?* Vale asked Bonnie once, screaming, pounding her fists against the coffee table, and Bonnie put her face in her hands. Held them there for a long time. Whispered — and Vale believed her — *I don't know.*

Vale thinks now of Danny's green eyes. Of Bonnie's green eyes. Of course. Her mother's father.

"Neko," she says.

"Yeah?"

"Hold me."

DEB

December 13, 2011

Vale is outside Hazel's door in a damp rain, midafternoon. "Did you know about Lena and Lex?" she says when Deb opens the door. "I don't know why I'm shaking. I don't know why I'm so cold."

"Come in, honey," Deb says, closing the door, bringing Vale a blanket.

She brings her niece a cup of coffee, sweetened with cream, and Vale tells her about the drawings on the wall. LW + LS. Those green eyes. The birth of a baby who never knew who her father was. Whose mother died before she could be told.

"Jesus," Deb whispers, sitting down. "Who else knows? Hazel?" They both turn to look at her, sleeping in the living room.

Vale shrugs. Sips her coffee and closes her eyes.

"The secrets of a hillside. The goddamn

316

damage silence can do," Deb says, putting her arms around Vale.

She thinks of Bonnie, whom they cannot find to tell.

She wants to ask Hazel, to find out if she knows, but she can't risk the possibility of breaking the news on her deathbed.

And then Vale rises, dumps the rest of her coffee down the sink, says she has to go, and heads out the door, and it is just Deb and Hazel again. This quiet old shell of a house. Lex and Lena's ghosts filling the air.

Hazel makes a sound from the living room, and Deb goes that way.

She's been growing steadily worse. Is only managing to swallow broth and juice and water when they bring a cup to her with a straw, say, "Drink. You must."

Her eyes are open now. Deb brings a cup of apple juice to her lips. Holds the straw still while Hazel sips. Her eyes glaze over again. She closes them. Turns away.

Deb goes to the couch. She is exhausted. She misses her solitude. Misses her cabin — she's been spending nights here on the living room couch. She checks her phone and finds there's an e-mail from Danny in Guatemala: *See you in five days,* he writes. She stares at the screen for far too long.

Can barely breathe.

Five days. Can she stand it? Danny — Stephen's limbs, Deb's cheekbones, Stephen's green eyes. The one she loves more than anything in this world and the one she has not been able to make happy despite it. That is the curse of motherhood, she thinks: they make us happy and yet we cannot make them happy. And so we suffer, doubly so. She laughs out loud. Had she done it wrong? Her quiet rage, her expectations. But enough of that. She is long done with guilt. Those thoughts are thirty years old now, and she is done having them — scraps in the wind she tosses.

In the early evening a visiting nurse comes to relieve Deb for a couple hours. She walks back to her cabin and throws logs onto the fire, turns on the light next to the kitchen sink. Lex and Lena. How long? How often? She thinks of Stephen as a boy, and what he knew, or didn't know.

She goes up the loft stairs, the ones she so rarely climbs, and puts clean sheets onto Danny's bed. Smooths down the wool blanket. The distance of all of their woods and fields and cities closing — Danny, Hazel, Deb, Vale. How tragic that it takes catastrophes, she thinks — storms and deaths and missing bodies — to do so.

"My birds, coming home to roost," Hazel had said a few days ago, looking at Vale and Deb by the bed beside her, a glint of recognition in her eyes.

The hole-in-the-heart pattern repeating. The patterns always repeating. And yet Vale — Deb feels spikes of hope there. Vale unraveling these truths from the past, unspooling a revisionist history in which love existed, too. What does that mean for this hillside and this family and the future? she wonders. She thinks of Vale's bright, fierce, solitary beauty. That poppy tattoo, petals strewing. Those owl wings in flight on her left shoulder.

Deb goes to the canvas — Ginny's painting — hung from two nails on the wall. A rust-red field, wine-colored trees.

The canvas is almost the height of Deb — ridiculously large. "Really, you want something this grand in your living room?" Ginny had asked, grinning, carrying it to Deb's truck a week ago. "Yes," Deb said.

It still smells of Ginny's turpentine. Deb scans her fingers across the thin lines, the scraped-away thicker chunks of paint. She loves this painting. Vermilion, burnt sienna, umber. A fine line of bright white in the center. Startling if you look at it for long enough. She needs this painting somehow. A writer friend of hers once said that you have to find the story that only you know how to tell.

This is the story Ginny knows how to tell: this painting.

And what is Deb's story to tell? Deb can't keep apocalyptic visions out of her head — images of what will happen when New York becomes submerged: bunkers, food scarcity, the hoarding of weapons.

But she turns that part of her mind off. Returns to the visions she chooses to let nest instead: community, resilience, coming together in small circles. Palliative care — maybe that is her thing. In the concrete and the abstract: wood stove, candlelight, straws in water, catheter bags, music, stew. Guiding one another through the dark times.

Deb goes to the record player and puts on Billie Holiday's *Lady Sings the Blues.* Bird would tuck a plastic gardenia behind her ear, shimmy across the kitchen floor, the quote from Frantz Fanon she wrote across the wall: "Each generation must discover its mission, fulfill it or betray it, in relative opacity."

Billie sings "I Must Have That Man," and Deb closes her eyes. Wool socks on pine floor. A smile across her lips. Deb has faith that they will find their way back toward one another, the women of this mountain. Vale and Vale's daughters. Danny's daughters. Find some place — here or elsewhere — to call their own.

When the song ends Deb closes the damper on the stove, slips her coat over her shoulders, and heads back down the hill to relieve the nurse of the bedside burden of a woman dying. That is another asset of middle age, Deb thinks, pulling her scarf around her neck — a bitter wind picking up, tall grass tangling around her boots and knees and thighs — the willingness to care for others. The ego's willingness to surrender time — much of it — for the sake of another. Even the ones who never loved you, Deb thinks, walking toward that farmhouse with its woodsmoke, its company, its single lightbulb hanging from the front porch ceiling.

VALE

December 17, 2011

"Come, let's go for a ride," Deb says to Vale, nodding toward the door. "The nurse is here for the evening. We deserve a break, me and you. Plus, the news is unbearable. Too many repetitions of the same thing."

Vale nods. Two days ago, Tropical Storm Washi hit the Philippines: eight inches of rain in twelve hours. Flash floods and landslides: 1,200 people reported dead, half a million without homes. In Europe they are smothered under Winter Storm Joachim: 400,000 in France without power. Trains derailed. Ships destroyed.

They take back roads along Silver Creek, cross a bridge, pass farms and double-wides and new houses not yet wedded to the ground.

"Where to?" Vale asks.

"Ginny's place. Farther Heaven."

"The commune?"

"Yes. The commune! The landscape of my naïve youth."

She tells Vale that Ginny bought out the others years ago and lives there alone, solitary and stoic and dirt poor, "like the rest of us ex-hippies. Ha — success not our forte. But you'll like Ginny. She's fabulous and fierce, an absurd misfit."

Deb takes a right up a long and steep and deeply rutted driveway, the shape of a bent arm. At the top of the hill is a large farmhouse, an old school bus sitting on stumps, stone cairns, a snow-covered garden — kale rising from the sea of white. Vale smiles. She thinks about the United Nations Climate Change Conference, finished last week in Durban, looking at that garden of winter kale. They didn't manage to create a treaty but agreed to establish a legally binding deal comprising all countries by 2015. Vale thinks how maybe the slow arc of progress is untrackable: all of these back roads, good-hearted efforts, twists and turns, gardens full of kale.

They get out of the car and walk up the path.

Along the south side of the house sits a long porch. There's a couch covered in wool blankets, a collection of mud-caked boots, wind chimes, and a peacock — male — tail feathers spread wide — standing in front of them.

"Peacock?" Vale says, her eyebrows raised.

"Yes." Deb laughs. "Several."

Ginny opens the door and steps out. She's striking — nearly six feet tall in blue jeans and a black T-shirt frayed at the hem. Her silver hair flows halfway down her back. Her face is full of lines, and when she grins Vale's surprised to see two of her front teeth missing. Long turquoise earrings dangle from her ears.

"Friends," she calls out. "Welcome. What gorgeous incarnations!" She throws her arms out toward them, smells of lavender and woodsmoke.

She kisses Vale's cheek, pulls her body close, says into her ear: "I am so sorry. So sorry about your mother."

Vale whispers thanks. The peacock walks in the open door, and Ginny motions for them to follow.

Vale's never been to one of the old communes before, but their stories have resonated around these parts her whole life: babies born in school buses, rotgut cider in basements, too much fucking.

But this house has a wonderful light, shimmers as Ginny does. The kitchen counter and table are covered in books, ceramic mugs, jars full of peacock feathers. The walls are covered in art — drawings, a collection of clay sculptures, a large painting of a naked woman holding a pistol, a hushed landscape of trees and mist and sky behind her.

"Excuse my mess," Ginny says, going to the wood stove where a kettle simmers. "One can take up a lot of space when one lives alone."

"More majestic by the day," Deb says.

On the wall behind Ginny's table are some sketches: a deer, a stingray, a guitar with the words "This machine kills fascists" scrawled across it.

Ginny brings them unmatching stemmed crystal glasses filled to the brim with box wine. "What is one to do! Shit, I'm growing old, losing my teeth. Ah, well. But look at this," she says, passing Deb a print she's been working on. It's a woodcut of a creek, feathery hemlocks, a fox passing under a rising full moon, with a line from a Wendell Berry poem at the bottom: PRACTICE RES-URRECTION.

"It's the age of doing so, no?" Ginny says, looking into both their eyes and taking a sip from her glass. She passes the print to Vale.

325

Vale can still smell the wet ink — nearly smell the feathers of the hemlock tree and that fox, too.

"Practice resurrection," Ginny says, closing her eyes. "That's what I'm working on. Jesus, the storm," she says, her voice suddenly low. "My neighbors lost their double-wide. Everything." She looks at Vale, her eyes brimming. "I'm sorry, Vale. I read recently that in Cree one does not say, 'I am sick,' but rather, 'The sickness has come to me.' There's power in that, no? Our sick world to blame for so much suffering."

Vale nods, reaches her hand into her pocket and rubs the beads of Bonnie's blue rosary.

"But let's not talk about the storm," Ginny says, going to the wood stove and pulling out a loaf of steaming fresh bread. "Deb," she says, turning, "we thought we were saving the world, and we were wrong! So very wrong! We hid out in the woods here, growing our tomatoes and our green beans while the apocalypse brewed. Cut this bread, will you?" Ginny sets the hot loaf on the counter, reaches for a knife.

The peacock is wandering around by Vale's feet. She's never been this close to one before; she's mesmerized by its tail:

iridescent jade and turquoise eyes and swords.

The bird shits on the floor next to Vale's boot and Ginny laughs.

"Apologies. My birds are tactless. The world goes back to wildness every day," she says, downing her wine. "I'll clean that up later. Oh, but my stew. Beans, leeks, potatoes, kale, rosemary. My stew is practicing resurrection." She goes to the cupboard and pulls out three white handmade bowls.

Vale takes a sip of her wine and looks around at the books littering the table. Langston Hughes, Leslie Marmon Silko, Monique Wittig, Edna St. Vincent Millay. She wants to crack each and every spine. She imagines what it would be like to live a life surrounded by books like this; to grow old in a house that tells the story of your life — your early idealism, your found eccentricity wedded to pragmatism, a life of too many people, and then too few.

"Our idealism wasn't entirely for naught, was it?" Deb asks, going to the bread.

Ginny shrugs. "I don't know. But art," Ginny says. "Where would we be without art? We have to show other ways of living, right? Write the stories for the future. Do so, blindly, and with love. Offer solace when and where we can."

Vale thinks of Neko and his photographs — not solace, but truth telling. A necessary act of art, too. She thinks of her body moving, with intention and fluidity under lights. What is her story to tell? What language will she tell it in?

Ginny serves the stew into bowls, brings them to the table. "Here," she says. "My humble offering."

Deb brings the steaming bread and a bowl full of soft butter.

Vale lifts a spoonful to her lips. Closes her eyes and breathes in. The woods; the soup smells like tree bark and balsam and woods.

"Délicieux," she says. "Thank you."

Ginny looks up from her soup, her eyes sparking, a rosy drunk shimmer in her cheeks. "Dried chanterelles," she whispers. "Dried chanterelles."

After dinner they clear their dishes and move into the living room, a large space with a vaulted ceiling. "This room used to be an attached barn," Ginny says. "Before the hippies came."

The peacock follows them, suddenly greeted by two more: a male and a female in the corner, shuffling around in a pile of leaves.

There is a second wood stove in this

room; Ginny goes to it and puts a log on, opens the damper. She puts a record on the turntable in the corner, and Edith Piaf's voice rises into the rafters.

Vale smiles; Piaf's voice reminds her of earthy French wine, of cigarette smoke. She thinks of her mother dancing barefoot to Patti Smith in the darkened kitchen. Of Shante singing in French in her apartment in New Orleans. The voices of these women: strange medicine.

From the ceiling hang clutches of drying mint. Under the table in the far corner sit baskets of apples, potatoes, winter squash. "This room stays cold enough all winter — ideal cold storage," Ginny says, refilling their glasses with wine. "I'm preparing for the post-oil world. I've been doing so for forty years. Who knew my skills would turn so phenomenally useful?"

"The hippies were right," Deb says, falling into an ancient mustard-colored couch, tipping her head back and closing her eyes.

The hippies *were* right, Vale thinks. Maybe this is the answer. This honing. Going inward. These root vegetables and wood stoves and drying herbs. She would not mind being like these women as she approaches and enters sixty — their gray-haired ferocity and resilience. Life didn't go how they'd imagined, and yet they hung on, made lives here, quixotic prisms.

"And look here," Ginny says, pulling a long piece of purple fabric from the wall that's attached to the highest point of the ceiling with a bolt and a ring. "I've taken up trapeze."

Deb guffaws from the couch. "Trapeze?"

"Don't laugh," Ginny says. "I may be wrinkled and losing my teeth, but I am practicing resurrection."

She slips out of her shoes and takes off her T-shirt. She wears a loose, silk tank top, no bra. Her shoulders are freckled, aged, brown, strong. She propels herself upward, twenty feet into the air, abreast this purple fabric. The muscles of her arms flex and quiver up there at the highest point. She tips her head back, a cascade of silver hair falling down her shoulders, lets out a long throaty laugh.

"A queen!" Deb calls out. "That's what you've been reborn as, Ginny. A fucking queen!"

Edith Piaf sings "La Vie en Rose," and Vale smiles. Feels an odd shiver. Hopeful: that's what she feels right now, watching Ginny up there at the top of that fabric, this sixty-five-year-old woman living a life of continuous trying. "You want a shot?"

Ginny says, lowering herself to the floor, turning toward Vale.

"Yes," Vale says.

She strips off her sweater and grabs onto the fabric. Ginny shows her how to knot it around her foot. How to pull herself up. How to climb. Vale's dancing muscles put to work.

"You're a natural," Ginny calls out. "Be safe."

Vale keeps climbing, all the way up to the top of this barn turned living room — cobwebs amid the rafters, Ginny and Deb grinning below her, the fabric slowly spinning.

"You're amazing," Deb hollers from below.

"Goddess!" Ginny crows.

Vale twines in slow motion and wishes Bonnie were here. Bonnie would have liked these women, this night, this house, this music. She throws an arm out into the shape of a star and listens to Edith Piaf sing words she doesn't understand in a nightclub in Paris. The motherfucking art of good company, Vale thinks, a pain she can't explain rising in her chest.

My mother will not see this, Vale thinks. Bonnie will not knock on the door and come in, see her daughter spinning, phenomenally high, head tipped back, a rare and extraordinary bird among the rafters.

HAZEL

December 17, 2011

There is someone in her driveway. Hazel can see the large blue-and-white van he or she drives, can see the box he or she carries (the shape of a gun case, or a fiddle case), can see the person cross the yard and walk toward Hazel's front porch.

Lex?

But it's a woman's voice. "Hello," she calls out, knocking on the door.

Goddamn, Hazel thinks, but what is she to do? The woman lifting the latch, opening the door, stepping inside. "Hello," she calls again.

Hazel hears the woman talking to the stranger in the kitchen — the nurse who is sometimes here. Then coming toward her. Where is Lex? Where is Lena? She doesn't walk tentatively, this woman, like Deb or that nurse. Her footsteps are heavy, determined on Hazel's solid pine floor. She comes closer and Hazel is surprised by the youthfulness of the woman's face and by the light that emanates from it — an orb, a moon, wrinkled, not young — piercing blue eyes and rosy cheeks. Some kind of china doll. But not flimsy — not at all flimsy — sturdy with long, beautiful hands and —

"I've come to sing you some songs," the woman says. "Deb thought you might like that."

The gall, Hazel thinks, but cannot say. When you are dying you no longer have any choice about who visits you, or what they say to you, or where and what happens with your body, it seems. Right, Mother? Her mother is beside her. Sleeping on the same pillow. Their hands wrapped in each other's.

"All right then," the woman says, opening the black box that looks so much like the box her father used to keep his rifle in, only this glowing, tall china doll of a woman pulls out not a gun but a dulcimer. She slides a chair over next to Hazel's bed, sets the instrument on her knee, and glances, for a moment, out the window with those blue-gray eyes, and then she begins to play.

It's not at all what Hazel expected.

The woman's voice isn't vague or weak or plaintive. She isn't singing a sad or melan-

choly song to ease Hazel into death, or a
gospel tune full of false joy. It's a song about
coyotes and stars and cowboys, and the
woman's voice is deep and clear and so loud
it seems to pierce though the stale air of
Hazel's room. It's utterly surprising. She
didn't expect this. She didn't expect to like
this, to have the air parted like this. Coyotes
and fish and Lex with his fiddle, sixty years
ago, at the barn dance, that first night when
he took her hand and led her out onto that
dance floor and spun her around until
blisters formed on her heels. What is this
song about? *Them stars, how often I've laid
on the prairie and watched them go spinning
around.* The woman sits bolt upright, looking out the window, only occasionally glancing down at her fingers; beautiful, young-
looking, graceful fingers.

> Some clusters is branded, the Dipper, the
>   Lion
> The Eagle, the Serpent, the Bear
> The Horns o' the Bull and the Belt o' Orion
> And Cassia o' What's-her-name's Chair.

The words of the song seem to go on and
on; how can this woman remember them
all? And sing them so clearly that a painting
appears in Hazel's mind: swirling stars and

deserts she's never been to and all the creatures up there. Her grandmother Marie used to know the constellations, and when Hazel was a girl she would take Lena and Hazel out into the middle of the field on clear, moonless nights, and tell them their names.

Hazel is that girl again, standing in that field, her grandmother's warm and thick hand in hers, under that big swirling, timeless sky that moves only in circles, not in straight lines.

The northern lights, her grandmother tells them, pointing, are caused by a group of people who play games with balls of light. And then a word rolls off her tongue that Hazel has forgotten until now, a word that sounds like some strange and familiar music, there in that field: *Wassan-mon-haneehla-ak.* "That was the name of the people," Hazel's grandmother Marie says, squeezing Hazel's hand.

She moves her other hand to the left. "And that," she says, "is Big Bear. *Kchi-awasos.*"

Kchi-awasos.

A terrible tangle in Hazel's chest.

Those words: Indian.

She thinks of what her father called them: *Indian niggers. Gypsies.* Voice copper and silver, tinged with hatred.

The music stops. "That song is called 'Them Stars,' " the woman says, looking straight into Hazel's eyes. "Are you okay?"

Hazel's lips won't move. She looks toward the window.

The woman nods and looks out the window as well, as if trying to see what Hazel sees. "Would you like another song?"

"No," Hazel says, trying to sit up but unable to.

A knot in her chest, making its way upward. Did she ever show Stephen the stars? Or Bonnie? She can't remember doing so. Stephen, a boy, standing in that very same field, his hand in hers.

"Okay, then," the woman says, rising and putting her instrument back into the black box it came in, clasping it shut.

Hazel doesn't want her to go; she doesn't know why. She is so sturdy, and that voice: deep, clear water. The water at the bottom of the pool in Silver Creek that she used to dive into when she was a girl.

"That's what boys do, not girls," her father had said every time Hazel came home dripping wet from head to toe, wet underwear, wet dress, creek water streaming down her thighs. But she had loved to swim. She had loved that cold, clear black water, the stones glistening at the bottom, the way she would reach her fist down and grab and then drift back toward the surface of the water — gasping, splashing — and open up her fist to find what was there: a quartz, a whetstone, loose gravel.

The woman turns back toward the room. "It was a pleasure, Hazel," she says. "Thank you."

Hazel lifts her hand. It doesn't come close to touching what she wants to say. To describe that clear dark water she used to dive into when she was a girl, to describe the stars her grandmother pointed out to her at night, that word — *Kchi-awasos* — to tell someone how she wishes she could go back in time to when Stephen was a boy, to hold his hand in hers, and keep it there in the cup of her palm, to point up to the sky and say, "Look, Stephen. Aurora borealis. That wash across the sky . . ."

Hazel can hear the woman going to the front door and letting herself out. She turns and sees the woman through the window, walking along the muddy path toward her van, and climbing in. She will never know the names of all the stars. Or dive into that water. But when she closes her eyes she can hear the woman's voice singing. It's in her head. Ringing there — clear and bright and loud.

DEB

December 18, 2011

A knock at the door, the creak of it opening, and they all turn. Danny!

Deb runs to greet him. Danny — her tall boy. The one who did not die in the landslide two months ago. The one who was in a nearby village but did not die. Tender-eyed and reaching his arms out toward her just as she reaches out for him. She holds him, this boy of hers. Hair thinning. Face sunburnt. His arms, his back, his slender chest. Smelling of wool and woodsmoke and sweat and the dust of another land. He holds her, too. She is weeping, foolishly. "Danny," she says, pulling away and looking at his beautiful face, his bright eyes, his toothy grin. "Come in."

They meet Vale in the kitchen. "Vale, valley, vibrant, Vale," he says, going to her, putting his arms around her. "I am so very sorry," he says.

Vale whispers, "Me, too."

A long hold, and like that they are all here: Hazel's chickens miraculously come home to roost.

Danny goes into the living room, stands next to Hazel's bed, and watches her sleep. The sky a hushed blue now, first stars visible.

Deb heats up the soup on the stove; Vale slices bread.

He comes back into the kitchen and puts his chin on top of Deb's head. Holds it there.

"How you be, my boy?" she says, wrapping her arms around him.

My God. Back to her. She thinks of the devastation in the Philippines, Haiti, Japan, Guatemala. You never know, Deb thinks, squeezing her son's body tight.

They set the table, something they haven't done here in Hazel's house since the Thanksgivings before Stephen died. Three settings. Bowls. Cups for water. Jars for wine.

Spoons. The bread and the butter.

What a communion this feels like, Deb thinks, while lighting the candles in the brass candelabra that's been in the cupboard for twenty-six years. Brought together by

341

disaster, natural and human, this son and this daughter. How many dinners have been had at this very table by the ancestors of Danny and Bonnie and Vale? At this same oak table. Lit by this same three-tiered candelabra. Zipporah and Ezekial, Henry and Marie. Their spirits feel very much in the room. They bustle around her, watch from the corners, and from behind the plaster walls. This house the colonizers built with their blood, sweat, ignorance, righteousness, and tears. The one Danny and Vale will most likely have to sell — how will any of them be able to afford it? Divide the land and save what they can — the perches on the outskirts, the cabins in the hills. We're going back in time, Deb thinks, picturing the original homesteader, Zipporah, who bore and raised thirteen children in a one-room cabin uphill of here somewhere while the house was being built. We're getting poorer, this family, Deb thinks. Our houses smaller.

Danny goes into the living room with Vale. Deb goes to the sink to wash the dishes. Refills her glass of wine.

She can hear Danny's gentle voice talking to Vale and Hazel. Vale's occasional laughter. How is it she found them, or they found her, this mountainside and its people? She dips her hands into the warm, soapy water.

How she loves each of them, their flaws and all. That is an essential part of beauty, after all — its pockedness, its darkness and its light. *Glory be to God for dappled things . . . all things counter, original, spare.* Those words have run in her head for thirty-something years now, ever since Ginny read Gerard Manley Hopkins to them all by candlelight in the kitchen at the commune. That long winter. Ringing in her head all these years when her cabin seemed too dank, too dark, too quiet, too dim.

Pied beauty. Her own gray hair, stretch-marked stomach and thighs, sunspots on her forehead and hands. Stephen's dappled love and fallible heart. *Whatever is fickle, freckled (who knows how?),* Hopkins wrote. Like this family of hers, here in this two-hundred-year-old farmhouse on Heart Spring Mountain. Deb holds her hands still in the soapy water and thinks of Bonnie, her pied beauty. Praise her, Deb thinks, looking out the dark window. And praise her — Hazel. And her — Vale. And him — her son.

VALE

December 18, 2011

"Danny," Vale says after dinner. "Shall we go for a walk? It's too quiet in here."

"Yes," Danny says, grabbing the half-empty bottle of wine from the table. They slip into jackets and scarves, hats and mittens, and head outside, the steam of their breath lit up by the light pooling from the kitchen windows.

Danny looks up at the sky. "Jesus. The stars in winter in the Northern Hemisphere. I'd forgotten."

"A luminous sphere of plasma," Vale says, quoting the definition she learned in fifth grade, a line that has reverberated there ever since. "Come. I want to show you something."

She clicks on her flashlight, starts walking up the hillside, and Danny follows. It's dark but there's enough moon to see by, a dusting of new snow beneath their boots.

She doesn't want him to know where she's taking him, that cabin where his father died — *near the sickness also lies the cure.*

"You believe in ghosts, Danny?" Vale asks, breathing hard from the climb, the cold air sharp in her lungs.

He pauses to look out over the farmhouse below, nestled into its valley. "Of course. You?"

"I'm beginning to. My mother's, Lena's."

Danny nods and looks up at the tree branches above them.

"And Hazel is half-ghost, too, at this point," Vale continues. "Hey, Danny. Are the stars the same in Guatemala?"

And so he tells her about the stars near the equator. The different constellations. About watching them while smoking a joint on a rooftop in Quetzaltenango belonging to a woman named Luz.

"Luz, like light," he says, and Vale does not allow herself to feel jealous of Danny's lover. She takes that feeling from her chest and sends it out toward the stars now popped above them: Venus, Mars, Orion's Sword.

She thinks of Neko, watching the stars from a rooftop in Iraq one month from now.

Vale starts walking. "Come."

■ ■ ■ ■

As they approach Lena's cabin, Danny stops in the path behind her. "Why?" he says quietly, his voice a near whisper.

Vale says, "Trust me. Please."

He looks her in the eyes, half-visible in this moonlight, and follows.

Vale pushes the door open with her shoulder, opens a box of matches, and lights the candles on the table.

Danny stands in the doorway breathing.

"Look," Vale says, shining her flashlight on the two cups hanging from a nail above the sink: pink roses, tea stains.

"And here," she says, lifting the flashlight to the feathers and stones and animal bones lined up on the windowsill, and farther up, to the photos tacked to the walls.

"Lena?" Danny says, moving toward the windowsill, reaching out and touching an animal's skull with his fingers. "I never knew all this was in here."

"Me either," says Vale. "But she's here. Her ghost is badass. Very much alive."

Danny sits down in a chair in front of the cluster of lit candles. He looks at the floor, the place where his father died one winter night. He nods. "She's here, your matriarch.

Her life written in these things."

"Yes," Vale says, sitting down next to him. "Also: I'm pretty sure we're part Abenaki."

Danny raises his eyes to her. "Really?"

She tells him about Marie, their great-great-grandmother. About the photo from Lena's attic. About that note scrawled in the town ledger: *Indian.*

"No shit," Danny says, rubbing the pine of the table with his thumb.

"Not that it really matters," Vale says. "But it matters to me. It seems important to know who you are. Bonnie never knew who she was."

Danny reaches across the table and puts his hand on top of Vale's.

"That's the tragic part," Vale says, her voice cracking. A branch breaks outside. "She had to get lost in order for me to — end up here. Get found." Vale puts both hands on the pine table. She looks at the photos pinned to Lena's wall.

"I'm so sorry, Vale," Danny says quietly.

Vale puts her fingernail into the soft wax of the candle. "It happens all the time, to people everywhere, you know? They die. Get lost."

"I do," Danny says.

Vale takes the two teacups off the wall, cleans them out with the wool of her mittens, and fills each of them from the wine bottle Danny brought. She places one in front of Danny and brings the other to her lips.

"Maybe that's why my dad came here, too," Danny says. "Lena's ghost here." He closes his eyes and takes a sip of his wine. "He told me a story once."

Vale looks at him. Doesn't say a word. He's never spoken about Stephen to her before.

Danny tells her the story of the woman who married an owl. Of the woman who chose that singing, that half-human world, over all else. Just as Lena did with Otie, Vale thinks. The woman who married an owl.

"Danny," she says. She's been waiting a long time to tell him. Her voice is shaking, a near whisper.

"Yeah?"

"Your grandfather came here, too."

He eyes her from across the table. "What?"

Vale's heart is loud in her chest. She fears it isn't true, but there is the drawing on the rafters. There are Bonnie's green eyes.

Vale moves the flashlight up the wall to her left and shows Danny the inked drawing above the bed. The naked lovers with their exaggerated proportions, the man with a fiddle in his left hand. Their ridiculous and goofy grins. LW + LS.

Danny looks from the drawing into Vale's eyes. "Lex and Lena?" Danny says. To Vale the cabin walls suddenly feel too close, too dank, too dark.

Vale nods. "He disappeared just after my mother was born."

Danny downs his teacup of wine and puts his face into his hands. "Jesus. It's a landscape full of holes and half-truths."

"I know," Vale whispers. The candlelight throws their shadows across the wall.

Danny looks up from his hands. A dry laugh. "Well, shit, Vale. At least there was love."

Vale smiles. Feels a streak of warmth shoot from her chest to her toes. "Yes, there was love."

Vale pours Danny more wine. Touches the rim of her rose teacup to his. "To their fucking and their love."

Danny shakes his head. Smiles at her. "To their fucking and their love."

They walk back in the dark. At Hazel's porch Danny opens his arms and she falls against him, lets him hold her.

Danny heads back inside to find Deb, and Vale goes to Hazel's car. She will drive to Neko's room. She will climb those stairs and let herself in. She will undress while he is sleeping, and slip under his sheets and down comforter, wrap herself around his thin and war-familiar body. The warmth of another human body: how badly we all need it, she thinks as she drives, headlights rippling across the bare bodies of trees. How essential, that coupling in the dark of winter.

She reaches for her phone and puts on John Lennon's "Love." A song Bonnie loved. Reaching: her mother's arms reaching on that bridge. She loves Danny. She thinks she might love Neko. No matter, it's him she will reach for. That warmth, that touching. The way he looks into her eyes and says hello as if surprised every time. She parks her car. Climbs the stairs. Opens the door and lets herself inside. Finds his body in the darkness. Finds herself there, in that touching. In the morning the sun rises. Lights the room. Luz. If she has a daughter, she will name her Luz, Vale thinks, watching it come.

LENA

May 23, 1957

Lena whispers, "Adele" in her sleep, dreams of those jars of herbs. Hemlock. White pine. Bloodroot. What would be the remedy for this? The only cure she knows, for sure, is her child, nursing. Her girl-child! Feathered, pink-eared, blue-veined. Easter egg, bird. Bonnie. And Otie — where is he? She smiles thinking of him, hopes that Adele will go find him. Oh my goddamn, "Bring me my child!" she tries to yell, but her voice is weak and the house still, the cooling tin roof ticking, a sliver of moonlight sliding across the white-washed floor.

She yells again into the night, but her voice is thin. Not what it should be. Her head spins. She's on the dance floor, spinning; those streaks of alizarin, streaks of crimson. She is so hot. She throws off the covers, throws off the sheet, rips the gown off her chest. She reaches for the cloth beside her, dips it into the bowl of cool water on the bedside table, rubs it across her chest, across her throbbing breasts, spurting milk into the sour sheets and sour pillow.

Where is her child? Her legs won't move. Won't rise. She can't get up, and yet she must, and then the door is opening, and she calls out into the darkness, "Baby B?"

But it is Lex.

He comes to her, puts his hands onto her shoulders. "Shh, Lena Bird," he whispers, sitting down on the edge of the bed beside her.

Lena lies down. Feels the sheets underneath her. Lets his hand touch her brow, her hair, her neck, the burning skin of her chest.

"Lena," he says, and she can smell the whiskey on him. "You have to get better. You have to sleep."

Sleep. She reaches for Lex's hands, holds them to her. Puts them on her swollen breasts. "Squeeze, Lex, please," she says, and so he does. He pinches one nipple, and then the next, releasing the pressure. Milk squirts down her side, pools beneath her ribs. Lex finds the cloth and mops up the pooled milk. Squeezes more. Gently, but firm enough.

The release. The burning pain. "Suck them, please," she pleads. He looks into her eyes, meets her there, then leans over and puts his lips onto her nipple, gently sucking the milk out, swallowing. One breast and then the other. And Lena can breathe. Oh, sweet Jesus, she can finally breathe.

"Sleep, my love," Lex says when he pulls away, the side of his face lit by the moon's milk-white glow, his fingers on the cloth cooling the fever from her freckled chest.

"Where is Otie?" Lena asks.

"Adele took him."

"And Bonnie?"

"Hazel is caring for her."

"Lex."

"Yes?"

"There are letters. In the cabin."

"Okay."

"Burn them."

"Burn them?"

"Burn them." Lena smiles.

Lena sleeps. She sleeps for the first time in days, while Lex sits and wipes her brow with a cool cloth. In her dream Bonnie is in her arms, and they are walking. The side of a mountain, snowcapped, but they are warm in layers of wool, hats stuffed with feathers.

Her girl-child Bonnie is two, or three —

apple-cheeked and strong-limbed. They walk and they sing. They sing and they walk. The trees around them — hemlock and spruce — quiver with their footsteps, join their singing with a feathery hum. "Where are we going?" Bonnie calls out, laughing, and Lena laughs also, calls back, "To the top of the mountain!"

They are hiking to the top of the mountain, this mother and this daughter. Snow-capped. A dome of white light. Treeless. A flock of gray birds circling its tip.

"What's at the top of the mountain?" Bonnie calls out, her voice cherry red, joy-filled, a bell, and Lena responds, "Love, my love! At the top of the mountain is love!" And so they hike together. And when the girl-child tires, Lena picks her up and carries her, singing, and wraps her in her woolen shawl, and when she falls asleep in Lena's arms she carries her still, humming, until they reach the highest crest of the highest peak. Otie is with them, wing-repaired, flying in circles. Hooting. Fierce. Angry. To the very top of the mountain. Ablaze with white light, snowflakes, frost-flecked moss and granite. At the top Lena lies down in a bed of that frosted moss and snow and holds her daughter close to her, closes her eyes, and sleeps, all the while humming, and her girl-child smiles. She smiles! Otie sitting nearby. Bird-friend. Girl-child. Apple cheeks, smiling. Bonnie, the Bonnie in the month of May, the last light fading on her apple lips, Bonnie.

HAZEL

December 19, 2011

The light is strange this evening, or nighttime, what is it? — candlelight flickering,
firelight from the wood stove, the sounds
unfamiliar, here in the front room where
she lies on the hospital bed, facing the
darkened view. Her father's view, the one
Ezekial Wood, her great-something-
grandfather, chose two hundred years ago.
The view the Indians saw, back when the
trees were native. Those hills! Them stars.
That was the song the lady came and sang:
*Them stars, how often I've laid on the prairie
and watched them go spinning around.* Hazel
cannot move her head, but she can hear
voices from the kitchen, occasional laughter.
The women are here. They are always here.
She calls out with what voice she has left:
"Mother?"

And then her mother is by her side. Or

356

not her mother but the girl who looks like her. Vale. Eyelids painted with a splash of silver or blue that somehow looks like moonlight.

"Hazel? Hello. I'm here."

Hazel can't take her eyes off those blue sparkling eyelids. Flecks of silver in there, and maybe purple, too. It must be the flickering light, making those colors blaze so. The blue of morning hoarfrost on the windows. Blue sky reflecting on ice in winter.

"Hazel?" the girl says, standing there looking down at her like a tall and unfamiliar bird. "You want something?" She blinks and the blue powder shimmers.

"Yes," Hazel says.

The girl leans closer. Smiles. Touches Hazel's hand. "Tell me," she whispers.

The words are fibrous in her throat. They force their way out, slowly: "I want my eyes done."

The girl looks at her for a moment like she hasn't heard, or understood, and then she smiles. Steps backward. "You want your eyes done, like mine?"

"Yes."

Just do it, Hazel thinks.

"Okay," the girl says, going to the corner for her bag, returning with it and sitting down on the chair next to Hazel.

Hazel feels Vale's fingers on her cheeks, then on the loose flesh below her eyes.

"Close your eyes," the girl says, quiet, and Hazel does.

Like a baby. When was she ever touched like this? She can suddenly smell her mother: that combination of flour and egg whites and milk that hung on her for years. Her mother must have touched her like this, stroked her forehead, her cheeks, oh God, her temples like this.

Mother, Hazel thinks. What will happen to our house when I die? What will happen to the land? Heart Spring Mountain. Eternal water. The girl puts her hands on each of Hazel's cheeks and rubs a cool cream into them. Ah! It is like fresh air, like breathing the quiet song of snow. Hazel can feel Stephen at her breast, his small fingers holding the heavy skin, his one visible green eye shocking her with its gaze. What did that eye want? Even then she couldn't be sure. My baby, my one and only baby, she sang to him, in that rocking chair, in that house, that whole long winter.

She hears the clicking of jars, the unscrewing of a lid, and the girl reappears above her holding a jar of blue.

"Blue okay?" she whispers, and Hazel nods.

"It looks beautiful," the girl says, dabbing the sparkling paint onto Hazel's eyelids. Blending silver and blue so it looks, Hazel imagines, like moonlight over a snow-covered land. But for the first time in a long time Hazel isn't thinking about the land. She's thinking about those fingers, there on her cheeks, her eyelids, stroking the soft skin below her ears. She's thinking about Stephen up there in the woods. My boy. She's thinking of that morning she entered Lena's room so many years ago. A tray of tea and hot oatmeal.

She entered and the tray fell to the floor by her feet. Her sister's damp face. An unfamiliar hue.

"No," she said. That's all. That quick word — *no.*

Later, that afternoon — after the doctor, and the casket, and Lena's body being carried away — Hazel walked into the nursery to check on Bonnie and found Lex there. Bonnie in his arms, his finger clenched in her miniature fist.

"You have to leave," she said.

"Please, no," he answered, his eyes bloodshot, his body stinking of sweat and alcohol. He put his lips on Bonnie's brow, sang: *My*

Bonnie lies over the ocean.

"Leave," Hazel said, her voice cool and strong as granite, and he stared at her for a long minute, then turned and set Bonnie in her cradle. Placed his lips on her forehead, a deep breath, before leaving the room.

He did not write. He did not call. It was the last time Hazel saw him.

Hazel looks up into those eyes above her — what a beautiful child. Beautiful child! There are tears in her own eyes, and for a moment she worries that this girl will see them, and then she is not worrying about that at all. They come fast and silent, the tears, stream down her face and pool in the valleys of her cheeks. She is thinking about that translucent blue powdering her eyes, about light filling her veins, about the beauty of sunlight reflecting on snow. Why did she wait so long for this? Was it this easy, all along, simply lying down and letting herself be touched? Hazel thinks for a moment she is dying, that she will never be able to breathe again, that her heart has seized, but then she does breathe, and a sob erupts from her chest. A single one.

"It's okay," the girl whispers, love and terror in her eyes. "It's okay."

VALE

It's late — ten or eleven. Danny climbs into the passenger seat, and they drive the few short minutes to Neko's. He is, by some miracle, awake, and Vale takes his hand and leads him to the door. Slips a hat on his head. Says, "Shhh."

Neko puts on his coat, grins, follows her to the car.

Neither of them knows where she's driving. She puts on Leonard Cohen's *Best Of* in honor of Danny's hayloft serenades. Danny turns to her. "You remember."

"Of course," Vale says, smiling. They drive the back roads, covered in a slim sheet of snow, the moon full or nearly so, the barns and fields near fluorescent in the night light, the landscape lunar.

Cohen sings about lonesome and quarrelsome heroes, and Danny sings along at the

361

top of his lungs, and Vale and Neko join in. Shouting. Singing out of key. Vale driving too fast. Intoxicated by recklessness and moonlight.

He sings about turning into gold, and they all do, too, their voices awful, all rage and laughter.

"This song," Danny says, slamming his fist on the dashboard. "Too damn good."

"Cohen salvation," Neko says quietly, leaning in from the backseat and kissing Vale's neck.

Vale accelerates. Gives the finger to the full moon.

She doesn't know exactly where she's headed until she finds herself passing the driveway to Ginny's Farther Heaven. Of course. She puts the car into reverse. Backs up and turns up the driveway.

She has to gun it with the snow; at the last hill the tires spin out and the car slides into the ditch.

"Shit," Vale whispers. "I guess we walk."

They climb out and scramble up the rest of the driveway in the dark. There are no lights on in the farmhouse. Vale hasn't thought this through entirely, but she has a hunch that if Ginny wakes, she won't mind.

She leads them to the backside of the

house, to the attached barn converted to living room, slides open a window, and they all climb inside. It's cold in there — the wood stove unlit — but the purple trapeze silk is still hanging, a streak of dark in the center of the moonlit room.

Peacock feathers litter the floor. "The promised land," Danny says, picking one up, smiling.

Neko is quiet. Eyes the trapeze silk and then Vale.

Vale throws off her hat and coat. She pulls off her boots and socks and goes to the fabric. She slips her sweater over her head. Steps out of her jeans so that she's wearing just her black lace bra and her gray long underwear. She lifts herself up — climbing — animal, creature-esque there in that moonlight, to the very top. She ties a knot below her foot and finds her balance — holds her left arm and left leg out, swivels her hips and neck until the fabric begins to spin. Slow. Then faster.

She doesn't look down at the faces she knows are there, looking up. This isn't about being seen. Or is it? She closes her eyes and imagines Shante's voice floating up from below — the syncopated strum of her ukulele, her voice, thick and beautiful, twining up through the air. There's a skylight amid the rafters, the moon bright in it, and every time Vale spins, that moonlight flickers across her face. A strobe light in that old barn.

The radiance falls on all of us, Bonnie, Vale thinks, spinning. Those men she loves below her, looking up. Those men who love her, looking up. Ginny's wild spirit, asleep in the next room, eyeing her through the walls. The peacocks, asleep in their corners. *On every one of us,* Vale thinks, spinning, feeling every muscle in her body work. *Every fucking one.*

DEB

She is half-asleep on the couch in Hazel's room. This vigilant tending. Hazel's breath uneven, ragged. Rising and falling. The dark brown of the catheter bag, its sour, human smell. Her body occasionally arcing in what Deb can only assume is unbearable pain. Deb's been giving her a dose of morphine twice a day, but it doesn't seem to be enough. The nurse from hospice brought her into the kitchen yesterday, said quietly, "This is up to you. How much pain you want her to endure. How long this journey lasts." She looked pointedly toward the jar of morphine on the table. "You know what I'm saying?" she said, her voice tender, and Deb had nodded. She understands.

And so it is up to Deb and Danny and Vale.

They slipped out an hour or more ago and

have not yet returned. Cousins. Old friends. She is grateful they have each other as the world transforms into something other. Apocalyptic or just plain harder than before.

And who will she have as the great world spins? Deb pours herself some more wine and thinks of Stephen and the darkness that must have lived inside him. That quiet suffering. She thinks: it is good to approach sixty. The doors open. The birds fly out or in. The light in the painting quivers. The music becomes more expansive, essential, quixotic.

"Stephen," she whispers into the dark. This room he grew up in. Its airs his own. "Life gets better. Less pungent. I wish you were here to find that out with me." One's suffering takes on hushed tones, Deb thinks. Becomes peppered with light.

But he is long gone. Twenty-five years she has been alone. Who will she fuck in the last half of her life? She would like to fuck Bird again. She would like to fuck the man who drives the town plow. She would like to fuck Georges Brassens. Oh how she would like to be found again! She would like to make love to Stephen in their bed, their sleeping child above. For so many years she has been waiting for Danny to come home and make her whole. And now Danny is home. And still she is alone.

Deb throws her head back against the cushions of the couch. "It's never too late to want to be fucked," she says out loud to Hazel, whose eyes flinch for a moment. "Never too late to learn to want something." How drunk is she? She will go out looking next Tuesday, after work. She'll go to the bar and sit there, like she did when she was nineteen, freshly washed, looking to get fucked. She'll ask Ginny to join her. Deb laughs, moonlight streaking across her face and cheekbones. "Never too late to want to be fucked," she whispers.

The dying woman takes a breath in, lurches to her side slightly, exhales. Those cheekbones, Deb thinks. Those beautiful unloved and dying cheekbones. Like Sandra Milo's. Like Lena Olin's. Like Grace Paley's, and Georgia O'Keeffe's and Sandrine Bonnaire's in *Vagabond*. "May your journey be peaceful," Deb says out loud, rising and going to Hazel, taking her hand in her own.

DANNY

December 19, 2011

Danny stands outside the door of the farm-house where Hazel, his grandmother, lies dying, and where his mother — aged, beautiful, bent-shouldered — sits drinking her wine alone. He can see her through the glass windows of this house that has sheltered for two hundred years, will shelter still. This house that his great-great-grandmother Marie moved to while her culture went silent, became unknown, disappeared into the trees.

She looks beautiful, his mother does. Serene. Not yet finished with this life and its living. Her head tipped back. Her eyes closed. A fierceness there he'd forgotten. She would tell him anything. He thinks of the French and Russian and Italian and Scandinavian movies she showed him when he was young. Jean Seberg and Brigitte Bardot and Ingrid Bergman. Her uninhibited weeping. Her laughter and dancing. The sex scenes that made him cringe, turn away, embarrassed, and her laughter and bright voice: "Gah! Ridiculous. Also: deep pleasure, my son. Deep pleasure."

Those movies carried them out of the silence of their life after Stephen. Danny saw himself in every single one; in every one there was a version of Danny, and in every one Danny found a pathway into the future, via a landscape or a train or a book or a body. Those movies told him that he, too, would make it through. That suffering makes you wiser. That those who *don't* make it, the versions of his father who also lived within those screens, didn't not make it because they were unworthy, or stupid, or cruel, but because their suffering was greater. That is all. Through those films he forgave his father. And loved his mother and her kind — the warm-blooded, surviving heroines.

Like Vale.

Danny shivers in the dark, looking through the window at his mother. He thinks his time of leaving the people he loves is done.

He knocks the snow off his boots and goes inside.

The dishes are washed, a kettle of water

simmers on the wood stove. He places mint tea bags in two mugs, pours the hot water, brings one to Deb.

She opens her eyes on the couch, smiles. "Danny," she says, patting the cushion beside her, taking the cup in her hands. "Thank you. What time is it?"

He sits down beside her. "Two A.M."

She lays her head on his shoulder and closes her eyes again. "I'm so glad to have you home."

"Glad to be here."

"Really? It's not terrible for you, this hillside?"

Danny looks at Hazel's bone-thin body on the bed by the window. Breath rising. Falling. "Yes. Terrible. And terrifying."

Deb nods. "So full of ghosts, eh? And so bloody solitary."

Danny takes a sip of his tea. "Yes. Ghosts and solitary. Hey, Mama."

She opens her eyes. Looks at him.

"Did you know about Lena and Lex?"

"Yes. Vale told me."

"Unbelievable, right?" He tells her about Lena's cabin: the stones and feathers and pictures pinned to the wall, the drawing of the fiddle player and his lover in braids. LW + LS.

"It kind of changes everything, doesn't

it?" she whispers. She looks at Hazel, dying there in that bed by the window.

"Yes," Danny says. "And nothing."

"Right. What power does a story have at this point?"

Danny pictures Vale spinning at the top of the barn rafters in moonlight and how that story might have made that spinning possible.

Deb squeezes her son's hand. He squeezes hers back. She closes her eyes and he feels her drift back into sleep.

There was a night when he was, what — eight? Nine? Stephen climbing up to the loft in the middle of the night and shaking Danny's shoulder, waking him. "The northern lights," he whispered. "Come see." He took Danny's hand and led him downstairs, put a hat on his head, boots on his feet, a coat over his shoulders. Outside it was cold — ten, at least. Maybe colder.

And then Stephen pointed up. Said, "Look."

Danny had never seen anything like it — the sky turned blue, purple, pink, and green. Unnatural colors, there amid the pointed tips of hemlock, spruce, and pine.

More beautiful than anything he'd imagined. Stranger.

Danny's cheeks were cold; he curled his

fingers inside his mittens, squeezed his body against his father's legs, listened to his father's breath rising in and out in that dark night.

"We should show Mama, don't you think?" Danny said after a few minutes, and Stephen had nodded, and so Danny went back inside to wake her.

"Oh — wondrous," she said when she came out, wrapped in Stephen's down jacket, walking toward Stephen, and then Danny stood between their two bodies — these people he loved most in the world — a bridge made of his limbs — as they looked up in silence at that perplexing and astounding show made of gas and light.

He likes to think of them that way, always, his parents.

Danny leans his head against his mother's shoulder. Closes his eyes. Lets his body give way to sleep there.

VALE

December 20, 2011

Vale is alone in her camper when she gets the call from the police. A farmer's dog has found a shoe. A white Reebok sneaker that matches the description of the one Bonnie was wearing. Dragged up from the farmer's east field that runs along the river, a couple miles downstream from the bridge. An officer has gone there to look but found nothing. She tells Vale, "There's no telling if it was hers. But it matches the descriptions. Not hard proof of course, but . . ."

Vale thinks of the bodies from Katrina she's heard about from Moe and Monty: bloated and stinking.

Vale thinks of coyotes. Of what buzzards will eat. Of carrion crows.

"No. No telling," she says over the phone. She thinks she might vomit. The field is quiet and still around her: frostbitten. The coffee mug burns her hands.

At the station they let her into the same back room where she watched the video.

The shoe rests on a pile of newspaper.

Size 6 1/2 like Bonnie's. Waterlogged. Mud-caked. Growing algae.

Vale wants to fall onto her knees. She wants to grab the shoe and hurl it at the window — the quick satisfaction of shattering glass.

"Can I?" she asks, reaching her hand out toward the shoe, thinking of the weathered, gray-flecked bones lined up on Lena's windowsill.

"Of course," the officer says.

Cool. Dank. Wet. The length of her hand.

It hardly seems like a shoe at all. Vale feels like she is holding a damaged creature of some kind. That dream she had in Lena's cabin: the dead barn swallow in her hands.

"Can I have it?"

The officer stares at the shoe for a moment, then glances at the office door. "Sure," she says quietly, handing Vale a plastic bag.

Vale asks for the location of the farm where the shoe was found, and the officer tells her.

"Thank you," Vale says, tucking the bag

under her arm, heading to the door, stuffing her hands in the pockets of her jacket to still them.

The bridge her mother stood on has been rebuilt out of thick concrete slabs and reinforced with steel I beams, but if you stand in the center of it, like Vale does now, on the narrow ledge of sidewalk, and look down, you can see the ruins of the first bridge — a monstrous tangle of cracked concrete piers and green iron. It's snowing slightly, and Vale tucks her jacket collar up around her ears, pulls her jacket sleeves down over her hands. The snow falls on the still-raw banks. The snow falls on the green iron. The snow falls on the new concrete bridge beneath her. Cars pass slowly, windshield wipers flapping, headlights on.

Vale walks to the far end of the bridge and scrambles down the bank, slipping on frozen ground and snow-covered rocks. She walks past the tangle of green iron. Walks downstream for an hour or more, past the backsides of Victorian houses, past mill buildings and abandoned industrial spaces, looking into the pools of the flood's detritus. When the creek joins the Connecticut, the mother river that will take the water south and east to the ocean, Vale turns south and keeps walking, for another quarter mile until she reaches the farmer's field where the shoe was found.

Vale roots around at the water's edge. Kicks at a pile of fallen leaves.

Snowflakes. Dead grass. Leaves drifting across the water.

She's about to turn back when she finds the deer bones.

A tangle of bone and hair, lodged under a pile of downed trees and creosote-soaked railroad ties.

"No," Vale whispers, going toward it, scraping away the branches and leaves with her frozen hands: a rack of ribs, sharp shinbones, skin that looks like dark, caramel-smoked leather, and then a skull appearing beneath her hands: deer-shaped.

"It's not a human skull," Vale says out loud, to no one, her heart racing.

She takes a deep breath. Looks at the carcass.

Not Bonnie. And yet: Bonnie.

Vale sits down there by the water's edge, holds the deer skull in her frozen hands.

"My mother is dead," she says out loud.

"My mother is dead!" she screams.

There is no smell. No maggots, no swollen flesh. Vale picks up a vertebra, the shape of a miniature female pelvis, and holds it in front of her. Her hand is shaking. She thinks of wasps, worms, buzzards, crows, beetles, yellow jackets. The things that will feed off these bodies, live inside them, turn them back into earth.

Vale thinks of a body being washed downstream, downriver, all the way to the Atlantic Ocean.

Bonnie bringing Vale cups of tea in the morning in bed when she was young. Soft lips on soft cheek. A smoker's whisper, scented with coffee: "Love you."

Bonnie's body Jesus-loved, eyeballs picked out by ravens and crows. Skin melting into pools of grease and smoked leather.

Vale looks out toward the calm river, wide and graceful, almost holy, floating past.

"Bonnie," she whispers.

She didn't know such a pain was possible.

"She's dead," Vale says, pushing open the door to Neko's room. "And I won't ever find her." She's shaking. Her clothes wet, snow-covered.

Vale goes to the bed and lies down on it. She closes her eyes and sees Bonnie on the bridge in white, her arms spread wide. Sees Bonnie's body lodged twenty feet below a dam.

Neko brings her blankets. Brings her tea.

Sits beside her, not speaking.

Her limbs won't stop shuddering. She tells him about the shoe. Tells him about the deer bones. Her breath isn't coming right. Too quick, shallow. "Damn you and your loving mother," Vale whispers, her eyes closed, her body unable to still itself. "Damn you and your job you love."

Neko puts his hand on her leg. Bends his head. Whispers, "I'm so sorry."

"Damn you," Vale whispers. Vale cries. Vale rages into the sheets. Vale sobs, Neko by her side.

She undresses him. He undresses her. Her mind tangles with the images of the deer's decomposed body, the bodies of children in Iraq, and the body of Bonnie, washed out to sea: night swimming. He puts his lips on her nipple. Slips his fingers inside her and Vale gasps. A long ache shooting through.

"Neko," she whispers later, her breathing slowed, her body stilled.

"Yeah?"

"Why are you leaving?"

He takes a deep breath, looks toward the window — a few snowflakes still falling — says quietly, "The only hope we have of people understanding war is if they see it." He tells her that there have been 45,000

Iraqi casualties, 3,900 of them children. He says that yes, the U.S. has formally withdrawn all combat troops, but that the violence is far from over. He says, "People need to know that."

Vale picks Lena's hat up off the floor and holds it over her eyes. "Yes, they do," she whispers, throwing the hat across the room.

Neko goes to a pile of photographs lying on the table and brings one back to Vale. It's a four-by-six print of the collapsed barn on Cedar Street, taken from the ground looking up at the web of fallen rafters, ribs launched against steel-gray sky.

The rafters look like a church.

Of the kind Vale might actually want to attend: light-filled, porous. "I took this a few days ago. For you," Neko says.

"Bonnie's barn," Vale says, sitting up, taking it. How ironically beautiful wreckage can be, she thinks. The colors rust and burn, a flock of birds lifting off from the power lines. She thinks of Leonard Cohen's bird on a wire, of his famous line about cracks being where the light gets in. Of Danny singing both those songs in the hayloft of the barn like they were gospel, eight years after his father died.

"Vale," Neko says.

"Yeah?" Vale turns to look at him.

"I always come back." He's looking straight into her eyes. Doesn't turn away. "I travel, yes, but I'm loyal as a fucking dog."

He puts his face on her thighs. "I like you, Vale. I'm not fucking around," he says quietly. "Are you?"

"No," Vale says, putting her hands on his head. Putting her cheek against his hair. Turning her eyes to the window, the slow light that filters through. "I am not fucking around."

DEB, DANNY, VALE

December 21, 2011

The rain turns to snow, then back to freezing rain, and the ice on the trees, windows, and roofs thickens.

Severe storm warning, the radio says, advising people, once again, to fill bathtubs, fill jugs, collect candles and batteries and flashlights. One-half to one inch of ice predicted. Widespread power outages, dangerous roadways, falling trees.

Of course, Vale thinks. The next storm. How bad will this one be? The apocalypse, or just another blip on the screen? How do we ever know? She was hoping to go see Neko tonight, to bring him here for dinner with Deb and Danny, but the roads are already too slick, the woods impassable.

She sends a text: *ROADS BAD. STAY WARM.*

She stares at her message for a long moment. Types: *POUR A GLASS FOR ME,* and hits Send again.

She wants to see him. She wants to hear him laugh. Cook steaks over a camp stove in his attic room. Touch his ribs. Kiss his chest. Find him.

Vale puts on Bonnie's silk dress over her long underwear and jeans. "My dead mother's dress," she says to Lena's photo on the wall, practicing the words, trying to wear out the sting. It's a party, after all — the winter solstice. She wonders how they're celebrating in the steamy streets of New Orleans; Vale misses Shante's voice this darkest night of the year. She puts on Lena's wool fedora and slips Bonnie's rosary around her neck. "My dead mother's jewels," Vale says to Marie. She dabs her eyelids with glittering silver and blue — in honor of Hazel — and reds her lips. The darkest night of the year. An ice storm. A party! She puts on her warmest boots and coat, gathers the champagne she bought three days ago for this occasion. She's about to leave when she sees the deer vertebra and her mother's sneaker on the kitchen counter. An unbearable shrine. She places them in a paper bag, tucks it under her arm, and sets off up the hill to Hazel's house.

She has to punch through the crust with

the heel of her boot to not slide, barely makes it up the already ice-slicked field. But if there's going to be an ice storm, the old house is the place to be. She wonders how many ice storms its bones have stood through. And isn't this what people have always done — will continue to do — during dark times: gather?

At the big house Danny has filled the bathtub and old milk jugs from the wood-shed with water, has collected flashlights and candles.

"Classic party favors," Vale says, placing the champagne, the deer vertebra, and her mother's shoe on the side table. "Happy solstice."

"Happy solstice to you," Danny says, looking at the items, touching Vale's arm. She told him about the shoe earlier this morning.

She opens the bottle of champagne and fills three canning jars, adds sprigs of dried lavender from her jacket pocket, passes them around. Deb fills a plate with apples and cave-hardened cheeses from halfway across the world. Danny takes the glass, closes his eyes, breathes in. His face is beautiful, as always, Vale thinks, watching him. Radiant and tortured, her cousin —

trying too hard to do well for the world.

"Cheers," she says, and they raise their glasses.

They move to the table, eat the apples and cheese, sip their drinks. The radio is on, tuned to an old-time country music station. Danny tells them about the festivals of Guatemala, about all-night dancing in the *zócalo*. "People are so much more alone here," he says. "The curse of puritan New England's stubborn self-reliance. Stoicism."

He looks at Vale. Raises his glass, says quietly: "To our heroine: Bonnie."

"To Bonnie," Vale whispers. The rain sounds like pellets on the roof and windows. The branches outside bend, lower themselves to the ground.

"To Bonnie," Deb says, raising hers. "And Hazel."

They can hear her sleeping breath from the next room. Slow and shallow. She hasn't opened her eyes in twenty-four hours. Every three, Deb gives her more morphine and immediately her body relaxes. Falls back into ease. How quickly one can go from all here to nothing, Vale thinks, watching her through the open doorway.

There's a cracking sound from outside — a large branch breaking — and the power flickers once, then goes out. The radio goes silent.

"Here she comes," Vale says. "The next great storm."

Deb rises and lights the candles they have set out on the table, lights an old kerosene lantern and brings it to Hazel's bedside.

"Of course," Danny says, rolling a joint and slipping it between his lips, "with global warming will come extreme poverty. Maybe these woods are the best place to be. Go back to the old ways of survival."

He passes the joint to Vale, who puts it between her lips and breathes in. Global warming: the unraveling future. The unraveling present. She exhales and tells them about *No Word for Time,* about a way of living in which the past is in the present and the future, too. About the words in Lena's notebook: *Near the sickness also lies the cure.* The sickness: wars, addiction, these storms, Bonnie's body washed downstream. And what, then, is the cure? She thinks of Marie's and Adele's ways of knowing and being: of seeing our human lives as part of a much wider and wilder whole.

She says, "We need Marie. We need to know what she knew."

Danny nods. Closes his eyes.

They sit quietly: pieces of ice hitting the

roof, Hazel's ragged breathing from the next room, candlelight jumping across the walls.

Vale hands the joint to Deb, who holds it between her fingers, takes a deep breath, and shrugs her shoulders. "Why not," she says, breathing in.

Deb's never been a pot smoker. Even at the commune, and in college, that wasn't her thing. She never liked the unhinging it brings on. But it seems like the thing to do here in Hazel's kitchen next to the lit Stanley, here with the two people she has come to love most in the world — Danny and Vale, these survivors — on the darkest night of the year, while outside the world cracks and glistens. Danny and Vale. They are the future: the bloodline of this Heart Spring Mountain. New creatures — wise and feral and truehearted. Have they failed their puritan ancestors or freed them? And Danny's children and Vale's children: Who will they be, and what world will they inherit? Will there be apples for her unborn grandchildren, here where the winters have been so unpredictable — no snow or too much? Warm Decembers and late freezes, destroying apple crops and peach crops. The dry springs and dryer summers. Will there be potable water? She thinks of refugees seeking shelter. Droughts. Famines. Wars. Bonnie floating downstream. The world will become something completely other after her lifetime, and she aches to think how she will not be here to save the ones she loves.

"Pass the joint, Mama," Danny says with a smile, and Deb's heart alights, grows warm again. Danny. Her son. His live face and green eyes like Stephen's. Like Lex's, the fiddle-playing grandpa none of them knew.

He takes another hit, gets up and grabs Vale's phone off the counter. "We need music, my friends," he says. He puts on Ruth Brown's "5-10-15 Hours." "Ruth!" he says, beginning a slow shuffle. Vale smiles, puts her glass down, and joins him.

"Dance with us, Mama," Danny says, reaching out to her, pulling her up off the chair. And so Deb dances, too. She feels like a fool, here in this kitchen, her old white body in wool socks, dancing next to the wood stove on these creaking pine floors, surrounded by these many-paned windows, while Ruth sings. My God, music — isn't there something to it? Deb thinks. A house that knows music — a house that fills with it, swells with it, is broken and made whole with it? She feels her grief for Bonnie and for Hazel flooding through her body, finding outlet in every crevice and every pore.

When the song ends, Vale goes to the phone and puts on Missy Elliott's "Party-time."

"Just what you might have heard in this very kitchen fifty years ago," Danny says, grinning, moving his sun-kissed bare feet across the pine. Vale raises her arms above her head, closes her eyes, shimmies her hips back and forth to Missy's syncopated thwack. Missy's unapologetic presence in the world. Missy's fury, sex, self-love.

Deb laughs, but there's a deep pang in her chest. What glorious creatures, she thinks, pouring more wine, watching Vale and Danny bust their young and beautiful asses. Fierce and resilient, she thinks, as a large crack comes from outside, rattling the house, making the candlelight flicker.

The joint is passed to her one more time, and she sits down and takes another hit, at once sure that they are not alone in this kitchen. She is sure that Hazel is here, too, only a younger Hazel, in a flowered apron and loose cotton dress, pulling bread from the hot oven. And Lena is here, too — Vale's grandma — with her long hair and one-eyed owl on her shoulder. Yes, she's sitting in the corner, tapping her foot and singing along. The owl blinks, closes his one good eye.

And Lex is here, too, with his fiddle, playing along, his left foot making its own percussive rhythm. What a crowd!

But there's another here, too, Deb is suddenly sure. Stephen, walking toward her. The Stephen Deb first loved — twenty-three years old. Blue jeans. Worn flannel. His too-soft heart. Not ever sure of itself. And then he is behind Deb. She smells him before anything. Warm heat. Wool. He bends and puts his hands around her waist. Puts his lips to her left ear, that particular tingle of wet lip, prickle of beard, whispers, "Hello."

Deb closes her eyes. A deep breath she hasn't allowed there for years.

But now Danny is calling her name and motioning for her to get up and start dancing again, and so she does. All of them do, across the pine floors: Danny, Deb, Vale, Stephen, Lena, Lex, Hazel. Their bright, best, young faces. Their fearlessness and inhibition. They are lighting up the night, moving their elbows, bending their knees, while the ice falls and the trees crash. While the world begins its great unraveling they are all there, dancing, their love and their joy on their shoulders. Their best-intentioned, misspent love. Oh, the impossibility of it. The sheer impossibility of doing it right!

"Don't stop now, Mama," Danny says, reaching his arms out to her, and so Deb two-steps across the floor with her son. They stumble into one of Hazel's one-hundred-year-old wooden chairs and right themselves at the last minute; they trot back across the floor the other way and crash into the refrigerator. Deb is laughing so hard, she thinks she might piss her pants, might cry. They open their arms into a ring and slip them over Vale's head — they circle around her, the outer petals of a flower — and Vale raises her arms toward the ceiling and closes her eyes and smiles, a beautiful spinning stamen, an unbearably gorgeous queen, and Deb thinks — this is it. This is how to face the end of the world. Like this: heads tipped back. Dancing. Laughing. Drunk and stoned in homage to the great beasts on their shoulders, on every shoulder, always — death and love. Death and love.

The song ends and Vale picks another. Nina Simone's "I Wish I Knew How It Would Feel to Be Free." Sweet Jesus. Deb's all-time favorite. She stands still, heart pounding in her chest, breath slowing. She falls back into her chair. If there were a singular voice of God, Deb thinks, it would be Nina Simone's. Danny pulls Vale to him and they slow dance, Vale's face against his chest, a smile across her lips, momentarily happy, and Deb is surprised by the tears that fill her eyes.

How Vale deserves to be happy.

They pull apart, and Danny sits down in a chair next to Deb, and Vale dances alone in the middle of the room. Her eyes closed. A streak of pain across her brow, limbs in slow motion, intoxicating. She's got something there, Deb thinks. Something being said with this body. Moving to Nina's piano. Nina's snaps. Nina's drums. Moving to Nina's voice right in her ear — singing, a near moan — a timbre that seems to set them all momentarily free.

HAZEL

December 21, 2011

She can hear their laughter. Boots across the floor. That awful music.

None of them notice the woman climbing in through the window: dark hair, a thin face, watery eyes.

Hazel can smell her from here — mud? Cigarette smoke? Piss? Who is this woman, and why is she here? She smells like an animal in pain, a dying cow at the back of the barn. Her clothes wet, mud-stained.

Hazel stares at this woman's face, the one that is easing toward her. This woman's cheekbones look so familiar. Her eyes a deer's eyes — dark and tender.

She comes to Hazel's bedside and sits down on the stool beside her. Hazel stares. What has happened to this woman's face? Rings under her eyes. Scabs across her cheeks, like she's been picking. Dark hair swirling around her brow and cheeks and ears.

Hazel glances toward the kitchen, at Deb and Danny and Vale, dancing like fools to that unbearable music. Why don't they see this woman who has broken into the house? Hazel wants to call to them, but her tongue won't move. Parched — her mouth is. Her throat unable to swallow. The woman seems more ghost than human. The woman reaches for Hazel's hand, and Hazel lets her touch it. Warm hand. Remarkably so. Beautiful small fingers — near-child size, all bone. Why are the pockets under her eyes so dark? What are those scars, up and down her thin arms, below her sweatshirt sleeves? The woman's sweatshirt: white with a wolf emblazoned on its front. Streaks of brown across it. Swamp water.

Oh. For a long moment Hazel cannot breathe, but then it comes, volcanic, her chest filling once more with air. Bonnie — this is Bonnie.

Bonnie come home. Hazel folds her fingers over Bonnie's fingers. Squeezes them as tight as she can, every muscle in her body straining to do so. Bonnie, who has been missing. She remembers that now: a storm. Hazel mouths, with her dry lips and dry tongue that won't move, "Bonnie."

The woman squeezes Hazel's fingers. Smiles at her. Her smile is bright — a beam of sunshine. "Hello," she whispers. "How are you?"

Hazel tries to say, "I am terrified," but the words don't come.

Why don't the others see? What a racket from the kitchen: their ridiculous bodies, angry sounds.

Bonnie, Hazel thinks, squeezing her hand. Wild child Bonnie running barefoot across the yard, squatting to pee on Hazel's periwinkle, seeing a cow, yelling out "thow!" and smearing her face with jam. Motherless child whom Hazel taught to pick ripe blackberries and gather eggs and shell peas.

"It's cold out there," Bonnie says. Laughing. "Dreadful."

Hazel nods. Squeezes the hand tighter. It's not about the land, she thinks. It's going to that baby, that baby girl, fat thighs and dirt in the rings of her neck, pee dribbling down the inside of her thighs.

Bonnie bends down and kisses Hazel's brow. "Sleep tight," she whispers. Her sour smell overwhelming. She lets go of Hazel's hand, goes to the window.

Hazel tries to reach for her. To call her back. But the words don't come. Bonnie slips outside. Closes the glass behind her.

Great light. Great panic. Oh my God. Great light. An astonishing pain. Hazel reaches for the bed sheets. Opening.

BONNIE

She looks down into the swelling and churning water and watches all the things passing below, picked up from the shore along the way: branches, barrels, a green rubber boot, trees, a refrigerator. She blinks, disbelieving. Laughs.

"Fucking beautiful!" she calls out, the sound of her voice swallowed.

She thinks back to the farm where she grew up, ten miles upstream, headwaters to this creek and all it harbors. "Wash us all clean," she whispers, her arms outspread toward the roiling water. The roar of the water is all she can hear. The rain covers her face, her hair, soaks through her sweatshirt, her pants, her white sneakers. She tips her face back and faces that rain. So cool. Effervescent! She wishes Vale were here to see it. Why aren't you here with me, Vale?

That perfect mole at the back of her neck, dark curls. Bonnie hears the crack of something breaking. She looks down — the concrete ripples below her feet. A black thing floats by. Wings. A large bird! Raven? Hawk? Owl? Her mother had one. An owl. Otie. Bonnie laughs, just thinking of it. Her mother and her owl. But what is happening? Electricity through her body. Water all in her white sneakers. The ground under her shifting. Another crack like thunder. Jesus, what is happening? Jesus: *Above all, love each other deeply, because love covers over a multitude of sins.* Ain't that the truth, Bonnie thinks, looking down at the water below her feet. The love of Jesus! *As the Father has loved me, so have I loved you.* The bridge is cracking, breaking, but Bonnie's body does not fall. It doesn't crash with the concrete into the roiling water below. Instead she walks across to the other side. To solid ground. To cool, black earth beneath her. Arms spread. A smile across her lips. Cackle of high laughter. The love of Jesus pounding in her chest and everywhere. She turns and watches the bridge crash and crumble and break, bones of green iron and steel and concrete disappearing into white water. Sweet water! Oh, Vale, baby. *Whoever drinks the water I give them will never thirst.* Vale, baby, Bonnie thinks, laughing, walking, I've always loved the motherfucking rain.

VALE

A thundering cracking sound comes from outside, and Vale goes to the window to look out. A large branch has fallen two feet from the house, missing it, miraculously. Vale turns and walks into the living room to check on Hazel.

There's a new stillness to the room. Sheets tangled around Hazel's legs, eyes closed, dry lips parted, lantern light flickering across her brow.

"Hazel," Vale whispers, going to her. She reaches for Hazel's hand and wrist.

No pulse.

She puts her hand to Hazel's chest: no breath.

"She's gone," Vale calls into the kitchen, an ache shooting through her chest and legs.

Vale's never held a dead hand before. She's never held Hazel's hand before.

Sunspots. Long bones. Thick veins, the warm blood stilled. "Hazel," Vale whispers, her breath lodged.

Maggots. Bees. Carrion crows.

Night swimming.

Deb and Danny come running from the kitchen. "Oh," Deb whispers, putting her hand on Hazel's chest. Danny stands close behind her, places his hand on Hazel's leg.

"We should sing, no?" Deb says after a few minutes, tears streaming silently down her cheeks, and Vale and Danny nod, and so she starts singing the words to the Nina Simone song still ringing in their heads. "I Wish I Knew How It Would Feel to Be Free." It seems absurdly fitting. Vale and Danny join in. When they don't know the words, they hum.

Vale's voice keeps breaking up — she finds it hard to breathe — their voices accompanied by the incessant peppering of ice on the glass windowpanes, the occasional crash of a branch falling.

With every one: mothers in El Salvador, mothers in Iraq, mothers in Syria and Somalia. The finality of every single death unbearable, Vale thinks, stroking Hazel's still hand.

"I'm here with you, Hazel," she whispers.

And she is: here. She's been without roots for so long. But she's here. Now.

While so much in the world goes wrong, and so many good things rise, too: Occupy, poetry, hospice. Good deeds, large and small. Counterpoints of magnanimity and altruism.

Vale puts her head against Hazel's bony chest.

The house is silent except for the refrigerator rattling in the next room.

"I'm here," she says. Cheek on Hazel's pale cotton nightdress.

Vale stands, goes to the door, puts on her hat and boots and coat.

She picks up the deer vertebra and slips it into her pocket. Grabs the white Reebok sneaker from the kitchen table and tucks it under her arm.

Outside, the trees are coated in a near inch of quivering ice. There is no light — star or moon — just a faint wash from candle and lantern drifting out the windows.

Vale scrambles down the driveway. She can hear branches cracking from the woods; the rain and sleet and ice drip under the collar of her coat. Her feet slip out from under her, and she lands on her ass, uprights herself, slides the rest of the way down on her feet.

At the bottom of the driveway, at the bridge crossing Silver Creek, Vale stops. She walks into the center of it, pulls the bone out of her pocket and holds it above the stream of still-open water.

She stands there for a long time, feeling the rain freeze to her cheeks, the rain freeze to her eyelashes, mingling with the tears that stream down her cheeks, a line from *No Word for Time* ringing in her head: "When you have learned about love, you have learned about God."

Vale raises the bone above her shoulder.

"You're free, Bonnie!" she yells into the wind and rain. The branches around her bend, shudder, arc, crack. Vale tosses the bone into the swirling water. It spins for a moment, caught in an eddy, then disappears downstream.

"Baby girl," Bonnie says, climbing out of the water, collapsing onto the sandy river-bank next to Vale on that day the photo was taken. "This is too good, honey-cakes! This river. This sunlight. You by my side? Too goddamn good." Closing her eyes. A smile across her lips. Touching Vale's toes with her own.

Vale reaches into her coat and pulls out Bonnie's shoe. She brings it to her face.

Puts her cheek against the cracked leather. Lifts it above her head and launches it with her best pitcher's arm into the dark water. "I've missed you," Vale says, watching the shoe disappear slowly, white thing bobbing on white crescent waves.

Vale pulls her arms to her chest, feels the water thunder past below her feet.

She would like to go to Neko, let down her hair, undress him, find their song, streaking. She would like to walk up-creek and find Marie, learn everything that was forgotten. To face the future, Vale thinks, turning in a slow circle, closing her eyes, heavy sheets of ice falling on the water, on the trees, on Vale, one must look both forward and back. The past and the future existing at once in the cup of her wet and shaking hand.

And then there's a sound from the trees uphill near the swamp. An owl, barred — *who cooks for you?* — and Vale opens her eyes, laughs. "Fucking of course, Bonnie," she says, standing still, looking into those upstream woods. "An owl: the death of something old, the start of something new."

Bonnie puts her wet cheek against Vale's dry one, grins. Whispers in Vale's ear, sand on her lips: "The mother is the love factory."

Vale tips Lena's hat toward the woods and the birds that dwell there. "Hoo-hoo-hoo-hoo!" she calls out, joining in, a near howl, her body exhausted.

Love songs, Vale thinks. Amid the squall they are seeking one another. Deb, Danny, Neko, Vale — seeking one another. Vale turns toward the house and the people in it — these night creatures she's been given. She holds her arms out wide in both directions, her body freezing, a block of ice, her lips and jacket and cheeks coated in it. Seeking one another. Amid these great and wilding storms that are our own. And in the dawn? Vale moves her arms up and down slowly, near wings. Luz. The thing that comes with every morning.

ACKNOWLEDGMENTS

Gratitude to the Vermont Arts Council and the National Endowment for the Arts for their generous support of this work.

Gratitude to the various cabins, living rooms, and cafés throughout southern Vermont (especially their beams and windows) where these words were written.

Gratitude to the following books for expanding my understanding of time, place, hope, and the lives of birds: Evan T. Pritchard's *No Word for Time: The Way of the Algonquin People*; Frederick Matthew Wiseman's *The Voice of the Dawn: An Autohistory of the Abenaki Nation*; Trudy Ann Parker's *Aunt Sarah: Woman of the Dawnland*; Robin Wall Kimmerer's *Braiding Sweetgrass: Indigenous Wisdom, Scientific Knowledge and the Teachings of Plants*; Rebecca Solnit's *Hope in the Dark: Untold Histories, Wild Possibilities*; and Tony Angell's *The House of Owls*.

Gratitude to my friend Judy Dow for teaching me about the Eugenics Survey of Vermont, forever shifting my sense of place.

Gratitude to Julia Kenny, agent supreme, for keeping my (mercurial) spirits above water.

Gratitude to Megan Lynch, editor supreme, for the brilliance, the clarity, and the unflinching faith.

Gratitude to the heart-strong and capable team at Ecco (a ship of dreams), especially Sonya Cheuse, Miriam Parker, James Faccinto, and Emma Dries.

Gratitude to Sara Wood for the matchless cover art.

Gratitude to Margaret Wimberger for keeping my lines true.

Gratitude to Jennifer Bowen Hicks, a phenom, for being there, always.

Gratitude to my parents — optimists, pragmatists — for getting back to the land.

Gratitude to my grandmother Margaret for her songs, her spunk, and her beautiful time of dying.

Gratitude to my grandfather John for his love of owls, his knowledge of stars, and his beautiful time of dying.

Gratitude to Ty, my rock, my roll, my poet supreme.

And last (but never least), gratitude to my

children, A and O, wild at heart, for being my reason, my cause, and my hope in the dark. I write for you, darlings.

ABOUT THE AUTHOR

Robin MacArthur lives and works on the farm where she was born in Vermont. She is the author of *Half Wild: Stories* (winner of the 2017 PEN/New England Award), the editor of *Contemporary Vermont Fiction: An Anthology*, and one-half of the indie-folk duo Red Heart the Ticker.

The employees of Thorndike Press hope you have enjoyed this Large Print book. All our Thorndike, Wheeler, and Kennebec Large Print titles are designed for easy reading, and all our books are made to last. Other Thorndike Press Large Print books are available at your library, through selected bookstores, or directly from us.

For information about titles, please call:
(800) 223-1244

or visit our website at:
gale.com/thorndike

To share your comments, please write:
Publisher
Thorndike Press
10 Water St., Suite 310
Waterville, ME 04901